ALEX'S REACTION WAS LIGHTNING QUICK, and he cut the tether before Zurah realized what he was doing. He shoved her to the side, and he grimaced as the crystal pulled itself up along his legs.

"Go, get out of here." He groaned.

"No, I'm not leaving you." Zurah turned her gun to aim at the base of the crystal holding him in place.

"Don't be a fool," he hissed as the crystal spread across his thighs. "The others have to be warned."

But Zurah fired. The bullet fractured the crystal around his feet, and for a brief moment, she thought she would be able to free him. But the shards reformed and created another layer on top of what was rapidly consuming Alex. Desperate, Zurah flipped the gun around and knelt, bashing the butt of the gun against the crystal. But her efforts had no effect. She spun around. "Let him go. We've done nothing wrong."

"The Timeless Sleepers see all. Justice has been called."

Abandoned Echoes

The Black Gates of Objer
Book 1

by

ELIZABETH KNOLLSTON

LEWIS BROS PRESS

Copyright © 2024 Elizabeth Knollston

Abandoned Echoes
The Black Gates of Objer Book 1
All Rights Reserved

This book, or parts thereof, may not be reproduced in any form without permission.

This is a work of fiction. All characters and events in this book are fictitious. Any similarity to real persons, living or dead, is coincidental and not intended by the author.

ISBN Paperback: 978-1-959159-12-4
ISBN Ebook: 978-1-959159-13-1

Cover Art and Interior Design © Elizabeth Knollston
Editing by Red Adept Editing Services

Published by Lewis Bros. Press
PO Box 261
Larned, KS 67550

www.elizabethknollston.com

for those who march
to the beat of their own drum
never stop

1

"It's your turn," Nissa called out as the dark-red orilic cube sailed through the air.

Zurah held her breath as she watched the cube bounce off the back panel, twist, and land in one of the uppermost baskets. All in all, the toss was decent. "Bets laid out at twenty to thirty. I'm up by twelve. Bet you can't beat that."

"Bet I can." Zurah Winters slammed her glass of ipp on the bar counter and turned. With a wide grin on her face, she snapped her fingers at the Neetho gaming vendor for her next cube. One of the vendor's eyes rolled in her direction, while its twin monitored the other customers. A bright-pink tentacle with soft-blue undertones snaked out from behind the gaming table and dropped the hefty die into Zurah's outstretched hand. The edges were well-worn from countless customers who'd believed in luck and had downed too much ipp to know better.

Zurah tossed the orilic cube into the air, feeling the weight and considering her next-to-last toss. She bit her upper lip, stepped up to the line, and watched the bouncing golden basket as it wove its way through the stationary ones.

"Time," she called out, and a huge countdown clock sprang to life above the baskets. The timer started off at fifteen seconds, providing the player with just enough time to lull them into figuring out the best strategy. The clock ticked… Fourteen… Zurah rolled the orilic cube in her hand, finding the best grip… Thirteen… Doubt flashed through her eyes… Twelve… Eleven… She pushed away the doubt. She needed the win. The pot was well above normal, and the credits would help make a dent in repaying Nissa. With laser focus, Zurah zoned in on the golden basket with the Neetho symbol for prosperity. *Come on. All I need is an extra three points to push ahead of Nissa.*

The commotion of rapid movement and chairs being flung back against the floor didn't faze Zurah. The golden basket had begun to rotate counterclockwise and was due to take a sharp U-turn.

Glass shattered as the timer hit three seconds… Two…

"Shut it down!" A gruff voice filled the room, along with the telltale whine of a speaker routed through suits designed for the InterGalactic Justice system. "Everyone, stay where you are and present your HalfLife chips for inspection."

Zurah's time was up. She stretched forward, releasing the cube as Nissa's hand closed around her wrist.

"Come on," Nissa hissed and jerked Zurah toward the back of the bar. But Zurah's eyes were fixed on her orilic cube. Oblivious to the commotion around her, she watched it arc through the air and land in the golden basket.

The timer exploded in a cascade of colors as Nissa lobbed a flasher through the air. A thunderous boom muffled the chaos, followed by a cheerful three-toned chime as smoke and nanobots rained down. Each nanobot was designed to seek and scramble a HalfLife biochip, masking its signal.

Nissa pinched Zurah's arm. "Focus."

"But I—"

"Winters," Nissa growled as she crouched and pressed her hand against the wall opposite the bar. A screen lit up, and she keyed in the code, gaining access to one of the hundreds of hideaway hatches tucked throughout Rockerton's All-In-One Resort.

"Thought Rockerton's was supposed to be IGJ proof," Zurah muttered as she slipped into the hideaway behind Nissa, making sure to close the hatch securely behind her.

Rockerton's All-In-One Resort boasted an IGJ-proof environment, no questions asked. A hefty amount of credits enabled free access to endless buffets, gaming, and entertainment venues. For a second unimaginable load of credits, Rockerton's had a wide range of upgrades that provided maps of emergency exits and access to the rotating codes needed to access the labyrinth of escape routes. Few ever complained about the cost, as it was implied the Rockerton family paid a ridiculous amount of credits to keep IGJ agents at bay.

Nissa and Zurah slid down the tunnel and landed in a smelly pile of refuse.

"Guess someone forgot to pay their bills," Nissa muttered as she rolled out of the bin, picking off the bits and pieces of rotting trash.

"This is the last time I let you talk me into coming to one of these places." Zurah flung a rather nasty and squishy piece of food at Nissa. "And I would've won."

Despite the severity of the situation, Nissa grinned. "Don't go all sour. You know I would've taken you in the last round. I always do." She winked then leaned to the left to look behind Zurah. "No more chitchat. Looks like they pulled out the big guns tonight."

"We should petition for a refund," Zurah commented, still working to pull some variety of fruit peel out of her braid. Then she silently added, *I would've won this time.*

"Doubtful we'd get paid. The IGJ has gotten a bit twitchy of late. Come on."

The two women moved through the shadows of docked shuttles, heading toward the rings that accommodated the smaller ships. The *HighTail Flyer* was a cozy craft for a small crew with ample nooks and crannies to smuggle a wide variety of goods. The ship wasn't the newest on the market. Its exterior was darkened in areas due to close calls, and the various knicks and dings provided a personality its small crew had come to admire.

"Open up," Nissa ordered as she banged on the side of the ship. "It's us, you fool."

"Bio ID confirmation required," a gruff voice replied.

"If I have to waste any more time on your crap, I'm going to grab a torch and pry this piece of junk open," Nissa replied calmly.

Zurah punched in to the trio's private comm line. "She isn't playing, Mexa." When Nissa stormed up and down the ship, kicked over crates, or even threw stuff, no one took her seriously. But when the woman was calm and collected, everyone hustled to do as they were told.

The small side door hissed as air leaked around the seals, then it popped open. The two women hustled inside, and the door slid shut.

"What was that? Thinking you could just fly off and leave us?" Nissa grumbled.

Zurah felt a small adrenaline spike as her heart skipped a beat. Normally, Nissa wouldn't joke about such things. In their line of work, being double-crossed was always a risk, no matter the crew. For a little over two years, Zurah had worked for Nissa, and she'd grown comfortable with their routine. She'd even come to admire the crotchety old man who was their pilot. Mexa was older than what most crews looked for, but his record was stellar. He'd been a top-rated pilot in his prime and had also earned a solid reputation as a mechanic hack. But the knowledge that there was always the slim chance of being left behind sent shivers down Zurah's spine.

"How was I supposed to know it was you and not some goon ripping off your HalfLife signal? You could've been caught in the raid," Mexa protested.

"And you could've been prepped and ready to leave," Nissa replied. "We need to get out of here."

Mexa looked everywhere but at Nissa. "Actually, we can't."

"Why?" Zurah asked. Her small spike of adrenaline rapidly got stronger. "You cutting a deal or something?"

Mexa scowled and made the motion of spitting off to the side. "Of course not. What do you think I am?"

"Spill it." Nissa sighed.

"We picked up a new gig. From Finn. She needs a ride and has… decided to use our services."

"A ride?" Zurah asked. "Finn? As in *the* Finn?"

Mexa nodded. "Can't turn it down. You know what might happen."

Nissa whistled long and low. "Damn. Wasn't expecting that. Either of you ever work with her?"

Zurah shook her head. "Nope, just heard the stories. And that's plenty enough for me."

"Once. Several years ago. Similar setup. Finn needed a ride, and I happened to be the pilot of the shuttle she picked out," Mexa confessed.

"Anything we need to know about?" Nissa asked.

"Not really. Just keep your head down and don't ask questions."

"What's her ETA?" Zurah started to pick at the back of the copilot's seat.

Mexa turned and checked the control panel. "Fifteen minutes."

"All right. Winters, secure our gear. Mexa, get us prepped," Nissa ordered.

But Zurah didn't move. "Can we chat?"

Nissa's cool blue eyes studied her.

Zurah's lips were pressed together, and her fingers worked at enlarging the hole in the chair's fabric.

"Sure." Nissa motioned for Zurah to follow.

Once tucked back in the rear of the ship, Nissa's posture softened as she waited for Zurah to open up.

"Taking on Finn is a big risk. You know the rumors as well as I do," Zurah said.

"Yes, as it is with any job or anyone who hires us. We don't exactly run in the best of circles."

"I know that," Zurah snapped.

"What's really bothering you?" Nissa asked.

"You're the boss. I get that," Zurah said. "And normally, I don't disagree with your choices."

Nissa crossed her arms. "Well, that's good, seeing as how I pay the bills around here."

"But the whisper nets say Finn's last job brought down a lot of heat. This might not be the best idea. How do we know she won't chew us up and spit us out?"

"I get it. I do," Nissa said, moving to lean back against the wall. "But we both know doing a job for Finn could open doors for us. Bring in a heap more credits and maybe let us have a moment to breathe. More than just a day or two at Rockerton's."

"Then you're sure?" Zurah asked.

Nissa nodded. "Yes, and I don't think we really have much choice in the matter either way. I listen to the scuttlebutt too, you know. If anything goes sideways, we'll figure it out. We've had to before."

Zurah nodded. "All right. You're the boss."

"You're damn straight I am," Nissa said with a large

grin. "You're just getting prejob jitters. We both know you fret and worry, then everything turns out all right in the end." Nissa pushed off the wall and headed back toward the front of the ship. "Get the gear stored and concentrate on the task at hand. Try not to think too many steps ahead, and keep it positive."

Zurah tried to smile, but inwardly, she felt a rush of unease. *Yeah, but one of these days, things will go wrong. And we won't be able to get out of a jam.* But out of all the bosses Zurah had worked for, Nissa had delivered on her promises every time. In fact, Zurah often suspected she wanted to trust Nissa—an unusual notion in their line of work.

Trust was an interesting word, one that Zurah had turned over in her mind thousands of times. As she worked to store what little gear had been left out, putting it away in the myriad of cubbyholes above the two passenger benches, she wondered if trust was something that eventually ran out. Or perhaps it could be worn down over time as little pieces of it chipped away. And it wasn't the trust she put in others that plagued her thoughts but trust in herself.

Zurah was well aware of how jobs didn't always go as planned and the stigma that could be attached to individuals who had been a part of crews who'd botched a job or worse. But Nissa hadn't cared about Zurah's previous jobs. And she'd defended her choice of security hack each time someone gave Zurah a hard time. She'd tried to ask Nissa why she defended Zurah on more than one occasion, but Nissa only ever smiled and said she liked working with someone who didn't give up.

The last of the equipment to stow away was a jammer lock and its components. Zurah picked it up and ran her fingers over the octagonal tool of her trade. Something had gone wrong with the jammer on a previous job—before Nissa—and Zurah was continually tearing it apart to find the reason why. But so far, she hadn't been able to figure it out. Her fingers curled around the jammer lock, the edges digging into her skin. The majority of their jobs went like clockwork, but when a job went sideways, the memories were hard to keep at bay.

The job had started off routine. Her boss at the time, a burly man with Telt and human ancestry who had run a small group of the Needles, had ordered her to stay on the ship until the all clear. But Zurah's curiosity had gotten the better of her, and she'd taken a peek at the cargo—med supplies. For Harold, that was highly unusual. The man regularly traded in high-quality goods, which brought optimum credits for him and his crew. Even more alarming was when Zurah had realized the drop was for Cloud-11.

Harold's orders had been clear. *Stay with the ship until I tell you.* But Zurah's curiosity had only grown—about the job and Cloud-11. She'd watched the vids and listened to the whisper nets concerning the destruction and attempts at rebuilding what had once been humanity's shining jewel in the stars. Within minutes of scouting the area on her own, she had come across the first dead body.

Zurah's forefinger found a nick on the edge of the jammer, and she looked down to notice a small dot of blood beginning to well up. She watched the blood trickle down the side of her finger, and the god-awful memories of that job filled her vision. That day, everything had gone to hell. Zurah had broken her cardinal rule. The moment she had realized Harold and his team weren't merely there to drop off goods but to run a kidnapping gig, Zurah had bolted. She'd wanted no part in that.

For a split second, Zurah felt as if she were cradling the face of a woman instead of the jammer. Blank glassy eyes stared up at her. Blood and dust were caked in the wrinkles of her skin.

No, Zurah thought. *I'm not going to go through this again.* She yanked open a cubby door and tossed the jammer inside. "Secure," she called out and stuck her bloodied finger in her mouth.

Zurah headed back to the front and took the seat behind the copilot's chair, watching Mexa as he finished prepping the ship. While the *HighTail Flyer* was a few years behind on the upgrades coming out of Confore Tech, it did boast quite a few black market add-ons, thanks to Mexa's consistent tinkering. The shields, weapons, and overdrive engine were kept in tip-top shape.

Nissa leaned back and said to Zurah, "This is a job like any other. Clear?"

Zurah gave her a tight smile. *Eerie how she seems to sense what I'm thinking at times.* "Sure, boss. Crystal."

"Winters." Nissa narrowed her eyes. The warning was clear: don't complain. Don't give anything away. Just sit there and observe.

Zurah rolled her shoulders. "I get it."

Before Nissa could admonish her one last time,

something hit the side of the ship. Then again and again, all in an irregular pattern.

"Mexa?" Nissa asked.

He raised a hand and shushed her. "Hang on… Yup, that's her."

"How do you know?" Nissa asked.

"Old-school code work." He twisted around to look at Zurah. "I'd move if I were you. She prefers that seat."

Zurah slid across the narrow aisle to sit behind Mexa, her hands sliding to the underpart of the seat, her fingers searching for any small holes to worry over.

There was a faint hiss as the small side door opened, then with a dull thud, it slid back into place. Nissa quickly got up and moved to greet their guest. Zurah strained to make out anything intelligible from the soft voices behind her. Then she realized it wasn't because she couldn't hear them well enough but due to the fact she couldn't understand what they were saying—neither were speaking standard.

The click of Mexa's safety harness distracted Zurah's eavesdropping just as Finn slid into the seat behind Nissa.

Zurah couldn't help but stare. She had heard the rumors just like everyone else. Everyone believed Finn was a part of the Little Asteroid Gang, but no one had ever been able to confirm it. And there were stories of a handful of individuals who had tried but had abruptly disappeared.

Zurah remembered looking at the posting with the Little Asteroids from time to time but had never really been tempted. The whisper nets were pretty confident about Miles High being involved with the gang, and he was one of the biggest players in the black market and smuggler leagues. She didn't want to get tangled up with someone who had once been in line to become emperor of Old Earth. Zurah was convinced that once someone was mixed up in that level of politics, they always were. There was no escape.

Finn's clothing was appropriate for a smuggling gig. The dull black leather was no doubt riddled with anti-everything, making sure scanners and goons couldn't trace her movements. Her hair was as dull and dark as her outfit and twisted up into an intricate series of braids. Finn turned to look at Zurah, and she cringed at being caught openly staring. But Zurah couldn't tear her eyes away, noting how Finn's lips were stained a dark blue and dusted with what appeared to be golden glitter. Dark-brown eyes watched Zurah, with a delicate eyebrow quirking up in curiosity.

"Prepare for liftoff," Mexa said. "Everyone buckle up. This might get a tad bumpy. Looks like the goons have set up some orbiters. Going to clear Rockerton's shielding then kick in the overdrive. You got coordinates for me?"

Finn nodded. She stood up and leaned over Mexa in order to key them in herself.

"Are you sure?" Mexa asked. "That'll take us—"

"I'm sure," Finn replied as she sat back down.

Nissa turned to take a look. "I'm all for helping fellow traders out, but these coordinates are going to take us to the edge—"

"I'll triple your normal rates," Finn replied.

The shock of such an offer caused Nissa's eyes to widen, and her mouth dropped open in shock. Then her expression changed into worry as her brow furrowed, and she bit her bottom lip. Her eyes flickered to Zurah then back to Finn. The moment of indecision passed.

"You've got a deal. And I want a fifty-percent bonus once we're safely back in normal space."

"Done."

Normal space? Zurah questioned. *Where in the hell are we going?*

The shuttle kicked as it lifted off. "Hang on, folks. We've got some rough and tumble coming our way." Mexa's piloting skills came to life as he ducked and wove through the IGJ's orbiters, taking only minimal damage. Once the *HighTail Flyer* was clear, Mexa kicked on the overdrive engine.

2

The *HighTail Flyer* stayed dark for two days as it moved through the emptiness of space, its small crew quiet and each one concerned with their misgivings about the job. Zurah and Nissa took turns handing out Zipper-Mates, a buttery pastry packed full of protein and nutrients when normal food supplies weren't available. Finn requested updates from time to time, but otherwise, she didn't engage with the others.

When Mexa broke the silence by announcing they should arrive at Finn's coordinates within nine hours, everyone breathed a collective sigh of relief. The pilot leaned back in his chair and glanced at Nissa, who turned to look at Finn.

"I want to be there within five," Finn said.

"Not without compromising the DTA converters," Mexa replied.

"Reroute through the inner conduits then switch over to the helioplex." Finn released her harness and moved back to the rear of the ship.

"Our helioplex is cracked. On the list of upgrades," Nissa interjected.

But Mexa had already taken the suggestion, posited a few different scenarios, and returned to the controls. "It's doable. As long as we don't mind losing the backup thruster panels."

"And if we get in a tight spot?" Nissa countered.

"I'll get us out of it." Mexa shrugged, confident in his skills.

"Fine. Do it," Nissa grumbled. Her bottom lip had suffered throughout the journey, and Mexa's response had solidified Finn's authority.

But there wasn't a solid reason to argue or to reprimand Mexa. If he had protested, Finn might have decided to take matters into her own hands. Zurah knew he was playing it smart, even if Nissa wasn't liking it.

Zurah glanced over her shoulder, noting Finn was busy working on something, and she slid over to her seat and whispered, "I've been speculating on our coordinates. Where are we heading exactly?"

"Nowhere you want to know. We'll get in, drop her off, and leave," Nissa replied.

"Trust me, I want to know," Zurah said.

When Nissa didn't give up the information, Mexa did. "We're heading to the gates."

"The gates? No one goes out there. That's the dead zone."

"And no one questions Finn's business either," Mexa hissed. "Keep those pointed opinions to yourself that I know are lurking in there."

Zurah was tempted to tell him a few of her opinions, but she decided it was wiser to err on the side of silence given the circumstances. Mexa was as calm as they came, a quality Zurah greatly admired in the pilot. If he was showing signs of unease, Zurah wasn't going to add to the trouble. She leaned back and considered the secrecy—a double-edged issue in the world of smuggling.

When, why, and how to keep a secret was the initial and most important lesson all smugglers learned. Zurah had been taught the lesson as an overzealous wannabe at thirteen. Abandoned by her parents at a way station not far from Mandarin's Rhine, full of the promises they would return after securing work, Zurah had run out of credits after two weeks. She'd played the "poor me" card to various business owners, earning a meal here and there, until resorting to scavenging before being put on the radar of local security.

The environment had been brutal, each hour filled with its own set of lessons. Pushed to the edges of society without credits or adults to vouch for her, Zurah found momentary comfort in the gangs that ran in the dark recesses of the way station. She was kicked out of one small-time gang to another until she landed her first solid job as a security hack. The skills she needed challenged her and sparked her desire to learn as much as she could. With each credit she earned, she bought every manual she could get her hands on. During every free moment, she pored over the manuals, making sure to keep up on the latest trends in security systems. Over time and through blood, sweat, and tears, she built a solid reputation for herself.

But too many secrets also meant Zurah had a good chance of missing out on vital information. She returned to her seat, pulled out her portable screen, and keyed in a search for the Black Gates of Objer.

Links to the whisper nets, along with a handful of fairly credible media outlets, filled the screen. But nothing Zurah scrolled through brought up anything she didn't know. Rumors about the gates were on every known world, and everyone agreed on one fact—the gates were firmly placed in the dead zone. It was the one area of the known worlds no one ventured to. Not because a ship wasn't able to handle the distance to the dead zone but because of what came after.

Zurah shut down the screen, leaned back, and closed her eyes. The *Eagle's Nest* was a familiar story, a favorite one to rehash whenever the subject of the gates came up. It was passed around during the long nights of little work and too much drink. A story used by the old-timers to scare the young, fresh blood of their crews into remembering there were limits to what a smuggler could do. Even the most ambitious.

"We've got to keep our heads on this one. No second-guessing. We work the job like we normally do." Nissa's reassuring words broke through Zurah's thoughts.

Zurah popped open one eye then the other. "Normal? This isn't normal."

Nissa shrugged. "It may not be, but just because the dead zone is enough to test anyone's mettle doesn't mean we have to go melting down before we get to the heart of the job. The credits Finn's offering is all we need to keep us focused."

But even that thought wasn't enough to assuage Zurah's concerns. "And so we'll just go down in history as another story to be bandied about?"

Nissa's face darkened. "If Finn is paying us for this ride, then I doubt there's much risk. You really think she'd—"

"Yes, I do," Finn said.

Zurah moved out of the way as Finn slid back into her chair. "Normally, I'd ensure the crew who questioned my motivations knew the cost of doing so." She let her words hang in the air for a heartbeat before continuing. "But given the nature of this job, I will relieve a few of your concerns. Mexa, cue up the area around the gate."

The nav screen blinked and was replaced by a star chart. Without needing to ask, Mexa and Finn switched places.

"We're here," Finn said, pointing at the screen. After a second or two, she moved her finger. "And this is where the researchers first observed the gates, or rather the rogue planet most people refer to as Objer." Her finger inched forward. "Here is where Captain Ujthout and his crew were lost."

Zurah leaned forward, making sure to pay attention.

"But this is where we're headed. Where, for no reason anyone can fathom, the gates have been located for the past three hundred and forty-nine years."

"So?" Zurah asked.

"Rogue planets aren't tethered to any specific

location. They are typically free-floating anomalies. But Objer hasn't moved from this spot. But there's nothing out here to slow it down or produce any kind of gravitational effect."

Zurah considered that. "Okay. So all the more reason to stay away. Leave this kind of exploration to the scientists."

Finn nodded. "Exactly. I have a team of researchers on Objer, and one thing we know for sure is low-value equipment functions. Anything above a three-star rating gives out after a week. No one knows why, and I'm not here to hash out theories with you. What matters right now is that team of researchers. There's been a critical dump of intel I need to evaluate with my own eyes. Your job is to get me there, drop me off, and get out. Do that, and you won't have any issues. But"—Finn sat back down and made herself comfortable—"get in my way, or think there's something worth hawking out there, then I'll make sure you never return to normal space. Am I clear?"

"We're clear," Nissa said and threw Zurah her best no-nonsense look. "Drop off, get out, get paid."

Finn nodded. "Exactly. Now, I've got work to do."

And so the silence returned.

Zurah's mind sorted through the new information. Finn's words had set off a few alarm bells, along with curiosity, which she immediately pushed to the darker corners of her mind. If there was indeed a research team on Objer investigating the gates, that information would have been at the top of the results of her earlier query. Instead, there'd been nothing but rehashed and recycled information. The Little Asteroid Gang—if Finn was truly involved—had a long reach across the known worlds, but Zurah doubted even they would be able to keep something like that a secret for long. A cover-up of that magnitude meant governmental oversight, as well as a staggering amount of credits and promises being exchanged. Finn had to be involved with someone or some organization other than the Little Asteroid Gang, something else with a lot more clout.

But that little seed of curiosity didn't want to be shut away, and try as she might to avoid it, Zurah's thoughts drifted back to why. *What could the gates be or do or hold or… an endless array of things that anyone would want?* The known worlds knew of the gates' existence because of the intrepid early explorers from multiple worlds. Those individuals had dedicated their lives and often their family lineages to mapping the galaxy.

Their imaginations and drive to push farther and farther into the unknown had been sparked by nothing but grainy images from long-range telescopes. Images that were refined as technology and science improved. Those brave explorers had opened up new horizons and paved the way for thrill seekers and individuals looking to carve out a better existence or to make a name for themselves.

When those individuals reached Objer, images, vids, and reports flooded the known worlds before their ships mysteriously went dark. Scientists and world leaders had formed interspecies committees to tackle the problem, then finally, the area was simply written off as danger-ous and was dubbed the dead zone. Warning buoys had been set, and for once, a multiworld project had come together instead of crumbling into a chaos of warring ideas and factions.

Zurah's mind spun up a handful of different theories. Most centered around a remnant of a long-lost species, while some implied the whole area was simply a quirk of nature, an aspect of science no one had come to understand just yet. Many tried to find a pattern in something that wasn't there. But they all boiled down to the simple fact that no one knew for sure. Not the Jumjul, the Glipglows, or a dozen other species. And that made it all the more appealing to the whisper nets.

Finn's need for a ride and her confession of a research team had confirmed at least one thing, Zurah realized. Whatever the gates were, there was something valuable there. Something important enough Finn was willing to risk her life for.

"We'll have comms within fifteen minutes and… twelve seconds," Mexa announced. "In three hours and twenty minutes, we'll be at the coordinates you provided. Anything I need to be aware of in landing? Is there a docking ring, or is this a free maneuver?"

"There should be a docking ring, but be prepared in case there are complications," Finn replied. "Signal the team we're coming in hot once we hit range."

"Yes, sir," Mexa replied.

The fifteen minutes passed in a blur, and Zurah's fingers made a significant increase in the hole she'd found on the side of her chair.

"This is the *HighTail Flyer*. We're headed your way with a three-hour ETA. Anyone copy?"

There was a pop and the sound of static. Then came a reply. "This is Alpha Team Six. We're picking up your signal. Confirm bio ID."

Finn stood up and hit the button. "Bio ID confirmation gamma, eleven, thirteen, roger, twenty-seven, star haven."

Zurah's ears perked up at that. *Bio IDs don't typically end that way. Who in the known worlds is she?*

"Please hold while we confirm Bio ID."

Zurah was watching Finn like a hawk and caught the subtle lifting of the woman's shoulders and the slight shift forward of her upper body at the response.

"Bio ID is confirmed. All teams have been downgraded to green status. Backup is not currently required. You are advised to turn around."

"Negative, a priority-one distress call was issued. I will be personally inspecting the site."

"All teams have been downgraded to green status. Backup is not currently required. You are advised to turn around."

With another slight shift forward, Finn replied, "Negative. Get me the team leader. Now."

"The team leader is currently in a meeting. Please be advised all teams have been downgraded to green status. Backup is not currently required."

"Prepare for docking. I'll confirm status with team leader—in person."

There was a slight squeal as someone on the other end must have hit the wrong button in their haste to cut the signal, followed by a few seconds of nervous chatter before the line went silent. Then abruptly, the comms flared back to life. "We read you loud and clear. Please note the docking ring is currently cycled down for maintenance. Please adjust your heading and prepare for manual landing at these coordinates. Repeat and confirm."

After a curt nod from Finn, Mexa did as requested and received the all clear.

Finn settled back in her chair. Faint furrows showed on her forehead, and her lips were pressed together.

"Weapons?" Nissa asked.

There was a pause—perhaps a bit too long—before Finn replied, "Yes."

"Right," Nissa mumbled. "Winters, prep our gear. Mexa, everything in working order?"

"Yuppers."

Zurah stood and made her way to the back, pulling out the hidden panel where the higher-grade gear was stored. She took stock of the conventional handheld guns and an array of Vulture and black market Jumjul knockoff tech. "Shadow play or up front?" she called out.

"Shadow play," Finn replied for Nissa.

Zurah settled on two Vultures and Nissa's latest acquisition—a DC-2-39 Growler, hot off the assembly line. The new line of weaponry incorporated the Glipglow's ability to cram multiple pieces of tech into an incredibly tiny space and piggyback off Jumjul weaponry and coding tech.

Slipping one of the Vultures onto her wrist, she saved the other one for Nissa. The Eagle was Mexa's baby. If the weapon had first-gen bugs to deal with, that was his area of expertise. Zurah glanced back at the hidden compartment, briefly considering grabbing something for Finn, but she decided Finn was undoubtedly equipped with her own style of shadow play.

"I'm reading a few other signals bouncing around out there," Mexa reported.

"Show me," Finn said, and Nissa leaned over to get a better look, as well.

"I can't quite get a firm grip on all of the signals, but I'd say they're playing fast and loose with their comms."

"Switch places with me," Finn ordered.

Mexa started to stand, but Nissa held out her hand.

"Hold on. You might be paying us for this little trip, and no doubt most of the rumors are true, but this is my ship. My pilot. If we hit trouble, I want someone at the helm who knows how to handle this bird."

Zurah tensed, ready for a potential confrontation. But all Finn did was give Nissa an appraising look and sit back down.

"Scan the area for other landing sites," Finn said.

"Looks like there would be two other suitable spots. Not far off from the original coordinates. Roughly eight hundred meters and…" Mexa paused as he redid the calculations. "And twelve hundred meters."

"The second site would work," Finn replied. "But only if there's trouble. If not, we head where we were told."

"Understood."

"What kind of trouble?" Zurah spoke up. "If we're heading into something you've got concerns about, a little heads-up would be appreciated. And if we need to crack a few shells, I need to have some info."

The polished and calm exterior Finn had clearly perfected over the years was beginning to show signs of wear and tear. "To be perfectly frank? I'm not sure. Just years of gut instincts, which have kept me alive." She adjusted a part of her suit. "My research team was handpicked and thoroughly vetted. The crews who provide the shipments of supplies—same deal. And they're under strict orders to hand off the supplies to the shuttles while in orbit then get out. No one hangs around. If their ships have issues, they limp out of the dead zone to find help. My team has orders to ensure no one stays."

"And the priority-one distress call?" Nissa asked.

"A last-case emergency. And I do mean last case."

None of Finn's words were comforting, nor did they provide Zurah with any information. She was about to ask a few more questions when Mexa switched the large screen over to real-time visual. A solid hunk of twisted rock sprang into view.

"I'm getting a strange reading coming off the landing site," Mexa said. "Nissa, can you confirm?"

"Rescanning the target," Nissa said. "Any chance of something in the area that can throw up gunk in the signals?"

"Not that I've been briefed," Finn replied. "Head off to the second site you mentioned. We'll land there. Any comms come through, keep silent."

"Will do," Mexa said.

"Winters, I'm sending you a copy of these readings. See if you can make sense of them and if they're something we need to keep an eye out for," Nissa said.

Zurah blinked and brought up her SeeClear tech, which was paired with a subdermal receiver node. *At last, something I can—*

"I'll add on a second bonus for you and your crew if you agree to stay on. I chose your ship because of its rating, below what might get crippled out here. You should be safe for at least up to two weeks." Finn's cool voice interrupted Zurah's concentration.

"Hold on," she said. "Two weeks?"

"Can it," Nissa snapped. "Is this truly an offer? One we can refuse? Or merely trying to soften the blow that you've stranded us out here?"

"A true offer. You have my word," Finn said.

Nissa gave Finn a shrewd look but nodded. "All right. Then allow us the courtesy to discuss for a few moments. Mexa, back off and hold position."

Finn didn't hesitate. She stood and headed to the back. Zurah was confident she carried bioupgrades that would allow her to hear their conversation, but the gesture of privacy was a small comfort.

"First up, Mexa," Nissa said.

He leaned back in his chair then swiveled around to be able to see both members of his crew. His pale-green eyes studied their boss. "No qualms here. But I'm an oldie. Bound to meet my maker on one of these jobs. Why not here?"

"Winters?"

Zurah wasn't sure what to say. *If I say my gut was telling me no, then what will the others really do?* It wasn't like they could drop her off somewhere then scoop her up after the job was done. But saying no also signaled she wasn't going to be a team player, and that could lead to cracks within the small crew. If Nissa had run a larger operation, they might be able to afford a few cracks here and there but not with only three of them. And not all the way out in the dead zone. Whatever was going down, they would have to have each other's backs.

"I'm in," Zurah answered. "But what about you?"

Nissa's left fingers tapped in a cascading rhythm against the console. "Not loving our odds, to be honest," Nissa confessed. "But this is what we do. The odds are never stacked in our favor." Turning back to face the front, she called out, "We're in."

Finn moved with a slow, measured pace back to her seat. "Good. I'm assuming your gear is suitable for thin atmo?"

"Yup," Nissa replied. "Latest coming out of Egor's Trade Shops. Suits hold a week's worth of charge and can be modded for a wide variety of scenarios. Including armor."

"Glad to hear it," Finn said. While Nissa and her crew were conversing, Finn had changed into a suit of her own. She adjusted the screen embedded on the left forearm of the suit, and a soft yellow glow appeared at the seams. "It shouldn't need said, but we go in under extreme caution. Whatever tricks your suits have, I'd start at the max. Once we've scouted the area, we can downgrade as needed. Agreed?"

"Agreed," the others echoed.

Mexa politely let Nissa and Winters change first. The suits were brand-new. Nissa had spent quite a bit of time trying to get Egor to come down on the price, but the merchant had insisted the tech was top of the line and clean. No bugs in the works—in fact, he had staked his reputation on it.

Zurah ran her hand down the smooth exterior of the ArmorTex Flex and Hold suit then slipped one foot inside, followed by the other. The suit didn't catch or bunch up on the biotech-infused undersuit, which was a step up from the previous model. For a split second, the suit hung off her body, but as it sprang to life, the smart material scanned her then tailored itself to her measurements. It was snug but not overly so. She twisted back and forth then reached down and touched her toes. She was pleased to find she still had her full range of motion.

Satisfied with the fit, Zurah brought up the schematics and noted how the suit was already taking into account her unique nutritional needs, setting up the output-waste-system converter, and pairing with the weapons. The system took into account her human anatomy, and when she plugged in to the ship's air valve, the suit's reserve tanks were filled with air suitable for her biology. The addition of reserve tanks was a comfort to Zurah, as she had always felt leery of relying on a suit's ability to convert unsuitable air into something breathable.

Before she and Nissa headed back to the front, Nissa reached out and stopped her. Her hand slid down to her thigh, where she tapped out instructions. *Comm 2 for the three of us. Tighten it up. Then tag Finn for Comm 3. Clear? Clear.*

As she and Nissa once more took their seats, Zurah

flipped through the rest of the setup. The suit had shielding capabilities, along with reinforced plating for critical areas or soft targets. Its system registered the Vulture and synced with the weapon's systems. Once the sync was complete, Zurah went through the options on customizing how she wanted to set up controls. Making a quick decision, she linked the Vulture's control through the suit and into her SeeClear tech, running through the blink and eye-movement commands. Once Mexa was suited up, they keyed their adaptable AI network and connected their suits. Then Zurah secured the comm channels.

"Preparing landing procedures… now," Mexa said. "Switching over to manual controls."

"Anything pinging?" Finn asked.

Nissa bent over the controls, scanning through the ship's readouts.

Zurah caught the faint furrowing of Nissa's brow. "What's up?"

"Not sure. May just be a ghost signal or some kind of strange interference since we're in the dead zone. But look—" She shook her head. "Well, whatever it was, it's gone now."

"Concerns?" Finn asked.

"No. Just a ghost reading. Everything reads standard, just those random comm signals we picked up on earlier and a variety of energy readouts."

"When we land, secure the shuttle and follow my lead."

"Roger," Nissa responded then turned so she faced away from Finn. "Winters? Once we're secure down there, I want you sorting through this jumble. We need to know about any traps before we spring them."

"Read you loud and clear," Zurah replied.

Mexa guided the ship down with only a slight lurch as it touched the ground. He powered down the main engines then flipped the ship over to standing security mode.

"Remember, follow my lead." Finn took up position by the door.

The locks disengaged, and the door slid open as Nissa and Mexa moved to stand just behind Finn on either side, with Zurah bringing up the rear. A rocky landscape opened up before them. The horizon was dotted with dark and strangely shaped hills. Scans revealed a barren landscape devoid of life. Finn gave the all clear, and the small group carefully moved out, following Finn as she took the lead. Less than a kilometer from the ship, a row of heavily armored individuals rose up out of the terrain to greet them.

3

Finn muttered a few unsavory phrases, while the other three brought up their weapon systems. "Behind me. Do not get in front of me." The air in front of Finn shimmered then rippled with an iridescent pearl-like coating.

Zurah was impressed. She'd drooled over the Trickster shield upgrade on more than one occasion. The bit of tech had been born out of pure human ingenuity, taking existing shielding technology and adding their own twist. When the tech had debuted, no one could keep it on their shelves long enough to get dusty.

A Trickster shield was designed to be visible to the wearer and those placed behind them as a clear marker of where not to breach or else destroy the entire ruse. Each shield could be customized with five different scenarios, able to project whatever images the owner or the situation called for.

As Zurah's attention was momentarily diverted, she

wished only one thing—that for a split second, she could be on the other side of the shield. She had never understood why the engineers had created the tech to project the images to only those in front of the Trickster. Anyone standing behind it had no idea what the images were. Except now, as her focus resumed, she wondered if that was a design flaw or a purposeful tactic. Because those behind the shield couldn't see the projections, they maintained a clear view of what lay ahead.

Zurah wished she was seeing something different. Each individual wore a top-of-the-line armored suit, and from her first sensor sweep, the gear was heavily peppered with military tech.

One of the armored individuals toward the middle raised a fist, and the unit stopped. "This isn't a designated landing site," a voice crackled through an open comm line.

"I have the authority to land wherever I see fit," Finn replied.

"That may be so, but your presence isn't required here. Apologies have been passed on that these orders were handed out too late."

"I'm funding this research team. I believe that supersedes any previous or future order."

"Your presence here isn't required."

Zurah glanced nervously at Nissa, but her boss was at full attention, weapons hot.

"That insignia on your suit means that you are under my authority. Stand down or be removed."

A bead of sweat formed on Zurah's brow, threatening to roll down dangerously close to her eye. She looked again at Nissa and switched over to Comm 2. "If this goes sideways, we don't stand a chance."

"This isn't anything we can't handle. Our suits can withstand quite a bit of damage. If anything happens, Mexa and I will cover you. Can you hack their suits?"

That reply didn't settle well with Zurah, but at least it gave her something else to focus on. She blinked twice to activate the SeeClear tech. She ran a quick scan, looking for a way to cut through the opposition's defenses. Codes and various programs the scan had detected scrolled through her periphery. There were a couple of ways she could attack the problem, but they would take time.

Just pick the fastest one. Give Nissa options.

Zurah looked again then identified a hole in the coding. It was a small glitch indicating the suits hadn't received an update in well over three months, but it was a vulnerability Zurah could take advantage of. As she got to work, the SeeClear tech brought up a new result—an unusual reading that didn't match anything she was familiar with. It hadn't come from the armored suits directly but was something they'd received. With a few rapid eye movements, Zurah set the SeeClear tech to keep a low-profile search running and to ping if there were any matches or more unusual activity.

As she continued to work, she realized that several of the suits were also showing erratic energy patterns, as if their power sources were on the fritz. She zeroed in on the reading and concluded the suits were failing.

Not being upgraded wouldn't cause that. And they're not showing significant signs of damage. Why am I seeing this? Zurah couldn't picture sloppy maintenance, no self-respecting person who signed up to come to a place like this would allow their suit to fall in such disrepair. "I think I've got a way in, boss."

"Good, we still might need it. For now, it looks like Finn is going to let them take us in," Nissa said.

"Why not fly?" Zurah asked, having missed a significant portion of the conversation.

"Finn didn't bring it up as an option. And I agree. Better to have something outside of… whatever this is. Looks like we're on the move."

Finn had holstered her weapon, while Nissa and Mexa had merely lowered theirs. Zurah briefly considered both options and decided to holster hers. She was a security hack, not muscle, and if she could get her hands on one of the suits in a worst-case scenario, she could do a lot more damage than wielding a weapon.

"Where's Turner?" Finn asked as the soldiers moved to flank Finn and the others.

"Currently unavailable," came the gruff reply.

"Doing what?" she pressed.

"A meeting."

"And Angelina?" Finn asked.

There was a brief pause, then the open comm line crackled. "This is Angelina."

"The moon hung low in the sky, its pale light casting shadows across the broad river of our ancestors," Finn replied.

"Correction," Angelina said. "The moon slung low within the cloudless sky, its pale light casting not a shadow across the wide river of the ancestors." There was a brief pause. "Your continual need for code work from me is growing—"

"Tiresome? As is receiving a distress signal then being told, 'Whoops, sorry, turn around and go away.' What the hell is going on?"

"Your people were simply trying to not waste your time. They know you've got multiple projects running, and they're not ready for you to come out and do some hands-on work."

"Bullshit," Finn snapped.

There was a pause. "Look, I'm—"

"I didn't just receive *one* distress signal. I was sent *two*."

"I don't see how that would be possible. Let me talk with IT and—"

"Don't you want to know who sent the second distress call?" Finn asked.

"I'm sure it was nothing more than a glitch in the system. I'll check with IT and get back with you. Should have an answer by the time you hit the perimeter. Angelina out."

The group walked in silence for a few minutes before Nissa switched to Comm 3. "Who sent the second distress signal?"

For a moment, it appeared as though Finn wouldn't answer, but then a single name came through the line. "Alex."

"Alex who?" Nissa quietly asked.

"Alex Goldsmith."

Zurah stopped in midstride, incredulous. "Goldsmith?"

There was a gentle but firm touch to the middle of her back to keep her moving.

"Yes," Finn muttered. "Typical, always thinking he has to watch over my shoulder." Finn stopped then changed subjects. "Look, the deal hasn't changed, but the parameters of this mission have."

"As we weren't clear on our jobs in the first place, I'm not sure how much of a difference that makes," Nissa said. "But I'm getting the feeling things are going to go from bad to worse fast. What intel can you provide?"

The flutter of unease in Zurah's belly turned into a hard knot in her chest. If she were Nissa, she would turn around and leave. Break the deal. They were wading into waters too deep for the team. Even if they disregarded the rumors surrounding Finn, getting tangled up with the Goldsmith Consortium was a bad idea. Everyone knew once someone was involved with the Consortium, they were hooked for life.

"Briefly. I'm currently running a team which is working on researching the gates and surrounding ruins. This team has been stationed here for over a year. I handpicked the best of the best from all over the known worlds. The mission was to unravel the secrets of the gates and, in doing so, figure out what happened to the *Eagle's Nest* and her crew.

"I've been pleased with the progress so far and had scheduled a run out this way in a few months. From the reports I'd been receiving, the team was getting close to a breakthrough. Then I received the distress calls and knew I needed to head out as quickly as possible.

This mission has to succeed." Finn stopped, and they walked in silence, each one digesting the information.

"But why use us?" Zurah couldn't help but ask, and she didn't need to look at Nissa to know the woman would be frowning at her question.

Finn shrugged. "Simple. I've been under surveillance for the past few months. A meet and greet for another project I have running had been set at Rockerton's. But the IGJ was alerted, and I had to make do with what was before me. And as a bonus, none of you have a vested interest in what's going on here, plus no ties to any of my competitors."

Another question formed for Zurah. "So why didn't Angelina cop to who the other distress signal was from? I'm assuming the level of security you have out here would've seen the ping."

"A good question, and one I need to figure out," Finn said. "At the best of times, Angelina is cautious with how and to whom she shares her information. So either she knows something and didn't want to say through the comms, or else she doesn't, and Alex is holed up somewhere out here. The implications of both scenarios aren't good."

"Any idea what we're walking into?" Mexa asked.

"Unsure. Could be a coup, a malfunction they don't want to have to admit to, or any number of scenarios," Finn said. "But as before, follow my lead. These are my people, and my choices for security and systems were put in place out here."

And that was that. Finn refused to answer any more questions.

"Boss?" Mexa asked Nissa on Comm 2. There was an edge of uncertainty in the single word.

"We stay on point… for now," Nissa replied quietly.

Zurah considered those words. Nissa never backed out of a job and had a solid reputation of seeing her commitments through.

"We follow Finn's lead. I doubt she's ready to kick off, and has a few tricks up her sleeves," Nissa added.

Zurah couldn't help but wonder who she was trying to reassure—herself or them.

"Doesn't mean she won't find a no-win situation at some point," Mexa said.

"But that's a gamble we all take with this life," Nissa countered. "If we weren't comfortable with that, then none of us would be here right now."

"I'll take your best guess as to what we're walking into then," Mexa pressed.

Nissa shrugged. "A competitor playing around with her workers? Alex possibly trying to set her up somehow? Maybe show Finn as incompetent or simply trying to offer a better payout. Credits talk, no matter who you are or what ideals you think you hold."

"If that's the case, then why are we sticking our nose in where it obviously doesn't belong?" Zurah asked. "I don't have any interest in adding the Consortium to my no-go list. Or any list for that matter."

"I'd have to agree," Mexa murmured, which was another startling revelation for Zurah. Mexa was usually solid. He rarely disagreed or raised concerns.

"We follow Finn's lead," Nissa said stubbornly. "Keep sharp."

4

Zurah sank her worries into sorting through codes, creating a solid back door into their escorts' suits. With a quick flip of a switch, she would be able to power down weapons for fifty-five seconds. In an extreme emergency, she could completely shut down the suits for at least thirty seconds before their systems would be forced to reboot. Both options would give Nissa or the others enough time to gain the upper hand or to find cover. Of course finding cover in the inhospitable terrain of Objer would be tricky. The landscape was nothing but dust, large boulders, and hills with the vast void of space stretching out before them. There was no atmosphere to scatter light, so there was nothing but black surrounding the small party.

Satisfied with one job completed, Zurah started to sort through the other reports. A lot of strange energy signatures floated through the air, along with comm chatter between their escorts. She was ready to tackle the strange readings she had picked up on earlier when the group came to an abrupt halt. Closing out of the list of files in her periphery, Zurah switched over to recording as the leader reached out and raised his hand. He held it steady against something she couldn't make out until a flash of neon-orange hexagonal netting sprouted from the ground, pushing out in all directions.

Holy smoke flares, a SmartTec 5.6 Security Grid. The latest in security nets from Confore Tech, with integrated comms and alert systems, the nets were said to have four different levels of deterrents and were even able to withstand heavy artillery for up to forty-eight hours. *Finn isn't playing around.*

Zurah scrambled to cast a dispersal net and capture the chatter between the suit and the security net, and she watched in fascination as one of the hexagons expanded, and a screen appeared in its center. The leader keyed in the code, and a narrow opening in the grid appeared.

As they slipped through, Zurah let her fingers brush up against the grid and added that data dump to everything else she was capturing. The grid had to employ a wide range of biometrics, and she needed to try to grab as much information as she could. SmartTec grids employed heavy security to enter and exit, and that meant there were no easy exits. If they needed to make a hasty exit, she would need to crack the grid. Nissa and Mexa would be depending on her being able to do that.

The challenge sent a small thrill of anticipation through her. With a confident grin, she started to contact Nissa to let her know she was already on top of a backup plan when her jaw about hit the ground. The empty landscape had dropped away, revealing the reality hidden by the security grid.

Looming off in the distance were the gates, monstrous blocks stacked on top of each other, gradually reducing in size as they stretched toward the emptiness of space. Zurah estimated the foundation of each pillar was at least the width of five or six of her lying out head to toe. The media and popular sites had only grainy pictures of the gates, always out of focus or with too little detail for people to really understand how massive the structure was. The curious and the dreamers had created a plethora of imaginative vids, but nothing anyone had dreamed up or tried to extrapolate from the historical archives did justice to seeing them in real time.

To the right were other impressive structures. Though not as tall as the gates, massive rocks were scattered about as if someone or something had been constructing more pillars then decided to topple everything over in a fit of rage. And to the left, single blocks of rocks were scattered across the landscape.

A hand touched Zurah's shoulder, and she jumped. Nissa huffed then glanced down at her hand. She tapped, *Did you get it?*

For a split second, Zurah felt confused then rather stupid. The first rule in their line of work was to not get distracted by shiny things. Zurah nodded and tapped back an affirmative. As she settled her mind and got back to work, she noted that her suit had continued to scan in the background and was relaying an overwhelming amount of information. There were hundreds of energy spikes, anomalous readings, and strings of code floating through the air. Zurah would have expected that type of chaos in the center of a major city or a trade area, but even then she doubted there would be quite as many readings.

She homed in on one of the stranger readings and noted that its signal was gradually getting stronger. "Hey, Nissa. Can you do a quick scan and see if—"

"Stay here." Finn veered off abruptly.

Two of the armored suits followed at a discreet distance, while the rest stayed with Nissa and her crew.

Zurah's programs chimed, indicating a new source of activity. She turned to watch Finn and realized someone was heading to meet her. Blinking, she zoomed in. Despite the distance, as her vision was enhanced, Zurah felt a knot grow in her belly. Whoever was wearing the suit moved with long, confident strides and had no escort. The suit appeared to be top-of-the-line, unlike the worn-down armored suits worn by those who'd greeted them, but it wasn't giving off any of the usual readings she would pick up from another suit. Zooming in once more, she initiated a routine sweep of the unknown suit.

The report was inconclusive. The materials were unknown, and the energy and strange signals bouncing around it were atypical. Another anomaly. The logical answer was modification to accommodate how Objer impacted tech. *But why aren't I seeing these readings from everyone?*

Zurah decided she would need to be closer to run a more thorough assessment. And despite her trepidation, a part of her itched to do that. The suit was impressive, with nearly invisible seams, and it appeared to fit like a dream. Both sleeves had embedded screens, and the slight haze surrounding the individual indicated the suit had its own personal shielding.

Probably another reason for mucking up my analysis. Clever.

"What do you think?" Nissa asked quietly.

"I'd say a quick survey ain't a bad thing," Mexa replied.

"Agreed," Zurah added.

"How's remote control looking?" Nissa asked.

Mexa glanced at the control panel embedded in his suit's left forearm. "Signal's at half strength but enough to do the job if needed. But we'd have to factor in leg time. While I can communicate with the ship, there's no way it's going to be able to punch through that shield."

"Winters?"

Zurah shook her head. "Not yet. I got as much information as I could, but that grid is going to take time to hack. And it might require a hookup into an actual system to do so. I don't know yet."

"All right. When you've got the opportunity, do what you need to in order to get into their systems. Untraceable. Create a back door for us."

"Will do," Zurah replied. "I've already got a small one in our friends around here if need be. Just give me the order, and I can flip the switch."

"Excellent. Mexa, keep us up and running. Minimal power drain, but I want options hot and ready. This credit dump is a dream come true, but I think we're all aware of how easily this job is going to go sideways. It's not a question of if but a matter of when."

Zurah turned her attention back in the direction Finn had gone, still curious about the mysterious suit. Finn was standing next to the unknown individual and was punctuating the air with her hands. Zurah's suit spit out another report, and she frowned. The anomalous signal was morphing into something she had never seen before. She tapped her screen and brought up the menu, making sure to capture the bizarre readings. She added a background analysis program with both her suit's programming and the SeeClear tech. When finished, Zurah glanced back toward Finn, but the enigmatic woman was standing alone on the crest of the hill. Slowly, Finn turned, as if considering something, and made her way back toward the group.

"Keep going," Finn's voice crackled through the comms.

"Intel?" Nissa asked. "We need parameters if we're going to be at all effective for you."

"Nothing verifiable, but behaviors aren't adding up," she responded quietly.

"That sounds more like gut intuition than intel we can actively use," Nissa said with a hint of a challenge. "You're continually asking my team to put ourselves at risk on scant little intel. How do you expect us to be of use?"

"And if I hadn't believed you were up to the challenge, I would have bailed the second we landed," Finn said. "We're headed to the base. I'll find Turner to get a handle on what's happening while the three of you gather intel. Three pairs of eyes with no prior biases is exactly what I need at the moment. Afterward, we'll debrief. Make sure to keep this comm channel clear, and I'll provide updates as needed. I need to assess the damage, and right now, the three of you are at the top of my list for allies. I've made sure all of my employees are well compensated for their time, but this type of work does lend itself to a nebulous gray area. I can't take the chance of believing everyone will remain loyal. What I do know for sure is that this is going to be a bumpy ride. So buckle up and stay alert."

"Understood," Nissa replied then switched comms. "As she said, stay alert. Winters, anything you need from us to help create some options, just let us know."

"Will do," Zurah replied.

Ignoring the massive blocks of stone as they continued to wind their way across the inhospitable terrain, Zurah returned to doing what she did best. She began sorting and isolating codes and programs she recognized, ranking them from the easiest hack to the hardest. Once done, she tackled the hardest hacks first, those that would require more time and attention. The easier ones, she knew she could do on the go if needed, and they weren't going to require any special hookup into a larger system.

Unfortunately, the one at the top of the list was the strangest of the lot. As she read through the information her SeeClear tech and suit had both provided, Zurah knew she had a puzzle on her hands. In the right place and with an infinite amount of time, she would relish the opportunity to crack something new—to take it apart, figure out how it all went together, and find the weaknesses where she could insert her own codes for future use. She considered the possibility that she was looking at an entirely new type of security system—a program that perhaps worked on scrambling or masking intel. If that was the case, then she would need some type of cypher. Of course, there was also the chance that what she was seeing was a result of being in the dead zone. The area affected technology, so it would make sense that the data she collected would also be affected.

"Whoa," Nissa said through the comms, and the party stopped.

Before them was a goliath-class cargo ship, half buried in the rocky landscape.

"I thought those things were defunct? Scrapped after Old Earth made nice with the Glipglows and tech significantly changed?" Mexa asked.

"The majority of the ships were, yes. But a few were maintained by select individuals," Finn answered.

"And by *select*, you mean *stinking rich*." Nissa snorted.

Finn turned and threw her an amused look. "Of course."

"And the fact that it's actually half buried?"

"A creative way to utilize its loss. Its systems have all been upgraded, and I was aware using it to haul my people and equipment out here would be a one-way trip. Now it serves as our headquarters and living area. Burying it like that helped to mask its signal from anyone who might happen to come by," Finn said as she started down the hill.

Zurah couldn't wrap her head around someone willfully doing that to a ship of that size. Or monetary value. The early goliath-class systems were legendary and therefore worth more credits than Zurah could imagine. The ships were an early testament to humanity's ingenuity as they moved beyond their solar system. Intrepid explorers had given up everything to reach for the stars. They were brave men and women who had known exactly what they were sacrificing when they set off in search of new planets and new life.

An image flashed before Zurah's eyes, and she quickly tried to shake it. She remembered her parents. Her mom had been a wizard with old tech, and she'd told Zurah stories about humanity's early ships, igniting Zurah's imagination. When it had been obvious her parents weren't coming back for her, those first few days she had told herself she was one of those early pioneers, braving the vast emptiness of space, waiting to find the perfect place to call home.

"Coming?" Nissa called out when she saw Zurah wasn't following them.

"Yeah, wouldn't miss it," she mumbled. She scrambled down the hill and joined the group as they headed toward one of the smaller cargo bay entrances.

As they got closer, Zurah noted that the doors had been reconfigured. Part of the ship's interior had been taken out and put to use as a small guard station. She targeted the station, taking note of the biometrics embedded in the upper arch.

"Where's the guard?" Finn asked on the general comm channel.

"Retasked," came the gruff answer. "Angelina's orders are for you to—"

Finn stopped. "I know where I'm going. Your duty is finished. Leave us."

Two of the armored suits flanking them raised their weapons.

"That's an order. Until it's her name on those contracts you signed, I'm still in charge."

Nissa signaled Zurah, and she brought up the coding to shut down the suits. Finn stepped toward the armored suit closest to her.

"Is this how you're going to play it? Remember Gray Rocks and what I did for you and your family, Montgomery," Finn said quietly.

There was a tense moment, then the guard waved a hand. The unit turned and ducked into the half-buried ship.

"I remember. But sometimes it's not about who has the most credits to sling around. There are other ways to motivate individuals." He turned and followed his unit.

"What have you got?" Finn asked them.

"Excuse me?" Nissa asked.

"Your tech. While I'm off debriefing Turner," Finn said as she walked past the guard's station. "I'm going to give you full access to my ship. Do what you do best. Break it apart piece by piece and find the secrets no one is telling me. Something isn't right, and I need to know what."

Nissa listed the gear they carried and the upgrades they had requested with the suits, but she was careful to leave out the more creative programs each of them had designed to suit their skill set.

Finn appeared satisfied. "Good." She touched a peculiar dent in the side of the ship then counted off eleven long strides. She stopped, turned toward the hull of the ship, then pressed her hand against its side. A small panel popped open. "Before we head inside, we need to spoof your suits. If your movements are tagged throughout the ship, it won't do us any good." She input a few codes. "Nissa, I'm going to tag you with command. That will give you full access to the ship. Mexa, let's set you up as a researcher. And you—" She turned to study Zurah. "We'll do medical. That will give you access to most terminals."

Nissa tapped her thigh, and Zurah stepped up first.

"Do you mind if I…?" Zurah asked.

Finn waved her hand and took a step back. "No. Do whatever you need to do."

Zurah looked at the program Finn had keyed up and double-checked the code. "Looks secure."

Once they were tagged, Finn closed the program and activated a small access hatch. "I'm going to go in through the front doors. I can set up my suit so it appears the three of you did so, as well. But I'm going to have you enter through here. You'll come out in a small engineering bay, and from there, head out into the main corridors. Clear?"

"Clear," Nissa said with Mexa and Zurah echoing her.

"Do what you need to. Figure out what they're not telling me. When I'm finished with Turner, I'll ping you with coordinates for a meetup." She started to head back to the guard's station, stopped, and turned to study the three of them. "I don't say this lightly. But right now, the three of you are the three I trust. Don't let me down." Then she spun on her heel and left.

5

"Not quite what I was expecting," Nissa muttered as they crawled through the access hatch. "Routine sweeps up and running."

Once inside, they got to work. Zurah made sure their suits' network was connected and secured before she set up an automatic update program. That way, any information they collected would be shared between the three of them.

"I count forty-seven within the ship," Nissa said. "Not many for the scale of operations it appears Finn set up."

"There could always be workers out at the site," Mexa offered. "I'm not picking up on much beyond this ship. It appears there is some type of dampening field at play. Could also be masking the numbers."

"Possible, but I would still expect a lot more personnel in the rotations," Nissa said. "Not only for the research but for all of the support personnel as well. This ship may not be up for traveling through space again, but there's still a lot of maintenance and oversight that would be required to not have things devolve into chaos."

"I'll need to move through the ship to get a better map," Mexa said. "Are we splitting or staying?"

"Winters?" Nissa asked instead of immediately answering her pilot.

"The security appears standard, even a bit subpar. I had expected more systems in line like the grid we came through. Finn doesn't strike me as someone who is going to leave things to chance," Zurah said. "I should have most of their systems cracked within the hour. Once I do, I can ping you guys what you'd need if you get in a jam." She sent them the coding to shut down the armored suits. "Here's something to use if all else fails. I'm guessing it'll work once, maybe twice, then the suits' systems should begin to compensate and undo my handiwork."

Nissa bit her lip and considered their options. "I'm not keen on splitting up when we have so little intel. But in order to get the intel we need, we'll have a better chance doing that reconnaissance on our own. And we don't know how much time we have until Finn pulls us back in. We need answers, not only for ourselves but for Finn."

"These suits' range should be adequate enough," Mexa said.

"Agreed." Zurah added, "Give me a sec… There. Our signal's boosted for the time being. You should see us on the map Mexa has provided."

"All right, then we'll split. Find out what you can and feed it into our system. I want us all playing with a full deck on this job," Nissa said. "Mexa, your first priority is to find at least two fallback positions and a couple of different ways out of the ship. Set up rendezvous coordinates not far from the grid. Winters, I want to be able to slip in out and of that grid, if need be, and to fully ghost this ship. I don't care what Finn said. We need a full whiteout. Meanwhile, I'll dig into personnel records and history logs, see if I can fill in everything Finn isn't telling us. Especially concerning this issue with the Consortium. Clear?"

Mexa and Zurah nodded, and they all headed off in different directions. Zurah considered her options. Ideally, she needed a terminal or workstation to gain access to the system. But finding a place to do so without bringing attention to herself would be difficult.

Casually, she wandered to the end of the corridor and, in a stroke of luck, noted a screen flare to life as she passed by. A directory. She smiled and shook her head in wonder. *Don't people know how easy these things make my job?*

She scanned through the files. Command would be ideal but was too out in the open and prone to risk being questioned. Even the research desks would be a considerable risk without any real knowledge about what Finn was doing here. Zurah wouldn't have the faintest clue where to start on bluffing her way into one of those work areas. She continued scrolling through the list until she saw the perfect location—the residential decks. This was a human-designed ship, and in her experience, all humans longed to maintain connection with their loved ones. There would, no doubt, be nooks and crannies tucked away on those decks where a person could slip in, check messages, and compose new ones.

When Zurah had been all alone, holed up in the rooms her parents had paid for after leaving her, she had recorded her fair share of messages to them. At first, she had been bright and sunny, pretending she was having a grand old adventure and documenting her discoveries. She had sat there, in a chair just a hair too big for her slight frame, and regaled her parents about the exotic food she had tried, the vids she had watched, and the various species she had bumped into on her explorations. After it had become clear her parents weren't returning for her, she had recorded messages for them for a time after that—heartfelt pleas for them to come and get her, concerns that maybe something horrible had happened. And as she'd become entangled with the different gangs and crews, she had gradually stopped recording messages altogether.

Zurah had also discovered how common that was. When she hacked into security systems, there would often be private messages awaiting delivery or private vid diaries. When a job was long and boring, with nothing for her to do for hours on end, she sometimes watched them, curious to see how other people had lived.

When she reached the residential decks, Zurah started to see a few personnel. She nodded and continued on. No one stopped her. Relieved to have passed the first few hurdles without any difficulty, she slowed her stride, and her shoulders relaxed. Hitting the junction to the next deck, she ran into a cluster of workers. At first glance, she thought they might beckon her over, but one of the taller workers—who appeared to have Telt ancestry—turned his back to her and bent over. The group's voices lowered to a whisper, and she caught more than a few nervous glances her way.

Shrugging it off, she kept going until she found a little nook tucked off to one side of the corridor. She took a seat, engaging the privacy shield, and powered up the station. It was a standard hard-wired comm station, connected to the neural network interlaced throughout the ship. There was a library of sorts, complete with ship schematics, how-tos, work-arounds, and general help desk information.

Satisfied the computer would meet her needs, Zurah reached into her pocket and pulled out a small disc. She stuck it to the underside of the station, and in a matter of seconds, Zurah was hooked into the network.

With ease, she bypassed the security measures, spoofing the system, and started to dig through the files until she hit what she needed. Despite the secrecy of what Finn was trying to accomplish, the ship hadn't been built with such duplicitous ideation in mind. Zurah didn't encounter too many buried networks or walled-off files, and what she did come across, she easily slipped through.

Sloppy, she couldn't help but think. If she had been in charge of security, no one would have been able to hack into the ship's systems. Then again, Finn had a reputation that screamed, "If you double-cross me, it'll be the last thing you do."

Zurah worked her way to the security files concerning

the grid. That was her first priority. Without a way to get out, they would be trapped. The first layer wasn't too difficult to hack. She embedded a few codes, created back doors, and moved on to the next layer. The experience was surprisingly easier than she had expected. Next, she worked on ensuring a complete whiteout for the three of them. Finn's spoof was helpful, but Zurah agreed with Nissa. Being able to move through the ship as a ghost would be far handier. Once she finished up with the part of her job that ensured they could escape with little pushback, Zurah leaned back and smiled at her handiwork, knowing she excelled at the work. Precious few other security hacks could do what she did.

Next, she pinged Nissa and Mexa, making sure they got the necessary access codes in case something happened to her or they were separated. Then she started to dig. They needed information, and in order to earn those credits, they all needed viable intel to bring to Finn. As she started to backtrack and consider where she wanted to start, Zurah caught a strange blip in some of the code.

In an instant, the confidence she had felt a few seconds ago vanished, and a flutter of anxiety tickled her thoughts. The blip wasn't her doing. She had created a clean hack—of that, she was one hundred percent sure. But still, she was staring at the unmistakable blip of someone having hacked through the codes. Someone had gotten into the system before her.

"Nissa?"

"What's up?"

"We've got a problem," Zurah said. "Someone else

has been snooping through the files, creating their own set of codes."

"Any idea who?"

"No. I don't recognize the handiwork. Might be someone on the team going off on their own, or Finn could have a whole other set of problems." Zurah kept digging and discovered two more strange strings of code. Cursing, she knew she should have caught them on the first go around. Picking apart the work, she felt sure the mysterious hacker had known what they were doing but had been either a tad bit overconfident—*I know the feeling*—or had been rushed. Mistakes were easy to make in the heat of the moment with the clock ticking away.

She made a note of the three blips and the files where they were located. One was the ship's internal biosensor program. The second was in a remote-access file, and the third was in the comms system. *Odd. Why would anyone hack that system?*

She continued to dig and noted how the hacker had overridden the ambient noise controls. *Was someone that pissed off about the background noises on the ship?*

Humanity had still been new to space exploration beyond their solar system when they discovered adding ambient noises that reflected the natural background noise of Old Earth greatly reduced the percentage of individuals who ended up with cabin fever or worse. The addition was easy to do and cost extremely little, and it had become standard across all human ships.

For individuals like Zurah, the noises were a minor inconvenience. Not quite a comfort but certainly better than the absolute dead silence of space. She preferred the noises all ships and stations created, the subtle whispers of recycled air, the soft continuous echoes of individuals moving about, and the gentle hum of the engines.

"Winters, update."

"Hang on." Zurah ripped into the code, realizing the blips weren't a rushed job but something entirely different. The first code she touched began to melt, causing a trickle-down effect. "Shit, shit, shit." She needed to wall off the codes, or else they would eat through the entire system, triggering a cascading failure. Melting codes weren't new to her, but they were finicky animals. Zurah weaved around it, building a wall to isolate the code, being careful not to touch it again. Not yet.

"Winters?"

Almost there… Gotcha. She breathed a shaky sigh of relief. "We're good, boss. But we need to let Finn know as soon as possible that she has someone on board who was ready to cause some serious—"

The code exploded, and the computer screen flashed up an error report.

"No, that's not possible," Zurah cried, trying to reboot into the system. But no matter what she did, she was locked out.

The soft-yellow lighting in the compartment switched to the harsh glare of red, and an alarm sounded.

"Winters!" Nissa yelled. "Fall back. Mexa's sending you the meeting—" The comm went dead.

"Nissa? Come in. Nissa?" Zurah scrambled out of the compartment. "Mexa? Do you copy?"

For a moment, she was alone in the corridor as she

emerged from the compartment, then someone turned a corner and came running down the hallway. They knocked into her, and she fell against the wall. Zurah stood there for a moment, the memories of another time when an alarm was triggered and people had begun to run rushed through her mind.

Keep it together. Come on. The sound of more boots pounding against the metallic floor filled the corridor, and Zurah turned to see a handful of people headed her way.

As the group surged past, one of the women reached out and grabbed Zurah's arm. "What are you doing? Get to your station. Now!"

Zurah tried to twist out of the woman's grip, but it was too strong, and she pulled Zurah along with her.

"Well?" the woman growled as she spun Zurah forward. "Station?"

"Medical."

There was a brief look of suspicion, then the woman shook her head and grunted. "Suppose someone has to. Come on then."

With no choice, Zurah moved with the group, and to her dismay, she discovered they were headed straight for medical. She needed a good excuse to disentangle herself from the others, but the blaring alarm and strobing red lights were triggering an anxiety attack. Even though she tried, all she could picture was the other place and time those two sights and sounds had been paired together.

"See you round the bend, Zachs," one of the men hollered and waved as one of their group split off.

"Same to you," Zachs called out. "Crossing fingers for a falsie."

"I think we all are," muttered the woman who was still tugging Zurah along with the group. Then she came to a halt and shoved Zurah off to the side. "I'd wish you luck, but—"

Then the woman was gone, and Zurah was left alone. She looked at the sign next to the double doors. Medical. She could head off in the opposite direction. Looking down at her suit's screen, she brought up Mexa's map, searching for the rendezvous pin. But there was nothing there. *Come on, Mexa. What are you waiting for?*

But before she could take off in the other direction, the door opened, and Zurah looked up at one of the strangest-looking Neethos she had ever seen.

6

A typical Neetho started dye-enhancing injections after their second molting, choosing the vibrant and often neon colors associated with the gaming pod they would eventually work for. No other species dominated the gaming and gambling industry like the Neethos, both in establishments that were wholly legit and those run within the black market and beyond. Zurah had never heard mention of a Neetho who had chosen not to go into the traditional line of work.

Yet, blocking the door to medical was a Neetho whose skin had never undergone the enhancement injections and had maintained their natural coloring. Dark browns and tans decorated a deep-gray background, along with the occasional streaks of black. Two of the heavier tentacles rolled and curled up along the doorframe, while two large eyes moved to focus on Zurah.

She shivered and took a step back. Neethos had a

disconcerting way of looking straight through someone, as if they could read a biological signature and
know exactly what a person was thinking and feeling.

"Come in. Come in," a deep voice boomed.

Zurah didn't move.

"Come in before the sweeps begin," the Neetho
said again then moved out of the doorway.

There was still time for Zurah to turn and run. She
glanced down once more at her screen and didn't see
any updates. Even the comm signal had gone offline.
The safe bet would be to return to the little compartment on the residential deck, but Zurah caught
sight of the workstations behind the Neetho. Those
computers would have more options for her to play
with, much better than on the residential deck. She
needed to figure out if something had happened to
the comms, if her suit was glitching, or if something
far worse had happened. The risk was worth it. Zurah
stepped into the medical bay, and the doors closed
behind her.

"Have you been assigned to assist with potential
injuries, or are you here to check up on me?" The
Neetho moved through the spacious medical facility,
its tentacles rolling out in front of it, grabbing the floor
to then pull itself forward. She watched as it made its
way to a strange bowl-shaped depression in the floor.

"I was sent to help," she answered quickly, assuming that was the better choice of her two options.
Zurah braced herself for the Neetho to realize at
any moment she wasn't a part of the crew. The spoof
was adequate for casually moving throughout the

ship, but Zurah wasn't sure what she would do if the Neetho decided to ask questions or press for personal information.

She eyed the nearest workstation and wondered how far she could take the bluff. *What would a medical personnel do in this type of situation?* She knew what she would do as a security hack prepping for a job—she would double-check her supplies. "I'll run a supply check, double-check which supplies might be low in case of a huge influx of injured." Without waiting for permission, she slipped into the chair and brought up the main menu.

Leaning forward, she scanned the list of options, selected medical, and moved through files until she hit upon the inventory lists. Bringing those up, she carefully slipped another disc from her pocket and attached it to the underside of the workstation. With a glance over her shoulder, she noted the doctor hadn't moved.

Thanks, Finn, Zurah thought. *Or maybe the Neetho just doesn't care.* Either way, Zurah wasn't going to complain.

But before hacking into the computer, she scrolled through the alerts popping up on the screen. The security team, along with engineering, had already discovered the hack and were working to isolate the code. And a mechanical team had been dispatched to ensure all the backup systems were still isolated from the main system and were ready to go if the main life support system failed.

Crews were being reassigned left and right, and—

"Winters?" a voice crackled through the comms. It was so scratchy, Zurah couldn't immediately identify who was trying to contact her.

She glanced down and noted it was coming from Nissa's suit. "What's going on?" she asked quietly.

"Compromised... We're heading to... Look for the..." The comm went dead again.

"Nissa?" Zurah started a back trace, but the signal had been bounced through multiple relay stations throughout the ship, and the farther back she went, the more corrupted the code became. "What in the worlds?" Comm signals weren't designed to degrade that like.

"An issue I can assist with?" a voice rumbled.

Zurah jerked and looked over her shoulder. "Um. No, thank you. Sorry, still double-checking the—"

"The supplies inventory? That is wise," the Neetho finished for her.

"Um, yeah."

Is he just toying with me? All of the Neethos she had known had worked in the gaming industry and weren't to be double-crossed. She needed to come up with a plan, and fast. Pushing against the mounting anxiety, she took several deep breaths, trying to get her mind to relax and focus. This was the risk of going in blind to a job. They'd had no sure-fire backup plan in place, a situation Zurah rarely had to face. The priority now was getting a reliable comms system back up and running. She needed her team's information, and she needed Mexa to send her the rendezvous coordinates. If the worst happened, and Zurah found herself on her own, she would send the codes necessary for the others to get through the grid, make her way back to the *HighTail Flyer*, and hope the others would too.

She ran a diagnostic on her suit, first double-checking

if the issue was on her end. Then she set it up to run a long-range check on Nissa's and Mexa's suits. As long as they didn't travel too far outside the ship, they should still be within range for her to try to figure out the issue. While her suit processed information, she began to dig through the medical database. Minimizing the inventory, she worked her way through the files, slowly and methodically this time. She easily identified the files and systems other personnel were working on and skirted those files.

When Zurah found herself engaged in her work, time became meaningless. Her suit let off a soft chime, alerting her to a spike in the unusual energy signatures. Startled, she glanced down and noted the signal was growing rapidly in strength. She also caught a flash of movement as a tentacle snaked across her feet then heaved itself upward, encircling her midsection. Zurah was yanked out of her chair, and for a moment, her brain had a hard time registering what was happening. But when it did, she pushed back against the thick, muscular tentacle, yet it didn't budge. Two suckers on the underside of the tentacle were stuck fast to her suit.

She slammed her fist against the soft flesh underneath. "Let me—"

Her words were cut off as the Neetho all but threw her down into the unusual depression in the floor, and to her horror, the Neetho moved the bulk of its body to hover directly above her. Disgusted yet oddly unable to look away, she watched as the Neetho lowered itself. Zurah considered all of the ways she could have died as a security hack, but being smothered by a Neetho had never been a possibility.

But she wasn't going to go down without a fight. Zurah blinked and activated the Vulture. Shifting her weight so she could have better aim, she lifted her arm and targeted the Neetho.

"Have you come to begin your experimentation?"

Zurah paused. *What?*

There was a reply, but it was unintelligible as the Neetho's body muffled the voice.

"Will you at least allow me the courtesy of monitoring the remaining crew's health?"

Zurah caught the sharp and definitive no.

"Then you have made your decision."

A lengthy pause followed, and Zurah wasn't sure if the conversation was still ongoing or had ended. But the tentacle wrapped around Zurah's waist relaxed, the suckers popping free. She took the opportunity to finish rolling over onto her side, making sure to keep her weapon trained on the Neetho's underbelly. The Neetho shifted, and a small gap appeared between it and the rim of the depression. Cautiously, she pulled herself forward to peer out.

The room was silent, save for the background noises of the ship and the medical equipment, but the person the doctor had been talking to was still standing just outside the door. Judging from what she could see, Zurah guessed the individual was a human male. His skin was a dark olive, with hair as dark as the void of space. There was day-old stubble along his jaw and the hint of a wound still healing on his cheek. He wore a tailored jumpsuit with the unmistakable logo of the Goldsmith Consortium.

Zurah watched as his eyes swept over the room. She ducked back down, her skin tingling all over, and was concerned he might have seen her—or heard her heart hammering away. She took in deep breaths, trying to control her racing heart, and crossed her fingers she hadn't been seen.

Then the Neetho shifted its weight and moved, leaving Zurah exposed.

"A cracked shell is but a sparse replacement," the Neetho murmured, and Zurah looked up into two pairs of eyes staring down at her. "I am Dr. Ordotham."

When no other reply or cry of outrage come from either the doctor or the unusual man, Zurah once more pushed herself up and looked toward the door. It had closed, leaving her alone with the Neetho. Realizing the doctor was waiting for her to introduce herself, she stood and climbed out of the depression, keeping her weapon trained on him.

Dr. Ordotham leaned back, several of his tentacles curling around each other and creating a sort of nest for him to rest upon. "Perhaps it would be helpful if I provide assurances that I am not in a position to alert security of your arrival. In fact, I'm hoping that you are a part of the team that arrived with Ms. Finn. I'm growing weary of being confined to medical."

Zurah saw two possible scenarios. This was either a clever trap or the real deal. Zurah glanced down at her suit, hoping to see incoming messages from Nissa or Mexa. But there was nothing but a new report detailing the results of trying to figure out what was going on with the comm system. As she scanned the report, her heart sank. The suit wasn't malfunctioning, and there was no apparent reason for the radio silence.

"I am aware of Finn," Zurah answered.

"Excellent. I will make the assumption that you have just recently arrived as I do not detect any biological contaminants, nor do I have your features cataloged."

"Cataloged?"

"One of the many benefits of my species—perfect recall—and a benefit to my chosen profession. I am aware of each individual who was assigned to this research mission."

Zurah tucked that little piece of information away for the next time she visited a Neetho-run gaming establishment.

"What do you want?" she asked.

"Nothing but your assistance."

"And what would that mean?"

"How much do you know about what is happening here?"

Zurah wished Nissa was available to advise her. Nissa's instincts for reading a situation were far better than hers. The temptation to trust the Neetho was enticing, but trust had to be earned, not freely given.

"I'm aware of the research concerning the gates," Zurah replied.

The dark-brown patches on the bulk of the Neetho's body turned to a deep inky blue, and a tentacle snaked out from under its body and weaved back in forth between them.

"A shallow cove can be far more dangerous than the depths of the great arm," the doctor murmured. The tentacle continued its strange dance, and Zurah started backing toward the door. But before she could take another step, the tentacle reached for her and from underneath one of the suckers, a cloud of coppery red dust settled around her.

Sensing a biological contaminant, the suit reacted before Zurah could. But even its reflexes weren't fast enough. She inhaled some of the unknown particles, and the cool warmth of a summer's day spread through her body. Her body immediately relaxed, a lazy smile of contentment spread across her face as she flopped down into a chair. As the dust dissipated, the suit retracted the helmet.

"The *sheiol* would normally be offered with consent, but I sense we do not have the time to build the rapport required for such an offering. I apologize for the intrusive nature, but I fear it is in your best interest to be able to openly communicate with me. We do not have time to dance upon the waves."

The Neetho rose and moved around the rim of the depression until he was on the same side as Zurah. "The effects will only be momentary, so I will first give you something of myself to show my sincerity in this matter. This is rarely seen outside of the shores of my pod, but I fear circumstances require such a gesture." And without any other preamble, the Neetho bit off the tip of one of his tentacles. There was no blood or resulting gore, just a fist-size piece of tentacle that dropped to the floor.

"Amongst the deepest recesses of the waves, this

offering would be consumed by the recipient. Yet, I am aware that most humans frown upon such things. So I do not expect you to eat the offering. I merely wish to convey my deepest sincerity and show the urgency which has settled upon us."

Zurah looked down at the piece of tentacle lying at her feet. She bent over to pick it up, the silly smile still plastered on her face as she slowly turned it over in her hands. The flesh was already beginning to cool and dry out. She saw that a small sucker was intact on the underside. She touched it gently, noting how it wasn't sticking to her skin. Lost in the haze, she heard the doctor's words and brought the flesh up to her face, gave it a sniff, then bit into it.

The flesh was rubbery, with a slightly salty aftertaste. On the third bite, the effects of the *sheiol* were dissipating, and in horror at what she had done, she dropped the tentacle and gagged.

"What the hell?" Zurah all but screamed, and she wiped her hands in disgust on her suit.

"I am trying to convey my deepest—"

"You just *bit* off a piece of *yourself,*" Zurah said. She stood and backed away from the Neetho. "Bit it off. Why would you do that? That's disgusting and... and... I... oh my god. I actually ate part of it. That's not normal!"

The Neetho's coloring swept through a variety of shades before settling on a pale white, which nearly matched the color of the room. "To offer oneself is the highest form of honor and respect I can show. I had hoped, since you are a companion of Finn's, that you would understand the gesture and in turn realize that

I can be trusted. But I see now I have made a grave mistake." Dr. Ordotham turned and moved across the floor to the depression. He pulled himself in, wrapping his tentacles around his body until all Zurah could see was a mound of suckers.

Revolted and alarmed, Zurah turned and fled. She raced into the corridor, and once suitably away from the door, she stopped to catch her breath. Her stomach rolled at the idea of what she'd just done, and she leaned over and dry heaved. Once the worst of the sensation passed, she stood and took several deep breaths.

She needed to get in contact with Nissa or Mexa. And so she needed a new place to work. A place far away from anyone else. Deciding to head back down a few decks to scout out a quiet place, she rounded a corner but stopped when she heard voices. She flattened herself against the wall and, as an extra precaution, engaged her suit's shielding.

"I don't care about procedure. I didn't sign up to become—"

"Careful. We don't know how he's keeping track. Or what he will do if he hears us."

Someone snorted. "And what's going to happen if he does? The odds are we're all—"

"I refuse to believe that," another voice cut in.

"And I refuse to believe that pink moths don't grow on yarbaa trees. But here we are. No, you know what, Phillips? Do what you want. But I, for one, am not sticking around for this crap. I didn't spend five years at my schooling branch to end up alone and forgotten on this miserable rock."

"But the word is she's coming, and we need to be ready."

"So, what? You're just going to sit around and twiddle your thumbs? Are you willing to die for her?"

"Die? No one's going to—"

"Hey, you three. Why aren't you at your stations?" a new voice barked.

Feet shuffled against the floor, and someone was slammed up against a wall.

"What did you just say?"

"Calm down, guys. We're all on the same si—"

The unmistakable sound of a weapon's fire rang out. Zurah sucked in a breath and held it. Her heart pounded as she listened. Fear coursed through her, freezing her in place, even as she was aware whoever had fired the shot could round the corner at any minute, take one look at her, and decide that she was the enemy.

Zurah squeezed her eyes shut. The enemy, a criminal. The words rang in her head, forcing her to remember the explosion. Alarms blaring. Lights turning red but unable to mask the blood as she ran and slipped in a pool of it. Her hands coated as she pulled back in horror, staring at the dead woman. Her eyes devoid of life but still accusing Zurah of stripping it away from her.

That's in the past. It was an accident. Not my fault. It is the past. This is the present. Focus on the present.

Nissa had encouraged Zurah to think of a mantra to help refocus her thoughts when moments like this occurred. But most of what she had tried had never managed to quite cut through the paralyzing fear.

A blast ripped through the ship, the aftershocks

running through the floors and wall, confusing past and present. *This isn't real. This isn't happening. It's all in my head.*

She forced herself to open her eyes and focus on the wall in front of her and its smooth, dull surface. The panel seams were fitted together with precision, rivets running down and across, holding the ship together. A scream tore through the air, followed by the sound of panicked voices. Then a second blast and a third rocked the ship.

Despite the confusion and the fear, Zurah forced herself to shift her weight, and she lifted her arm to check her suit's readouts. Relief flooded her body. Mexa had sent an update. Zurah opened the map and found a rendezvous pin had been dropped at the access tunnel they'd entered through. Without a second thought, she rushed off.

The access hatch had taken them up, coming out one deck above the main entrance to the ship in a sort of no-man's land between the upper levels and the midsection, which was devoted to research. When Zurah hit the deck with the main entrance, she was forced to slow down. Clusters of personnel clogged her way. There were workers coming in, trying to get past other workers dressed as security who insisted on scanning everyone trying to access the ship. But there were also workers clambering to get out.

A man, his suit stained with grease and other fluids from mechanics, bumped into Zurah. His bleach-blond hair, streaked with reds and blues, was wild and unkempt.

A hot retort was on the tip of her tongue, but when she glanced in his direction, she froze. His face was coated in grime and blood, his eyes unfocused as he stared off into the distance. A deep gash ran from his forehead to his neck and appeared to ooze something orange. The man bumped into another worker, and when they turned, a look of shock spread across their face.

"Harry? My god, what happened to you?"

The man didn't respond but continued trying to shuffle forward.

"Hey, we need help here. Hey!"

Zurah edged away from the growing confusion and took advantage of the distraction to push her way through the crowd and dart up to the next deck. She glanced down at her screen. The glowing green pin indicated she was close. She hit the intersection where she'd decided to head to residential, took the corridor to the left, and kept going. Within minutes, she was standing in front of the door leading to the access hatch. But the door didn't open, and the controls next to the door didn't respond. Frustrated, she pried the covering off the panel and, with a quick hack, forced the door to open. Smoke billowed out of the room, and Zurah's suit sealed itself against the poor air quality.

"Mexa?" she called out, peering into the room. Even through the suit, she could feel the heat. "Nissa?" Panic started to creep into her voice. *What if they were discovered or killed? Or severely injured?*

The temptation to turn around and run was overwhelming. Something had obviously gone wrong. When in doubt, the rule was to fall back to the ship. No matter the job. She could get through the security grid, and she'd sent them the same information. Something could have been jamming the signal, or interference she hadn't yet identified could have prevented Mexa's update from reaching her. When Nissa last tried to contact her, the signal had been broken up. Zurah's mind raced through the worst-case scenarios. Had Nissa been trying to tell her the rendezvous point had been compromised and that Zurah was supposed to fall back to their ship? Or even worse yet, would Nissa or Mexa would wait for her?

Zurah made up her mind. She turned and ran once more. She didn't care about the credits. All she wanted was to get out in one piece. When she was back at the entrance, there were even more workers this time. She got in line, bouncing on her toes and craning her neck to watch as she slowly crept closer to the entrance. If there was an issue, she could send the code and shut down the suits, at least giving her enough time to get out and make a run for it.

Zurah only half listened to the fragments of conversation around her, keeping her eye on the guards. She wasn't sure how Finn's spoof would work when it came time to try to leave. Zurah was concerned the spoof wouldn't hold or would trigger another set of alarms. As the line moved forward, she cursed her blind decision. Before she ran, she should have double-checked Finn's work. But it was too late. Tampering with the systems so close to the checkpoint would undoubtedly raise red flags.

"Do you know what's going on?" a voice behind her asked.

When Zurah didn't respond, she felt someone tap her shoulder. She didn't want to turn around and answer.

Getting drawn into a conversation meant more ways to accidentally reveal she didn't belong. But being rude and not answering could potentially draw a lot more attention.

Zurah turned and was surprised to see a Glipglow standing behind her. Its suit was a clever design, able to accommodate its girth, six limbs, and tail.

"Not much. You?" she said, trying to keep her voice relaxed.

"I was told engineering had a catastrophic failure, but from the vibrations, I'd say it was far more than—"

Zurah's suit chimed. See glanced down and saw there was a new message from Mexa. "Excuse me," she said and opened it.

Rendezvous site compromised. Proceed to command. We have control of the situation. Will provide information there.

Zurah reread the message and looked around. She had a hard time believing Finn had control of anything judging from the nervous energy flowing through the crowd. But then again, personnel were being rerouted to different workstations. Perhaps what appeared to be chaos to Zurah wasn't. Double-checking the coding behind the message, she confirmed it had been sent from Mexa's suit.

Confirmation required, she typed back but was already stepping out of line.

The confirmation code came back, and Zurah pushed her way through the crowd and headed up to command. *I'm coming.*

7

The first level of command was eerily quiet. Zurah slowed down and double-checked the coding on the message. Everything appeared to be in order. She couldn't find anything that looked or felt out of place, no glitches in the system. The message must have come from Mexa. If he had been under duress or forced to send the message, they all knew the trick Zurah had set up to alert the others that it was a trap, and none of her internal security systems had been tripped.

With several deep breaths, Zurah calmly made her way to the bridge, and as the door opened, she took a quick scan. No alerts popped up. Command personnel moved back and forth, orders and questions flying around the room. Mexa stood off to one side, deep in conversation with a member of command, and sitting in a chair next to them was Nissa.

Zurah's shoulders dropped, and a huge knot of

anxiety loosened in her chest. Nissa was there. Neither of them had been killed. She rushed over to join them. "What in the hell happened? Comms went down, and I couldn't—" She realized Nissa was sitting in the chair for a reason. Blood had trickled down her hair line and was already growing dark and crusty. The front of her suit was ripped to shreds. Her head was leaned back, with her eyes closed.

"Nissa?" Zurah whispered then turned to Mexa. "What happened to her?"

Mexa had continued talking with the bridge officer, and when he turned to face Zurah, she grimaced. He wasn't entirely unscathed. There were several minor lacerations on his face, and a large gash ran down from his left shoulder to just past his elbow. Someone had put his arm in a sling. On his right leg, the suit was ripped to shreds, and the edges were crusted with dried blood.

"This whole thing has been a mess from the beginning," Mexa said with an angry shake of his head. "I was working on mapping when I got an urgent call from…" He paused and rubbed his forehead, squeezing his eyes closed. "Nissa. That was it. The message was garbled, but I understood the gist. Finn set us up. None of this is what we thought. A rendezvous pin was dropped, and Nissa sent the codes for backup. We both got there at the same time, just seconds before the explosion. If we'd been any sooner, we'd both be in pieces right now."

"Why hasn't she been treated yet? And what about you? Why aren't the two of you at medical?"

Mexa gave her a quizzical look. "Medical? That level got hit. The reports are saying substantial damage. Best guess is Finn set up explosives throughout the ship while she sent us on our fool's errands. Everyone's scrambling to regain control." He reached out and pulled Zurah away from Nissa, bringing her in close to whisper. "Look. I'm not going to sugarcoat this thing. Nissa's in bad shape, and Finn lied to us. We got no tether, no backup. We got to play it smart and stick with the ones on the winning side. This Alex Goldsmith. He isn't so bad. I've already talked with him, and he's waiting—"

"Wait. You've talked with Alex Goldsmith?" Zurah asked.

"Beat me back a few breaths too. That's for sure. But that's not the point." He shook his head as if trying to clear his head then muttered, "I can't think with all this damned humming."

"Humming?" Zurah strained to hear it, but all she caught were the sounds of the bridge personnel and the background noise of the ship. "Mexa, what are you talking about?"

"Talking about? Talking about… What are we—" A brief look of confusion crossed his face, then he scowled. "Zurah, I'm talking about deciding what you're going to do. Alex offered a hefty bonus to help hunt down Finn."

Zurah twisted out of his grasp. "So, it's that easy, huh? You've just switched sides?"

Mexa scowled and leaned against the edge of a workstation. "You'd be best signing with him. Alex has a lot more to offer than Finn ever did."

"I thought you were the one to vouch for her? And what about your sense of loyalty to Nissa?" Zurah glanced over her shoulder. "She needs medical attention. Now."

"When security has things sorted and a triage center can be set up, I'm sure they'll do what they can for her. Nissa's been a decent boss, but this is a Goldsmith we're talking about. You do a favor for that family, and you've got it made. If you come with me, I can show you—"

Zurah whipped back around. "Show me? Show me what? I see our boss dying and no one's doing a god damned thing about it. Mexa…" Zurah felt like she was begging. "This doesn't sound like you. We've got to get her help. I was just down in—"

She abruptly felt sick to her stomach, and she looked over to watch the bridge door slide open. Causally coming to a stop just inside the door was the man she had seen in medical. He had changed into a multifunctional suit, but his face was the same. He took in the bridge and its bustling activity, then he stopped when he laid eyes on her.

"Ah, this must be the estimable Zurah Winters. Hello," the man said as he walked over. "Please, let me introduce myself. I'm Alex Goldsmith. I must apologize for the unfortunate set of circumstances that brought you here. And from everything Mexa has shared, I am aware you had no idea what you were walking into. But I know your unique talents could be put to good use here—if you would consider working for me, that is."

His smile was easy going, and there was a jovial gleam in his eyes. Alex held out his hand, but Zurah didn't take it. "What about Nissa?"

Alex's eyes flickered toward the injured woman. "The explosions have severely damaged our medical bay. I have surveyed what remains, and unfortunately, we're having to scramble and bring some of our smaller treatment areas online. There just isn't enough left of medical for us to use that area. So I've recalled the med teams. But unfortunately, we aren't sure who is playing for which team quite yet. There is a lot of chatter and codes that need to be sorted out before we can make that assertion. We do know that there are personnel still loyal to Finn, and they're trying to persuade others to join her cause. Once we've cleared who is left of our medical team, I can assure you we'll do what we can for her."

"Sir, we need to update you," one of the officers interrupted.

"Excuse me, please," Alex said with a small bow toward Zurah, before stepping away.

"Mexa, listen. I was just down—" But she stopped herself. Mexa had already given his allegiance to Alex. If she shared what she knew, he would feel obligated to run to Alex. But more than that, Zurah recognized the suit. The unknown material, the seamless construction, the unusual signal, and the unwelcome feeling in her gut. This was the person Finn had talked to before they had come to the ship. *Nothing is making sense. If Finn was organizing a hostile takeover, why would they have talked? Why would Alex have let her walk away and let us on the ship?*

They were small details, but pieces of information didn't settle well in her mind. Not to mention the fact that when Alex had visited medical, there hadn't been any damage. The explosions had occurred after she'd left medical, but she'd been close enough. Zurah was fairly certain she would've realized if that area had been destroyed. But she needed to know for sure.

"So, what do you say?" Mexa pressed.

Zurah didn't want to make a decision, not without more information. "I don't know… This whole situation is just messed up."

"I agree, but Alex is going to need to know. One way or the other. If you let me, I can show you why Alex is to be trusted."

"Just let me think, okay?"

Mexa frowned, rubbed his forehead again, but stepped away as Zurah slid down to the floor. She let her head fall back against the bottom of a workstation as she looked over at her boss. Nissa's chest still rose and fell, but her skin was pale, and when Zurah reached out to touch Nissa's cheek, the skin felt cold and clammy.

Carefully, so as not to attract attention to herself, she slipped her last disc out of her pocket and attached it to the underside of the workstation. *Might as well take advantage of being on the bridge.*

Then she paired her suit with Nissa's, updating files and looking through the medical readout. The news wasn't good. In fact, it was far worse than what she had feared. Nissa had sustained severe internal injuries, and without full-on medical treatment, she was going to die. Zurah ground the heels of her hands against her eyes. If she said yes and jumped ship to get into bed with the Goldsmiths, she would make an enemy of Finn but gain a powerful ally. But that didn't mean her chances of helping Nissa would improve. Nissa could be used as bait, forcing Zurah to make a hasty decision or further bad choices down the road.

She glanced over at Mexa, who had returned to his

conversation with the command personnel. Zurah had worked with him long enough to feel confused by his reaction. He was a good man who had proved loyal to Nissa. Zurah wondered if he was working an angle she couldn't see. Perhaps he was simply trying to ingratiate himself with Alex and his cronies in order to get Nissa help. *Or perhaps he sees how grim the situation is and is simply securing his own future.*

Zurah's suit chimed, and she glanced down to see she'd gained access to the workstation. The first thing she needed to confirm was what had happened to medical. She started to open the file, then another message popped up. Nissa's suit was sending an alert. Zurah edged forward and gently rotated Nissa's arm so she could look at the screen. At first, it appeared to be a jumble of codes. *Perhaps error messages due to the damage the suit had sustained.*

But as she stared at the mess, she started to see a pattern hidden beneath the chaos. Not wanting to twist Nissa's arm more than necessary, Zurah transferred the code to her own suit and gingerly placed Nissa's arm back across her legs. Then she scooted back into the shadows of the workstation to take a closer look. Glancing up, she noted that both Mexa and Alex were still engaged in conversation, but no doubt they would turn to her and demand an answer. She knew she didn't have much time.

Picking apart the chaos, Zurah discovered a message had been hastily scrambled and tucked with the coding. It took her only a few seconds to unravel. But when she did, she shivered.

The moon seeks its twin, its pale light consumes the past, present, and future. Run.

The words sounded familiar, and the time stamp indicated the message had been constructed only moments before Zurah had arrived on the bridge. Even more concerning, the message hadn't originated from Nissa's suit but from another suit.

"Well?" Mexa's question startled Zurah. She stood hastily, brushing her hand against her screen to hide the message. Alex had finished his conversation, as well, and stood a few paces behind Mexa.

"I'm sorry. It's just—"

Mexa's eyes grew dark, and he reached out to try to grab her again, but he shook his head as if to clear his thoughts, a look of momentary confusion written all over his face.

"Zurah?" he asked, but she shrank back, unsure what he expected from her. They had always worked well together, but there had been a distance between them that neither had ever tried to close.

"Everyone is free to make their own choices." Alex stepped up and placed a hand on Mexa's shoulder. "If Zurah decides not to get involved, I wish her no ill will. Nor will the Consortium. In fact, I value a person who has a hard time crossing the lines of a deal. It shows character."

Red blossomed across Mexa's cheeks, and he pulled back. "Sorry, it's just that time's running out."

"I understand your concern for your boss. I would feel the same if it was a member of my family on that chair. Perhaps…" Alex shook his head. "No, I shouldn't ask."

"What?" Zurah asked, wary.

"I want to provide medical aid for her, but we need to make sure the personnel check out. My people are spread thin right now, trying to triage the worst of the damage, and I have security teams working to find Finn and identify any other potential threats in the system. To put it plainly, I simply don't have enough people. No matter what you decide, if you could at least help me with this, I would be very appreciative. From what Mexa has shared, you are a decent security hack. If, perhaps, you were able to take a look at the coding, just to verify that there aren't any bugs or potential red flags that they've been in contact with Finn, it would help speed up the process and allow the medical team to start doing their jobs. I would make sure Nissa is a priority."

Zurah glanced at Nissa, at Mexa, and finally at Alex. She didn't trust him or his promises. But Nissa had done so much to make sure Zurah was taken care of and safe. At least she could return the favor.

"Fine. Show me what you need checked."

"Excellent. Come with me." Alex led the way, taking them up two decks. "Mexa informed me of how Finn commandeered the ship, and I want to apologize for how you've gotten tangled up in a matter between Finn and the Consortium. Please be assured if you choose to decline a contract with the Consortium, you will be free to leave and with no black marks in my book."

Zurah listened but didn't respond. The words were smooth and full of honey, almost too sweet for her liking. If she was going to make a deal with someone, she preferred an honest, upfront conversation, not veiled meanings and half-truths. Zurah realized she would much rather deal with Finn instead of Alex. While the lack of intel had been frustrating, Finn had been concise and upfront about what she required.

"I don't suppose you know much concerning the sordid history of the *Eagle's Nest*?" Alex asked, catching Zurah off guard.

"No. Just the standard gossip," she replied.

"That's unfortunate. It is an area of great intrigue. What exactly was Captain Ujthout doing in this area of space, when his mission logs clearly state he should have been in Glipglow territory? Was there some secret mission? Or a simple error of navigation? Or perhaps some kind of mutiny against orders?"

"I'm sure the whisper nets have a wide variety of possibilities," Zurah said.

"Yes, and I've read through many of them. I'm surprised Finn didn't share more with you, seeing as she was going to use the three of you for backup. But we all have our secrets, I suppose."

They stopped in front of a conference room door with two heavily armored suits standing on either side. "I'm afraid I must leave you. With all of the disruptions, there are hundreds of small fires to put out. Sanders here will escort you inside. All you need to do is a routine inspection of their suits and comm logs. If you don't find anything out of the ordinary, then they're free to resume their duties. If there is something we need to be aware of, let Sanders know"—one of the guards nodded—"and she'll make sure they're appropriately taken care of."

The threat was clear, and Zurah clumsily nodded her understanding.

Alex reached out and touched her shoulder. "Good. I appreciate your help in this matter. Now, I must be getting back to the bridge."

Sanders keyed in the code to open the door, and she followed Zurah into the conference room. Five medical personnel were seated at a long rectangular table. Each one looked hot, tired, and worn-out. When Zurah entered, everyone kept their eyes down, focused on their hands splayed out in front of them on the table.

"All right. Hector, get up. You're first," Sanders snapped.

Zurah walked up to the medic who had slowly gotten to his feet, eyes still focused downward. *Remember, you're doing this for Nissa. No matter what Alex tries to get out of you, your mission is to secure help for Nissa.*

Hacking in the suit's system didn't take more than a few minutes, and Zurah ran the routine sweeps, looking for unusual coding or encrypted files. Next, she turned her attention to the comm logs, scanning through messages, double-checking points of origination and destinations, ensuring nothing had been purposely bounced from scam locations. Zurah didn't find anything to raise a red flag with Hector's suit. "He's clean."

Sanders grunted and jerked her head to the door. "Head down to the bridge and report in with Ipoa."

Hector nodded meekly and shuffled out of the room. "Talli, you're up."

Talli and the following medic were clear, and Sanders gave them their orders. When the fourth medic stood, sweat had begun to roll down Zurah's face. Her nerves were getting the better of her, with Sanders standing at alert with her weapon held at the ready. And Alex's kind words had produced the opposite effect on Zurah. She wasn't relieved at the idea of having no strings attached. She was alarmed. Everyone always wanted something.

These routine checks are a joke. If Finn wanted to spoof the system, she is more than capable of doing so. It'd have to be a much deeper dive into the system to find and untangle any hidden codes. Zurah's thoughts troubled her. *What does Alex really want? Is this some kind of test?* She didn't have any answers, but she certainly wasn't liking the whole setup.

The comm logs checked out, but Zurah detected a strange energy spike coming from within the suit. Intrigued, she started to tap into the central command node, but the medic looked up and gave a slight shake of their head. The motion startled her, and she stopped, staring at the medic, who was now staring at her. Their eyes were unlike anything she had seen before, a mixture of a deep-emerald green and a bright fluorescent orange. Their bodies were angled so that the guard could see Zurah but not the medic, and the person in the suit silently mouthed, "Please. We can help."

Help me? Nissa? Finn? The possibilities of the simple statement were too many to know for sure.

When Zurah didn't respond, the medic silently said, "The moon is looking for its twin."

Zurah jerked back, stumbling against one of the chairs.

"What's wrong?" the guard growled, advancing toward them.

"Nothing," Zurah hurried to say before her mind could decide otherwise. "I just stumbled. I'm sorry. I didn't mean to alarm you. This one is clear." As the medic walked past her, Zurah wondered what in the world she had just done. Hastily, she worked through the last medic and cleared them, as well.

Why did I do that? But she knew why. If she had said she'd found something strange, the guard would have opened fire. And Zurah would have another face to haunt her nightmares.

The door to the bridge opened, and Zurah felt as if her heart were in her throat. She half expected to see weapons drawn, ready to fire. But everything was as she'd left it. Mexa was working calmly with command personnel. Alex stood off in the corner, hearing reports. Two of the medics who had been cleared were attending to Nissa. The one with the strange eyes looked up and motioned for her to come over.

"Her internal injuries are extensive. They've stabilized her and have given her a first dose of healing bots. You're going to have to get her to medical. I am confident Dr. Ordotham will see to her needs."

Zurah's head jerked up. "What?"

But the medic smoothly stepped to the side then exploded into a million pieces of glittering sand.

The sand swirled through the air as if caught in the midst of a terrible maelstrom. The minute particles whipped across organic and inorganic materials, leaving score marks and blood in its wake. Screams erupted from the command staff as they tried to fight back or find cover, but their actions were in vain. Zurah tried to shield Nissa from the worst of it and braced for the pain she was sure to come.

A terrible wail rose up from within the sandstorm, and for a split second, Zurah believed she could see those strange eyes looking out at her. A mouth formed beneath the eyes and said one thing. *Run.*

Zurah didn't hesitate. She threaded her arm through Nissa's and grunted as she hauled the woman to her feet. The surge of fear and adrenaline coursing through her body provided the strength she needed to move her boss. She was less than a meter from the door when Alex stepped in her way.

"I can't let you leave," he said. The sand concentrated its fury on him, ripping through his flesh. But where the sand tore through skin and muscle, Alex's flesh knitted itself back together.

Zurah could only watch in horror. "What are you?" she whispered.

Alex smiled and lifted his hand. His skin shifted from the deep olive to a beautiful orange-tinted crystal. "For the time being, I'm your potential boss. You can still decide to help me. I know you are simply caught in the dance between opposing forces."

Zurah wanted no part in it. Not with either side. "No. All I want is to leave."

Alex's smile didn't falter. "A pity. I had hoped you would join us. Your skills are quite impressive, and I will mourn the loss. But I can find another security hack to complete my vision." He fluttered his hand, and the crystalline tips disintegrated into small orange-yellow pieces of glass.

They swirled together in the air, like a flock of birds, then hovered for a mere second in front of Zurah. A strange ripple moved through Alex's face, and his smile fell. The flock of crystals rushed toward Zurah. With a cry, she turned, pulling Nissa down in front of her, using Nissa's body as a shield. She braced herself for the pain as the glass would cut through her suit and seek her flesh.

"I will destroy you!" Alex screamed.

When Zurah realized the pain had never come, she stood and looked over her shoulder. The swirling sand had gathered around Alex, swallowing him in a sort of tornado with the blue pieces of glass caught within its violet storm.

The path to the door was clear, and Zurah knew the opportunity wouldn't come again. With a surge of strength, she made her way to the door with Nissa. The sensor registered her presence, and the door slid open.

"I can't," Mexa's voice whispered in her ear. "I can't."

Zurah glanced to her right and witnessed a transformed man. Underneath the blood, his skin had turned ashen, and his eyes were full of fear.

"Please. I can't hold them back," he moaned. His left arm started to rise, but he clamped his right hand his other wrist to stop the motion. "You have to help me. I can't do this on my own."

Zurah was torn. Nissa's weight was dragging her down, but Mexa was a part of their crew, one of two people she had learned to trust. "Come with us. We'll get you help," Zurah said. "But we've got to go."

Mexa's face twisted in anguish, his lower lip angling

down at an impossible angle. His left eye flashed a brilliant aquamarine. "If you won't join us, then you must—" He bit down on his tongue with a vengeance. Blood spilled from his mouth. "I can't hold on. You've got to help me."

Fear gripped Zurah's heart as she shrank back from the grotesque sight. "I don't know… I don't know how."

"You do," Mexa whispered. "Look inside." He let go of his left arm and tapped his chest. Then he wedged his fingers into one of the holes created by the sand and pulled out a small Beaker's Knot. Zurah stared at the weapon in awe and trepidation.

"That's not possible. Nissa would've—"

"Worst-case scenario. But requires two activation codes," Mexa said, then his body spasmed. He bent over in pain. "Hurry. Can't hold out." He lifted the weapon and spoke the code. Then he held it out for Zurah to do the same.

Zurah pushed Nissa backward, and the blood drained from her face. "No. I can't. You'll die. They'll all die."

"I'm already dead, girl. They all are. They just don't know it yet."

There was a roar of triumph, and Zurah saw that whatever Alex was, he was winning. She looked back at Mexa, whose face was contorted in pain, his one good eye pleading with her. She leaned forward, gave her code, then ran as fast as she could with Nissa's weight slowing her down.

The blast was partially contained as the doors had closed once Zurah and Nissa were clear, but the shock wave sent them flying forward. A chunk of metal ripped through Zurah's suit, slicing her shoulder down to her elbow. The shock left her feeling weak and dizzy. Acrid smoke filled the corridor, and with the damage her suit had sustained, it wasn't sealing itself off and purging the contaminated air. But there was enough power left to send out the worm she had crafted to shut down any armored suit for thirty seconds.

"Zurie? My little Zurie?" a voice tugged at her through the haze.

Zurah crawled on her hands and knees, wincing as she put pressure on her injured arm, but she made her way over to Nissa's side. Fresh blood was welling up, and her eyes were open but cloudy.

"That's not the way to the market, Zurie. Come on, we've got to go find Mommy."

The words didn't make sense, and all Zurah could see and hear was that Nissa was dying. Nissa was going to die because of her. The pain melted away, and Zurah pulled Nissa to her feet, half supporting her, half leaning Nissa's body against hers. One step at a time, she forced her way through the ship. "Come on, we've got to move. I haven't bought us much time."

Workers were rushing to get out, and others were running down the corridor. But no one paid any attention to Zurah or Nissa. Everyone was too focused on either doing their job or trying to get out of the ship to save themselves. Blood streaked the floor where Zurah moved with Nissa, and by the time she arrived at medical, she was beginning to see stars. The door opened, and a vast world of calm and serenity flooded her senses.

"Help us," she groaned, and together, she and Nissa collapsed to the floor.

8

When Zurah woke, dried sweat and tears were crusted around her eyes, nose, and mouth. She struggled to sit up, and a wave of dizziness washed over her. The bright-white walls and floating lights were disorienting. Something tight was wrapped around parts of her body, and she tugged at its edges, wondering if she was having a fever dream. But the material was coarse as she ran her hands over her body, not the smooth exterior of the suit. As the dizziness passed and her eyes focused, she realized someone had taken off her suit and placed her in a QuickHeal wrap. The majority of the nanobot-infused material had done its job, and there were only a few layers left on her arms, torso, and leg. Realizing how exposed she was, Zurah blushed and looked around for some type of gown.

"Here," Finn said as she threw over an undersuit and a new outer suit.

Zurah grabbed them and pressed them up against her body, the cool material causing goose bumps to race across her skin. "What the actual hell is going on? Where were you?" Fury began to bubble to the surface. "Do you even know what's going on? Or what Alex did? That Mexa—" She almost chocked on the words. "That he just killed himself so we could get away?"

"Yes. And you have my sincerest apologies. But I was securing our future," Finn replied. "I'll guide you to an exit—"

"Apologies? That's it? You brought us here for no good reason other than to be a taxi service. Then threw us into this mess without the intel we needed to stay alive. Now one of my crew is dead, and Nissa isn't far behind. You had better do a hell of a sight better than an apology." In the moment, Zurah didn't care who Finn was or what the whisper nets theorized. All she saw was the woman responsible for tearing apart her world.

Finn clenched her jaw, and her gaze grew hard. "An apology will have to suffice for now. But if you like, I can walk away and let you figure out what to do next."

Zurah opened her mouth, a cutting remark on the tip of her tongue, but she snapped it shut. *Don't let your emotions guide you*, Nissa's voice said in her head. But Zurah wasn't sure what else she had left.

"No? Then as I was saying, I'll guide you to another exit hatch. From there, you will make your way to the beta site. Those who haven't been contami—those who are still loyal have set up a base camp." There was a brief pause, and for a moment, Finn appeared ancient.

A heaviness had settled on her face and pressed down on her body. "I had no idea things had progressed so far. If I had, believe me, I would never have brought the three of you here."

"None of this makes any sense. I saw a man *crumble*… crumble into *sand*. And then Alex—"

"I don't make a habit of saying this twice. But I am sorry. When I spoke with… Alex, I had no understanding of how insidious—" She shook her head. "None of that matters. We have to continue to move forward, and if our projections are correct, then we don't have much time. The doc and I have done what we can to secure—"

"No." Zurah slipped off the platform. "That's not good enough. You dragged us here into the middle of gods know what."

"We don't have time to bring you up to speed. It won't take them long to break through the barriers we've thrown up."

"I don't care," Zurah snapped. "I want Nissa patched up, then we're leaving. On our ship. No beta site bullshit."

"The doc has done what he can. But we've had to put her in a stasis tube. She needs top-level medical care. And right now, that's not something we can provide. But when this is over, we'll get you guys patched up and on your way."

"No," Zurah said. "I'm not leaving her."

Finn huffed, her patience already thin. "We'll see to it—"

"A pod does not easily abandon their own," Dr. Ordotham said as he turned to watch them. "There are a great many things I do not understand about the human species, but the fierce protectiveness of one's family is an attribute I can relate to."

Zurah's anger overrode her embarrassment of her last interactions with the doctor. She whirled around. "And you! What's all this nonsense about medical having been destroyed? All of this equipment just sitting here while people need help."

"The doctor doesn't deserve your ill-placed anger," Finn growled. "He's already risking far more than he should by having us here. Now get dressed."

Zurah's anger was boiling, and if it weren't for Nissa, she would have stormed out of the room and figured out how to get off the planet on her own. Biting her tongue, she got dressed, sourly noting the suit Finn had supplied was barely acceptable compared to what she had arrived in. There was a scratched-up antiquated screen, and when Zurah attempted to pair with her SeeClear tech, the two technologies wouldn't talk to each other. This inconvenience wasn't the end of the world, though. Zurah went through the steps to manually connect the two technologies. When the connection was established, she zipped up the front of the suit and secured the protective outer layer over the zipper. The head gear was old, as well, and the hard collar pinched her neck. She tested out the helmet, and it took a few seconds for the head gear to fully activate. The face shield was grimy but did have a lower field of information that mirrored what the embedded screen provided. The boots were heavy, and it would take some adjustments to get used to their weight.

"I'll take the stasis pod with me, or better yet, you

can help me get it to the ship. Then we'll be gone and not your problem any longer," Zurah said.

Finn shook her head. "Too risky. We'd be a slow-moving target at best. The pod is better off here."

"How? How is that better? You just said they could breach this deck anytime."

"While that is true, for now, they will not do anything to jeopardize my well-being," Dr. Ordotham said. "As it happens, my biology is resistant to the—"

"He's a valuable asset," Finn interjected. "And as such, they won't touch him. Not yet. We can mask the pod's signature and hide it in the doc's nest. Again, right now, that's her best option. And yours."

Zurah's resolve started to dissolve. Mexa was dead, Nissa almost so, and now she was supposed to blindly take orders from Finn. "How do I know I can trust you? That you're not… whatever Alex is or that medic?"

"For right now, you're going to have to take my word," Finn said.

"Come, see the pod and give your well wishes," Dr. Ordotham said. One of his tentacles reached out toward Zurah but didn't quite touch her boots. "This way."

Zurah was reaching the end of her tether, and the reality of what had happened to Mexa was beginning to settle in her gut. She shuffled toward the doctor and stopped at the edge of the depression in the floor. The tentacle unfurled, and she slipped down into the well.

"The second compartment on your left," Dr. Ordotham quietly said. "Here." His tentacle slid over and pushed against a small panel. Air hissed and blew out from behind a small door, and a medical stasis pod slid out. Zurah wiped the condensation from the view port to stare down into Nissa's face.

For a split second, she was staring at the bloodied and bruised face of a woman she had stumbled over. A woman laid out in a steadily growing pool of her blood. She squeezed her eyes shut, trying to keep her emotions in check. But the anger she felt toward Finn reared up and turned inward.

The wall Zurah had built over the years collapsed, and tears streamed down her face. Nissa had created a home for her, and until that moment, Zurah hadn't realized how much the feeling of belonging had meant. Now that she was facing the very real possibility of losing it, the realization was overwhelmingly painful. She wiped her face, embarrassed by the tears and the sensation of grief, loss, and abandonment.

Another tentacle slipped into the nest and gently touched Zurah's shoulder, but she couldn't bring herself to look up at the doctor.

"It is natural to molt such emotions when within the deep depths of losing a *kriepolo* member of your pod."

Zurah shrugged and tried to stop crying. "Nissa was a good boss."

"An admirable trait of the human species, to be able to extend the life of the pod and work with those of the same blood. It is not the same for my kind."

The words were soft and gentle, and undoubtedly, the doctor was trying to comfort her. But Zurah's emotions were spiraling. *I don't deserve your empathy. This whole thing is my fault. And why should he be nice to me after I treated his offering with such*—"Wait. What did you say?" Zurah looked up and stared at Dr. Ordotham.

"An admirable trait of the human species, to be—"

"No, the part about those of the same blood," Zurah interrupted. "What are you talking about? I'm not related to Nissa. I picked up a job with her, and she asked me to stay on. That's all."

The doctor's tentacles moved out of the depression, and his color morphed from pale blue to a deep pink. "You are incorrect. When entering your medical information into the system, it showed a familial match. I believe, in human terms, this woman would be considered a maternal aunt."

"No."

"I'm afraid I must insist. I am quite familiar with the program, and the margin of error is too small to be considered."

Zurah stared at Nissa. *My aunt? My mother's sister?* The revelation was too much to take in. "Nissa is my boss. She's a good boss. And I owe it to her to make sure she comes out of this alive. That's all."

"I get that family reunions are hard. Can't say I'm keen on ever getting together with my brothers—most especially my older brother—but we don't have time for this," Finn's voice cut through the fog. She had crouched on the edge of depression.

"Right," Zurah said, knowing she needed something else to focus on. She climbed out while the doctor tucked Nissa's pod back into its hidey-hole. The latest revelation was too much, and Zurah pushed it back, promising herself she would deal with it later. She would survive, and so would Nissa. Then, when they were safe, Zurah could deal with the mess.

"What do you need me to do?"

Finn gave her an appraising look. "I'm going to smuggle you out of the ship. I've got a few distractions set up, and you're going to head for the beta site. The team already knows there might be a few stragglers still heading their way. You'll have to go through some security checks, but once you're cleared, just tell them you're to wait there until I arrive. I need to take care of a few more things before I can head out."

"And Alex? Or whatever he is?"

"You focus on staying alive. Then I'll reconsider what you need to know." Finn held out a handgun. "We weren't fully prepared for events to escalate at this speed, but that doesn't mean we weren't preparing for the worst-case scenario. It's old-school tech, but it has been modified to work on Objer and to deliver a hefty punch—human or otherwise."

Zurah took the gun and was surprised at the weight. "Ammo?"

Finn nodded and handed her a belt with a holster and extra ammo. "Just remember we have almost no atmosphere, and things are going to move differently than artificial g's or planet side."

Old-school weapons weren't Zurah's specialty, but she was fairly proficient with most weapons. After a quick tutorial from Finn, she felt reasonably confident in its operation.

"Doc, you take care, and I'll see you on the distant shores," Finn said.

Dr. Ordotham reached out and touched the top of her head with one of his tentacles. "On the distance shores, we shall feast and bathe in the sun."

Zurah felt a twinge of embarrassment at watching the exchange. Finn gently touched the tentacle, and a sliver of color raced up the doctor's body.

"Thank you," Finn murmured, then she turned and headed off to the rear of the medical bay.

Zurah knew she should say something to the doctor but wasn't sure what was appropriate. An apology for her earlier affront to his customs seemed too contrite. Too easy. But despite her outright rude behavior, the doctor continued to show her compassion and was risking a lot to hide Nissa. An idea popped into her head. "Do you have some kind of cutting tool?"

Dr. Ordotham leaned to his right, opened a drawer underneath one of the medical platforms, and handed Zurah a scalpel. She took it and pulled her braid over her shoulder. She undid the band securing her braid and moved it farther up. Running her fingers through the end of the braid, she worked out a few knots, gathered it together, then cut it off.

"I don't claim to understand exactly what you were offering me before. But know that I do appreciate what you've done for me and what you are doing for Nissa." She handed the doctor the small bundle of hair, and she noted how his skin shimmered in a wide variety of colors.

He took the offering and gently wrapped one of his tentacles around it. "This is already more than most comprehend. I am pleased to have learned your name,

Zurah Winters. It shall be added to the shoals of my pod."

Zurah blushed, and at a loss for words, she bowed then turned to find Finn.

In the few minutes Zurah had thanked Dr. Ordotham, Finn had undone a panel and was crouched next to a gaping hole. The dark interior and shadows of conduits wouldn't be an inviting situation for most people, but Zurah took one look and was ready to go. As a security hack, she sometimes worked in the open, wearing a uniform of the local guards or impersonating someone of note. But for the most part, she worked in the shadows, tucked away in locations few individuals rarely dared to go.

"Here." Finn held out her arm. She transferred a map to Zurah's suit. "Come on. Let's go."

Zurah crouched and ducked into the small utility tunnel. Finn crawled in behind her, and they both switched on the lamps on their suits. Finn leaned out and pulled the panel back into place.

"There. The doc will finish it up. We need to go. Head on straight until you hit an intersection."

The air was warm and stuffy, and after a minute of crawling over conduits and avoiding exposed wiring, sweat was beginning to tickle Zurah's skin. She came to the intersection and stopped, twisting around to look at Finn.

"You will continue going straight ahead. Just follow the markers on the map. Bring up the timer on your suit." Finn paused. "Good. Now set it for a twelve-minute countdown. That's when you need to be at the exit hatch. Wait for another two minutes then blow the hatch. That will give me time to get set up. Once you're out of the ship, you need to head to the beta site. It's roughly thirty-five hundred meters to the west. Your suit has enough juice to help you get there in one piece. But not by much. Deviate too far off course or take too long, and it could get dicey. Got it?"

Zurah nodded. "Promise me."

Finn had turned and was already heading off to the right. "I promise. Nissa will be safe. Dr. Ordotham isn't the only one left on the ship who isn't keen on following Alex. Now go. You're wasting time."

Zurah listened to Finn crawl off into the darkness before continuing on. The tunnel was wide enough to accommodate her frame, and she checked the countdown on her suit. Eleven minutes and three seconds. Due to the cramped quarters and poor ventilation, sweat had begun to run down her face, working its way along the collar of her suit. She decided to flip on her helmet, seal the suit, and let it work at maintaining a cooler temperature.

When the timer hit seven minutes and twenty-nine seconds, Zurah ran into a section with rather large pieces of pipe cutting through the tunnel. "Dammit," she muttered. The fit would be tight. She had to scoot around to crouch, then she pushed herself up to try to squeeze over the top of the conduit. The pipe was warm, and the heat seeped through the suit. She pushed herself forward, the pressure along her torso growing. Wiggling a bit, she tried to continue to inch forward, but she felt something catch. Cursing, Zurah twisted her left arm around, trying to feel for the problem. Something had snagged the front of her suit. Her fingers fumbled with the heaviness of the gloves, and she wasn't able to free herself.

Six minutes and two seconds.

Zurah braced her hands against the pipe, and with a violent shove, she snapped free and rolled over the pipe. Turning over, she sat up, her back hunched over, and she tried to assess the damage.

"Shit." The tear wasn't bad, and if she had a patch kit, it would take only seconds for the application, and she could continue on. But Finn hadn't given her one, and the suit only had one pocket, which was empty. She glanced at the timer. Five minutes and thirty-three seconds. Even if she scrambled back the way she had come, there was no way she could fix the suit, start over, and have enough time.

"Come on. Think," she muttered. *I don't want to be stuck here.* She repositioned herself and, trying not to think about it, made her way over the next two pipes. With a sigh of relief, she noted the next bit of the tunnel looked clear. Pushing forward, she kept her eye out for anything she might be able to use as a makeshift repair. But all she saw were metal walls, metal pipes, and conduits that would be of no use.

If I could find a small access panel or an engineering hatch, there might be some sealant around the seams I could repurpose.

After another two minutes had passed, she spied a small maintenance hatch. "Yes," she hissed and reached out to pop it open. There was a rubber seal crammed into the seams, and as she pried it out, feeling a wave of relief. *At least something is going my way.*

The rubber seal wasn't standard but constructed from a press 'n seal material, indicating the panel had been replaced more than a few times. Once she had a significant chunk, she rolled it around in her hands, warming up the material, but then stopped.

There was no guarantee the material would hold to the suit or for how long. And judging from the map, she still had at least another two or three minutes' worth of crawling left. That meant she was barely going to make it. She tucked the press 'n seal into her pocket and kept going. *Once I'm there, I'll get in position. Then right before the final two minutes, I'll patch the suit and hope it'll hold long enough to reach the beta site. I'm really not keen on experiencing a massive ebullism due to decompression.*

By the time Zurah reached the exterior hatch, she was already thirty seconds into the final two-minute countdown. She scrambled into place, ready to blow the hatch and jump. Taking deep breaths, she watched the last timer run down.

One minute five seconds…

Fifty seconds…

Zurah took out the press 'n seal and rolled it around in her hands, warming it up so it would be pliable once more.

Twenty-seven seconds…

Squashing the press 'n seal into the rip for a makeshift patch, she kept one hand over the area while her other gripped the lever to blow the hatch.

Fifteen seconds…

Zurah took a deep breath. *Please. Let me live. Let Nissa live.*

Ten seconds…

The ship vibrated, and Zurah's gut twisted into an ugly knot.

Five…

Four…

Three…

Two…

One…

Zurah pressed hard against the patch, then she reached up and, with both hands, pulled the lever down. The hatch door swung outward, and without a second thought, she jumped and landed hard on the rocky surface. She glanced down, half expecting the patch to have fallen away and to feel the effects of depressurizing. But the patch was still there. *No time. Got to move.*

She glanced at the map then took off. After stumbling with the first few steps, she had to slow down some as she adjusted to the weight of the boots and how her body moved on Objer. She glanced over her shoulder and caught sight of a bright flash of light enveloping the front end of the ship then a second and a third.

Keep going. Reach the beta site. Stay alive.

She turned away, glanced down at the map, and took off.

The suit struggled to keep up, the air inside becoming warm and moist. Beads of condensation had formed on the inside of the face shield, and Zurah had turned off the bottom portion, relying on her SeeClear tech and the suit's screen. She was less than halfway, according to the map, and her lungs burned. Each breath was painful.

I'm not going to make it. The suit was failing, and the beta site was still too far away. Zurah stopped, struggling to breathe, and scanned the horizon. One of the large clusters of cut rocks was roughly a hundred meters to her left. Her scans picked up energy spikes, and once she'd analyzed them, Zurah concluded some type of shielding network had been established within the rocks. She reasoned it must have been set up by one of the research teams. *But would anyone be left? Would they be friend or foe?*

Yet Zurah knew she didn't have the luxury of options. She only hoped the researchers had been recalled, and she could figure out how to get her suit up and running in order to make it to the beta site. She changed course, and what should have taken only a handful of minutes stretched on for what felt like hours. Each step forward was a struggle, the boots feeling as if they each weighed a ton. Her vision started to blur, and she blinked constantly, trying to clear away the hazy fog.

Just a few more steps. Almost there. Zurah could almost reach out and touch the side of the rocks, but pain ripped through her body, and she fell to her knees. Nissa's face flashed through her thoughts, and she dug her fingers into the rocky surface, pulling herself forward. The SeeClear tech indicated the shielding was just inside the odd sort of doorway the jumble of rocks had formed. She only needed to crawl forward a few meters. But she couldn't breathe, pain filled her chest, and her vision went dark as she collapsed, her fingers only a few centimeters away from the edge of the shield.

A gloved hand reached out from behind the shield, grabbed Zurah's wrist, and pulled her into the cool embrace of the rocks.

9

Fresh, oxygenated air moved through Zurah's suit. She coughed then sucked in lungfuls of the sweet air. She rolled over on her side, her heart pounding as she waited for the wave of dizziness to subside. As her body and mind recovered, she sat up and took stock of her surroundings. Slow-moving orbiter lights rotated in a lazy clockwise circle above, and temporary workstations skirted the perimeter of the room. Behind a few of the workstations were crates haphazardly stacked on each other. In the center of the room was a long table and half a dozen chairs flung about. Except for one.

Zurah gasped and scrambled to her feet. She pulled the gun from its holster and aimed it at the man sitting in one of the chairs, watching her calmly.

"How did you get here?" she asked.

The man leaned back and raised his hands. "I'm not what you think."

"Bullshit. I saw what you did. What are you? Because you're definitely not human."

"I can assure you I'm fully human. And judging from my scans, you are too. But if you need convincing, please do what you need to do."

"No human could just dissolve like that," Zurah snapped.

"I agree. But that *thing* you saw, it wasn't me. A pretty damn good copy, minus the whole dissolving issue, but assuredly not me." Alex Goldsmith gently let his hands come down to rest on his thighs. "Go ahead. Run your scans."

Zurah blinked and went through the gamut of what the SeeClear tech offered. Every reading and test she could think of came back normal. The man sitting in front of her was human. "Tests can be spoofed. What if you're wearing some kind of interference shielding or projecting the biomarkers of a human?"

"Would you care for a more thorough examination?" he asked, the hint of a smirk on his darkly tanned face.

"Yes," Zurah said without hesitation. "Stand up and take off the suit."

Alex complied without complaint.

"Toss it over." When he did, Zurah kicked it behind her. "Take off your shirt too."

Alex quirked up an eyebrow but complied.

Holding the gun, Zurah took a few steps closer, running through the security sweeps one more time. She reached out and lightly brushed his skin, checking for any abnormalities in her vision that might indicate some type of projection field.

She stepped away, double-checking the data, and was only an ounce more satisfied. Scanning the room, she considered what tech might be used to confirm biological status with some flesh-and-blood samples. She kicked the suit back his way and considered the options as he dressed. In the end, Zurah decided to forgo that route. Even if she was able to get something up and running, she wasn't a doctor, and those types of tests could easily be spoofed without having an intimate knowledge of what to look for. She would have to rely on what she did understand.

"What the hell is going on here?" she asked.

"Are you saying you believe me?"

"Maybe," she replied, not used to having to do the upfront and personal part of a job. That was Nissa's domain.

"How much do you want to know?"

"Enough to get off this miserable ball of rock," Zurah said. "And in one piece."

"That might be more difficult than you realize," he muttered. His confident smirk vanished momentarily, and there was a flash of concern in his eyes. "If you really want to survive this, then it'll be easier if I show you rather than just try to tell you."

Zurah weighed her options. Everyone was working their own angle, and she needed to consider how to approach hers. Finn's instructions had been clear—getting to the beta site was priority. But Finn was light on answers and heavy on orders. Acquiring intel might provide Zurah an edge in whatever was to come and prove to be a valuable bargaining chip. Alex's comment wasn't a revelation; Zurah was increasingly aware that getting Nissa off Objer was going to be far more challenging than Finn or anyone was leading her to believe. But would it be a wise use of her time and resources to gather intel? Or should she simply ignore Alex, fix her suit, and head to the beta site? Nissa might be tucked away in the stasis pod, but there were so many things that could go wrong.

The thought she didn't want to dwell on wormed its way into her considerations. If Nissa died or was discovered, Zurah would need to rely on herself. Newfound revelations of familial connections be damned at that point, she had lived long enough without relatives. She could continue to do so. Zurah needed to ensure *she* had bargaining chips, as well.

Decision made, Zurah said, "Fine. Just know if you're trying to con me…" She flicked her wrist with the gun to make her point.

Alex blinked, hesitating for a split second. "I'm not." He bent over to reach inside one of the crates beside the table, and Zurah felt her stomach seize.

"Don't do anything stupid," she said, ready to fire if needed.

Alex huffed. "I'm only being polite. Here." He tossed her a zip. "Who knows when we'll get a chance to eat."

She let the zip land at her feet and watched as he took another one, quickly peeled off the wrapper, and started eating.

"Come on, then," he said around mouthfuls. "Follow me. Be careful, though. There are areas in here which aren't stable." He turned and headed to one of the workstations, where a steel door had been embedded in a gigantic piece of rock. Finished with the zip, he tossed the wrapper aside, gripped the handle, and swung open the door. Overhead lights flickered to life, illuminating a corridor.

Deciding she would rather face whatever was coming next with some food in her belly, Zurah quickly snatched up the zip and finished it in a couple of bites. While she ate, she ran a swift scan of the area. The SeeClear system flagged a multitude of unusual energy signatures then tagged those readings with the anomalous readings she had picked up on earlier. Not only that, but one of the energy signatures actually matched the strange readings emanating from the creature masquerading as Alex. Zurah was well aware of the risks, but this was the first concrete lead she had come across. Something she could chase and unravel.

Get the information then get out. Next up will be the beta site.

They wound their way through a spacious corridor, with telltale cut marks scoring the walls. After only a few minutes, it ended. Her SeeClear tech detected a standard shield perimeter alert, and the space beyond the corridor was full of dark shadows and strange shapes.

"You'll need to suit up. And don't worry. I flooded the oxygenation cells on your suit. I wouldn't advise trying to leave this outcropping, but for now, the suit will be adequate protection." Alex engaged the helmet on his own suit, and he turned to wait for Zurah to do the same. "Have to say I'm surprised anyone would use such a relic out here."

"Wasn't mine." Zurah shrugged.

Alex reached out and pushed his hand through the shield. The ripples of energy were picked up by her SeeClear tech. "See those larger pillars? The researchers have theorized this area was under construction when something went wrong and the site was abandoned. The resulting collapse of the pillars created a type of cavern, but there are too many nooks and crannies for the shield they installed. If they were going to expand the shielding, they would've needed at least two more generators set up."

"Who built these pillars? Do the researchers have an idea?"

"Don't know. One of the questions that the team was working on out here."

Zurah engaged her helmet as Alex stepped through the shield. She took a deep breath then followed.

The cavern-like space was massive, and after a few moments of scanning the area, she began to see the patterns where megalithic-sized rocks could have been placed as pillars sporadically throughout the space. But several of them were either chipped or appeared to have toppled over on top of each other. She wasn't a zenologist by any means but did feel a small spark of curiosity concerning who or what had built the space. Not to mention the question of why someone had decided to build on Objer.

Did the planet have an atmosphere at one time? Was it better suited for life? Or could there be species out there who could survive and thrive on a place like Objer?

"So, here's where it gets a bit sticky." Alex's voice cut through her thoughts. He had stopped in the center and turned to watch her. "It really would be better if you put away that gun." When Zurah didn't move to holster the weapon, Alex huffed. "I don't want to die any more than you do. In fact, I plan on making it out of this mess alive. There's too much at stake. So put the damned thing away."

"Why? What's going to happen?"

Alex didn't answer but continued to stare until Zurah felt an awkward blush creep up on her cheeks. Then he turned, took a few steps, and completely vanished.

Zurah gaped at the empty space. "What the hell?" she muttered, all of her senses on high alert.

Before she had time to initiate a sweep of the area, Alex's voice rang out from behind her. "That's going to happen."

Zurah spun around and found Alex standing casually on the other side of the cavern.

"Multiple tests and trials were conducted before the researchers started exploring these… portals, for lack of a better word. The risk was tremendous, but each researcher ended up returning to this cavern."

"Portals? As in long-distance teleportation? To where?"

"Yes, to the first and second. The third question, that is what is easier to show you than to tell you. I'm assuming you've got some variation of the SeeClear tech?"

Zurah nodded.

"You'll want to adjust the settings. Here." Alex walked over and held out his arm so Zurah could see the screen. None of the adjustments were a security concern, so she followed his lead, and when she rebooted the system, she gasped. Suspended around the room were shimmering diamond-shaped images. Each was slightly transparent and had an almost-opalescent quality.

"It's… It's beautiful," Zurah whispered.

"It is. On many different levels. The researchers believe each one to be connected to one of the megalithic stones. Don't ask me for the technical details. It's a deep dive into energy signatures."

Zurah opened her mouth, snapped it shut, and considered telling him about the matching signals between the cavern and his copy. But Alex could already be aware and keeping that tidbit to himself. And if he wasn't, Zurah wasn't sure it was wise to hand over the only bargaining chip she had discovered.

She blinked and scanned through the readings coming off the portals. There was a wealth of information, and most of it would require quite a bit of time to sift through. As she blinked the extra screen off, a wave of unease washed through her. This was a level of technology way beyond her understanding. And in Zurah's line of work, more often than not, things that appeared outwardly beautiful often ended up having an ugly truth buried at its heart.

"Tell me, how did the other you… the copy, come to be? And more than that, why are people following its orders? Can't they figure out the difference between what it is and a real flesh-and-blood human?"

"All good questions, and ones I've attempted to answer. But everything so far leads me here."

Alex began to pace, weaving between the shimmering

portals. Zurah kept a close eye on him, with the gun trained on him.

"Here's another one for you. Why are you *here*? And why are you alone?" Zurah asked.

Alex stopped, lifted an arm, and opened and closed his fingers a few times, as if testing the flexibility of his suit. "I'm here because I received a distress call from Finn. But as it turns out, she didn't send it. So I decided to lay low, do recon, and ascertain what was going on. The next thing I knew, comm chatter exploded about Alex Goldsmith taking over and forcing everyone to choose a side."

Again, Zurah considered providing Alex with more information. "Did you send a distress call to Finn?"

His head snapped up, and he stared at her. "No. I had considered it but didn't want to without more information."

"Then someone has purposefully lured the two of you here," Zurah said. "Because that's why Finn is here. A distress call from someone named Turner and one from you."

"Turner?" Alex stepped toward her. "Are you sure?"

Zurah nodded.

"Turner was the first person I tried to check in with, but he's dead."

That news wasn't a welcome revelation, and Zurah immediately traced back to her last conversation with Finn. She had questioned where Finn had gone when everything went pear-shaped, and she'd only given Zurah a cryptic answer. Zurah hadn't done a scan to check if Finn was still Finn. *Fool.*

"What's at the beta site?" she asked.

"The primary research field. Most of the technician's energies went into setting up that area. This site and a handful like it had only basic equipment installed."

"Even with a discovery of this magnitude?" Zurah asked.

"Yes. The beta site is focused on the gates."

"All right, riddle me this, then. Why the hell are you guys even here? What's the big deal with the *Eagle's Nest*?"

Alex shook his head. "For that, I need to show you."

He started to step toward one of the portals, but Zurah rushed forward. "Stop!"

Alex froze and turned to stare at her.

She huffed, unhappy to give up information at this point, but her logic was sound. "One of the energy signatures matches what I picked up on coming from your copy. Who is to say that going through these portals hasn't somehow made the copy? Or triggered something?"

Alex frowned. "Then why aren't there copies of all the researchers running around? Individuals have been coming and going for quite a while now as they've been studying these. But honestly…" He turned to look at the portal. "I don't know. But I can assure you, the only way to unravel this mystery is by seeing what's on the other side."

"I've learned that sometimes the risk isn't worth the reward," Zurah countered.

"If that was the case, then why are you here?"

Because I trusted my boss, who put her faith in Finn not getting us killed. But the words were stuck in her throat, and her thoughts circled back to Nissa. Trust. There was that slippery word. *Why didn't Nissa tell me the truth?*

"Your copy wasn't the only strange thing I saw," Zurah said, deflecting from Alex's question. "I was asked to help clear the medics, and one of them… they warned me and then turned into sand." She paused, gauging Alex's reaction.

He pressed his lips together and narrowed his eyes.

"I believe that whatever it is was fighting your copy. If it wasn't for that medic, I don't think I would've made it off the bridge." *And Mexa's sacrifice.* But that wound was too raw to speak aloud.

"That could explain a few things," he murmured.

"Like what?"

He sighed. "Again, it'll be easier to explain on the other side."

Zurah stepped back, her certainty wavering. "I need intel, but what guarantees do you have that this isn't the worst idea ever? I'm supposed to get to the beta site, my… boss's life depends on it."

There was a drawn-out pause, and her shallow breaths and rapid heartbeat filled the silence.

"Finn's team."

Zurah nodded.

"She's still alive, then?" he asked.

"Were you hoping for the opposite? So you could take over? Or was it that you could stop her from taking over? There seems to be some confusion around the matter."

"Neither. Finn reached out to me about this little pet project of hers, and I offered to help. She would run the majority of the teams, while I was free to check in and provide oversight as needed."

"Then why are you hiding out here?"

Alex scowled. "As I've already stated, I'm not hiding. I'm trying to understand what's happening before running headlong into a problem I can't solve."

"I think you're avoiding dealing with it," Zurah shot back. "People are dying out there, believing or being forced to believe that Alex Goldsmith has started a coup or is finishing one. You could tell them that's not true. Make them see that… that *thing* for what it really is."

"And until I have the proof that I need or a way to stop him—this copy—from forcing people… good people into following his orders, I will. Just, look." He huffed. "Everything will make a lot more sense if you would just come with me."

"You seem pretty keen on getting me to step through one of these things," Zurah said, pointing with her free hand at one of the shimmering diamonds. "Usually, that means it's something someone shouldn't do."

"I've watched horror vids, read those jute-store novels," Alex said. "And sure, this is usually when something pops out and eats you or disembowels someone. But this isn't one of those stories. At least not yet. But if you want to leave, fine. Go on. Take your chances out there and see if you can make it to the beta site. If you do, tell Finn I'm here, and I'll be waiting for her." And with that, Alex turned and stormed out.

Zurah watched him leave, and once he had disappeared into the tunnel, she lowered the gun. Indecision weighed heavily on her. The little that Alex had just shared, coupled with the possibility of the portals, was far more than she bargained for. Following him through a portal might provide helpful intel, but that was putting trust in a man she had just met. And not only that, this man was at the head of one of the most notorious organizations in the known world.

Whenever Nissa or another boss had accepted a job, someone was always tasked with digging up dirt—on not only the target but also the individual or group who had hired the crew. Jobs always went off track, and having leverage over others was an important part of staying alive. Zurah had never had to deal with that end of things, though. She might have helped by hacking into security systems or files, but then it was turned over to someone else to sort through the information. Even if she was able to figure out what was going on, Zurah wasn't confident she would be able to make sense of it. *And if I do? Can I find Finn's or Alex's weaknesses? And exploit them?*

Zurah was sure of one thing. Nissa would have a backup plan, and Zurah didn't. She took a long look at the shimmering diamond hovering before her. If the heir to the Goldsmith Consortium was willing to step through the portals, then that was worth paying attention to. *Enough dithering. Get the intel, form a backup plan, save Nissa, and get the hell off this planet.*

Zurah stepped into the shimmering air… and stepped out into the void. For a split second, her heart leapt into her throat, and she feared she was free-floating. But her boots were firmly placed on something solid, surrounded by the vastness of space. Off to her right was an explosion of color. Bright blues and greens with touches of reds and yellows stretched into long, thin strands, crisscrossing within the nebula. Space had never appeared to be so beautiful before, and Zurah couldn't tear her eyes away from the sight.

"Impressive, isn't it?" Alex stepped beside her.

Zurah didn't flinch at his presence, as she was so taken in by the mesmerizing scene. Alex remained silent, letting Zurah absorb the beauty and the impossibility of the situation. When she turned away, Alex cleared his throat. As he talked, Zurah realized they were standing on some type of platform—a structure that had sustained quite a bit of damage.

"I've read through the reports, and no one has come to a consensus yet as to what or who constructed these. Personally, I would lay bets on an ancient race we aren't aware of. Humanity forgets, I think, how infinitely tiny we are, even as far flung into the known worlds as we've become. You might even say it's a poor character trait of our species, always believing we're much bigger and more important in the cosmic order than we really are."

"Philosophy was never my style," Zurah said. "But in this moment, I think I can agree with you."

"If you look over there, you'll see a spire of some sort. Best guess is there is some residual technology still in play that's keeping these pieces together and anchored to this spot. And of course, allowing us to come and go. Here..." He motioned her over to examine twin pillars with a semicircle resting on top.

Suspended within the cradle of the curve was a diamond-shaped piece of metal with a strange symbol.

"These are what allow us to transport back." He reached out, touched the symbol lightly, and vanished. Zurah blinked, did a quick three-hundred-sixty-degree turn while recording the area, then touched the symbol.

Safely back in the cavern, Zurah reappeared a few meters to the left of Alex. "All right," she said. "I'll confess, I'm impressed. But that could have been explained to me. Teleportation technology isn't a new idea."

"True," he replied with a shrug. "But that was just the warm-up act." He moved to stand in front of a different shimmering diamond. "This is where the fun begins."

Zurah wasn't sure that was how she would describe their current situation.

"A word of caution, though—once you step through here, don't move. Just stay still."

She nodded and watched as Alex went through first, then she followed, her fingers involuntarily tightening around the gun.

Her sense of balance was immediately challenged, and she waved her arms, trying to stay steady.

Alex reached out, caught her arms, and helped her regain her footing. "I would still advise holstering the gun."

Zurah didn't argue.

The portal had taken them to a narrow ledge surrounded by nothing but the emptiness of space. No brilliant nebula or twinkling stars. Nothing but pitch black. Alex flipped on his suit's lights, and Zurah did the same.

"I continually marvel at the brave few who take the first steps into the unknown. Risking their lives in the pursuit of knowledge. The records indicate after the third individual to step through, they understood what was happening. Here, if you turn to your right—carefully, that's it—you'll see this ledge extends for several meters. This paneling behind us is sturdy, and you can use it to help catch your balance. Someone even attached a few handholds here and there. See?"

Feeling a tad lightheaded, Zurah tried but found her feet wouldn't move. "I... I can't," she whispered.

Alex turned back and studied the situation for a moment. "Think you can stay there for just a few minutes?"

Zurah gulped but nodded.

"All right. Don't move. I'll be back." With ease, Alex traversed the ledge and disappeared into the darkness.

"Alex?" Zurah called out but got no response. *What in the worlds have I gotten myself into?* She felt another wave of dizziness and closed her eyes, leaning against the panel. She felt sure she was going to fall and die floating along in the depths of space. Her legs began to tremble, and her knees buckled just as a pair of hands wrapped around her waist.

"Hold on. I've got you," Alex said.

Zurah tried to regain control, but all she could do was tremble at the fear of wasting away in the emptiness.

"Deep breaths, focus on the panel. Look for the next handhold."

Zurah followed his instructions, held on to the reassuring calm in his voice, and caught sight of a knob-like protrusion a meter or so in front of her. With Alex's hand holding her firmly, Zurah took a deep breath and slid a foot forward. She swung her arm and grabbed the knob.

"That's it. Just keep going. I've got you."

Little by little, Zurah moved forward, and when she saw that the ledge finally appeared to widen, she let out a deep sigh of relief. Alex continued to hold on even as they moved away from the edge.

"Thanks, I—" Zurah gaped. The platform was vastly different from the first. The dimensions were beyond comprehension, and it held gigantic megalithic slabs of rock placed at irregular intervals on the perimeter of the platform. In the center, a tall spire stretched up into the blackness of space.

But as grand and awe-inspiring as the view was, it wasn't what had stolen her breath. Lying on what she assumed was its side was some type of ship. Flat and full of odd angles, it had strange bulbous protrusions on either end. Its hull gleamed gold, as if bathed in sunlight, and bled soft-purple lights at what Zurah presumed were seams. As Zurah took it all in, she realized the ship was actually grafted *into* the platform. She turned and stared at Alex. "How is any of this possible?"

"Your guess is as good as mine. And this isn't even the half of it. Come on." He headed toward the ship, and Zurah hurried to keep up.

A small section had been removed from the ship's outer hull, but before Alex ducked inside, he pointed. "Look."

"No." Small drifts of sand were clumped up against where the ship and platform melded into one. "Do you think that has anything to do with what I saw?"

"From what I know, the probability is strong. It looks like sand. That's how we would describe it. But it isn't. Not really. The chemistry and compounds break down into things we don't have names for. There's more throughout the ship."

Alex ducked inside, and Zurah hesitated for only a second before doing the same. The walls were coated in petrified vines with large broad leaves and delicate flowers. Zurah glanced up, and instead of seeing either more of the same or some type of hull plating, wispy clouds drifted gently back and forth in a soft blue summer sky. Zurah shook her head, turned, and stepped out of the ship, craning her neck to look at the top.

Alex appeared in the doorway and grinned. "It's quite a trip, isn't it?"

"I've never seen anything like this. The level of technology, of engineering, it's…" She was at a loss for words to even describe how impossible it all was. She moved back inside the ship, disbelief crowding out any rational thought.

"Come through here."

As if in a dream, she followed Alex through the interior of the ship. The gentle blue sky never wavered, and all the side walls were constructed from the petrified foliage. Here and there were small piles of sand, some neatly clumped together, while others appeared to be spread thin across the flooring. Alex led Zurah through the ship, until they reached one of the odd bubble-like protrusions on the end.

Zurah understood why Alex had said it was easier to show her instead of trying to tell her what this was. A soft golden light flowed down from the sky, widening into a generous circle, where a replica of the *Eagle's Nest* was suspended in the middle of the room.

10

Zurah didn't have the exact layout of the infamous ship memorized, but from what she did remember, the model appeared to be well done. Moving slowly in a circle around the projection, she considered the model from all angles. When she finished, Alex leaned forward and passed his hand through the light. The image shifted from the ship to that of an individual.

"Captain Ujthout?"

"Yes," Alex said. "And that's not all." He passed his hand through the light again and again. Each time, a new image of a member of the *Eagle's Nest* crew appeared. "The entire manifest is in here, and once you've cycled through it, the images start over, beginning with the ship."

The improbability of everything she had experienced within the day was overwhelming. She reached out, searching for a chair that wasn't there, and stumbled backward. Her eyes fixed on the projection of the latest crew member, she slid slowly down the wall. "So, at least this much is true. Finn really is researching what happened to the ship and its crew."

"One of her goals, yes."

"But why? What's so important about it? It was lost over three hundred years ago. I get that a historian might be interested and all that, but there are hundreds of ships that have gone missing. What makes this one so special?"

"Beside the fact it and its crew have been logged into some unknown alien database?" Alex asked.

"Sure, but Finn couldn't have known that when the research began. They would have discovered this after the fact," Zurah said.

Alex grinned, and for a moment, the tension and weariness drained from his face. His dark-brown eyes twinkled with the delight of someone who knew more than they were sharing. "Who says that Finn is the one who started the research?"

"I thought you said there wasn't some kind of coup? That you weren't trying to take over."

"I'm not. But Finn wasn't the first to begin research-ing what happened. Her great-grandmother did. Even though the records were sealed, Finn discovered them and has been intrigued ever since."

"Right," Zurah muttered. "I find it hard to believe that *the* Finn is risking everything just because she's curious. What's the catch? What is all of this knowledge worth?"

Alex's good humor vanished. "Why does there have to be a catch?"

Zurah sighed. "Because there always is."

"Believe what you want." Alex schooled his face into a neutral expression and held out his hand to help her up. "There's one more place you need to see."

A twinge of guilt pinched her chest as she realized her flippant attitude had caused him to shut down. *That's not how you gather intel.*

As they made their way out of the alien ship, Zurah considered the man. Alex obviously held a lot of knowledge about what was happening, and he had shared far more than Finn had. Perhaps he would have continued to share if she had chosen her words a bit more wisely. Cultivating Alex as an ally would be a wise decision, and Zurah decided she needed to work on that. *Finn may or may not come through, and a Goldsmith would have the resources I might need one day.*

Despite Alex's cool demeanor, he held out his hand once they were at the narrow ledge. Zurah grabbed it, his fingers closed around her own, and she took comfort in the support. She had been too petrified and had missed the medallion with the strange symbol. There was no pedestal for this one, and Zurah assumed an earlier researcher had rescued it and attached it to the panel backing the narrow ledge. Before reaching out to touch it, she recorded the image with a quick look over her shoulder. Once back in the cavern, she took a few deep breaths, greatly appreciating standing on something firm and reliable.

There were no words exchanged. Alex simply glanced over at Zurah to make sure she had safely returned, then he passed through a third portal. With one last deep breath, Zurah stepped through, as well.

The portal took them to yet another platform, one riddled with scorch marks. Large sections of the structure were floating above gaping holes in the platform, each one rotating slowly. Along the edge of the platform were the splintered pieces of what Zurah assumed had once been a shell or dome. Several of the pieces were quite tall and still impressive. The only tangible difference between the new platform and the previous two was the unmistakable feeling of being watched. Despite the protection of the suit, a cold chill passed through her, and Zurah scanned the area. Her SeeClear tech didn't pick up on any living lifeforms, but as Zurah hurried to catch up to Alex—who was maneuvering through the jagged edges with practiced ease—she couldn't shake the feeling that they weren't alone.

Alex paused, waiting for Zurah, and when she was a few steps away, he descended into the platform. Zurah felt a surge of fear, then as she looked down, realized the hole was smooth along the edges. A wide staircase was casually winding its way down into the darkness. The lights on Alex's suit bobbed up and down as he took each step, and Zurah seriously considered turning around and returning to Objer. Her hand moved to the gun, firmly tucked in its holster, and she wondered if it would do her any good in a place like this.

Alex's lights were fading, and Zurah needed to decide. *I've come this far, might as well see this through.* She took to the stairs and headed down. Her suit's light illuminated more of the strange symbols carved into the massive pillar that held the stairs. The symbols were grouped together and placed at regular intervals. Even though linguistics wasn't anywhere near her skill set, she assumed this was the language of the aliens who had constructed this place.

At last, the staircase ended, and the floor extended out into a fully enclosed platform that showed no signs of damage. The area was far larger than the one above. Scattered along the perimeter were alcoves, and Alex was already heading toward one of them.

Zurah started to follow then felt the firm reassuring presence of the platform give way to something gritty and unstable. She immediately stepped back and looked down at a pile of sand. She swung her head both ways, also using the light on the undersides of her wrists to expose more of the space. Piles of sand were clustered up against the base of the staircase, and there were a few more throughout the space.

An unsettling feeling fluttered in her gut, and her chest tightened in apprehension. Zurah had only experienced a severe attack of sixth sense one other time. It had been during her second job with Nissa. They'd needed to break into an abandoned dwelling that had once belonged to a well-known Glipglow. The second they had stepped foot inside the atrium, Zurah had felt ill. Dust and cobwebs filled the space, and there were no signs of life besides their footprints in the dirt, which had blown through the growing cracks between the doors and windows. She had stopped Nissa and told her they needed to leave, that something horrible had happened there, and that it wasn't safe. Nissa had given her a peculiar look but had backed them out and set up a casting net. The report had revealed the house was booby-trapped. Not only that, but tucked away in the depths of the lower decks were skeletons. Glipglow and human alike.

Now, Zurah was experiencing the same feeling. "Alex, stop." When he didn't, she added, "Please."

Alex did and turned to stare at her.

"We need to leave," she whispered, sweat beginning to bead along her forehead. "This place isn't right."

"I thought you wanted answers."

"I do, but not here. We need to leave, now." She felt the surety of knowing something horrendous had taken place, and the stench of such atrocity clung to the space.

"Just give me a moment," he said and continued to head to the alcove.

"You can do what you like," Zurah said. "But I'm leaving." She started to leave, then her light caught something bright and glistening above the alcove Alex was headed toward. A gentle hum started, its vibrations gently moving through the floor. She froze then watched in horror as a crystalline structure began to shift. It fractured then expanded, new crystals emerging as they forced their way through the wall, heading toward the side of the alcove.

"Alex, run!"

He didn't move.

"Above you! Get back!"

Zurah wasn't going to warn him again. Nor was she going to wait. She turned and ran for the stairs. A flash of crystal caught her attention on the side of the pillar supporting the stairs. Then another on the edge of a step ahead of her.

"Go, I'm right behind you!" Alex yelled.

Together, they took the stairs two at a time, narrowly dodging budding crystals as they exploded out of the stairs and walls. At one point, Alex stumbled, and Zurah stopped to grab his arm and drag him back to his feet. They raced to the top of the platform and headed for the symbol to take them back to safety. When they were only meters away, a pale-orange crystal erupted up through the platform in front of them. They skidded to a stop then stumbled back a few steps, watching in terror. Crystals continued to explode, the chips rapidly expanding and growing into new, healthy pieces. Layers began to form, winding around itself, until the edges started to retract and reform. Within seconds, a human-oid-shaped creature was standing before them. There were no discernible features on its face, just a gaping hole where a mouth should be.

Alex moved to stand in front of Zurah, and she caught the subtle shift along the edge of the cuffs of his suit as he activated the weapon's system.

"What do you want?" he asked.

The creature's mouth opened and closed as if it were getting used to the sensation. "Justice." The word was as clear as a bell in the emptiness of space.

"Justice for what?" Alex asked.

"Desecration." Its mouth opened wide, small bits of crystal pushing out like teeth erupting. "Desecration of the tomb." Its words flowed effortlessly.

"If this is considered a sacred area, we were not aware," Alex said. "Please accept our apologies for walking where we do not belong."

"Contrition? It is in our experience your form does not possess this quality."

"I can assure you that humanity does, although it may not present itself in every single representation," Alex replied. "If you would allow us to leave, we can ensure no one else returns to this place."

"Your form was warned, and the same assurances given. Then you returned and harvested from our dead."

"I wasn't aware of any prior warnings, nor do I understand what you mean by harvesting from your dead. Can you explain this?"

Zurah watched in equal parts fascination and horror as the creature did far better than explain. It *showed* them. The lower half of its crystalline body crumbled and fell. The shards vibrated and expanded in an explosion of growth until they stopped to reveal an expertly rendered replication of the *Eagle's Nest*.

"But that was over three hundred years ago," Zurah blurted out.

"Years?" the creature asked, its strange head tilted to the side in a horrific mimic of human expression. "A construct of time, a linguist and cultural formation in order to orient your species within the *ov* dimension, is it not?"

"That sounds correct," Alex replied. "Are you telling us that the crew of the *Eagle's Nest* are the ones responsible for the desecration of your dead?"

The creature's head resumed a normal angle and

jerked down then back up. "Leniency was granted upon the first transgression. Then upon the second, a warning was issued. Now a demonstration is required."

The *Eagle's Nest* shifted, and a smaller craft took its place. Neither Zurah nor Alex recognized it. The small craft shifted, and a hatch opened. A miniature crystalline human stepped out. It walked forward, its stiff legs swinging its torso back and forth. When it stopped, another crystal rose then collapsed on the human figure, completely engulfing it.

"And now, justice has been requested, and justice has been dispensed."

"*Has* been dispensed?" Alex questioned.

"The situation will be rectified. The gateways to the dead will be closed, and all who hold this knowledge will be consumed."

"Holy shit," Alex muttered. "It's got to be talking about my—"

"Copy," Zurah finished. "This appears to be doing the same thing I saw your copy do on the bridge."

"We've got to get back, warn the others," Alex said. "Any intel on how to disarm or neutralize this thing?"

Zurah blinked and ran a quick scan. The anomalous energy spikes she had picked up on Objer and emanating from the copy of Alex were present. But that would take too long to work through to provide any actionable advice. The crystals had an eighty-seven percent match with Old Earth specimens that were constructed of hexagonal pyramid structures. But there were irregularities and differences, and Zurah wasn't sure what they represented or how to use the information. Electrical signals raced throughout the crystalline structure, and buried deep within the heart of the creature was a larger piece of crystal that didn't match anything in the database. Zurah zeroed in on that part, looking for anything she might identify as a weakness. But the information she was receiving was gibberish to her.

"No," Zurah whispered. She considered trying to link her SeeClear with Alex's suit, but that would require access to its system to bypass a few security issues. And they didn't have time for that. Her mind whipped through a dozen different possibilities, but none of them returned a viable alternative. The creature shifted, the crystal on its right breaking and falling to the platform, only to grow and thicken on that side.

Justice? What did it mean by justice? The question wormed its way into Zurah's calculations. *What was the copy of Alex going to do?* For Zurah, the thought of justice aligned more with retribution. Destroying those who had done harm or who threatened to do more harm. Instead, the copy of Alex was insidiously embedding itself with the researchers, forcing them to recognize his authority. Or perhaps, with this creature questioning their sense of time, it meant they didn't experience time as the majority of species within the known worlds did. *Could three hundred years be a blink of an eye? Or even less to them?*

Alex cleared his throat, took a small step forward, and raised his arm. Without warning, he fired. At the center of the energy burst, a part of the crystal liquefied, and as it dripped down the creature, the drops hardened into a darkened version of the rest. Alex fired again, and this time, the energy rippled across the crystal creature.

When he fired the third time, as the energy spread across the crystal, it created intricate geometric patterns and appeared to energize the crystal.

"Stop." Zurah tugged on Alex's arm. "You're not having any effect." His arm didn't move, and she watched the barrel of Alex's weapon grow hot. "Stop it!"

The platform vibrated, throwing both of them off-balance. Alex powered down his weapon. His arms shot out to grab Zurah and twist her around as a piece of crystal burst through the platform less than a meter in front of them. He grabbed her arm and started to pull her back toward the staircase.

"Come on," he snapped. "We need to find cover or a defensible position."

"Not down there, we don't. We'll just get trapped. We need exit strategies," Zurah protested.

"The Timeless Sleepers see all," the creature calmly said as it deconstructed then reformed to move itself across the platform.

Zurah shivered at the words, and Alex huffed at her refusal to move. "Then what?" he asked. "Down there, we might be able to take cover, find a defensible location. You didn't see what is in the alcoves. There's—"

"It doesn't matter. Don't you get it?" Zurah snapped. She was sure of one thing—if they went back down there, they were dead. "Just... just distract it and let me think."

"And how do you propose I do that?" he asked.

"I don't know. Throw some Consortium mumbo jumbo at it. Act like you're negotiating for a new planet or something." Zurah turned her attention to her suit.

She scrolled through the menu, trying to figure out what she had that could be useful. But the system was old, and the suit had originally been designed when long-term exploration was prevalent. The material was heavy, ungainly, and not meant for combat maneuvers or little else besides maintenance in the void. The rocket pack was antiquated, as well, designed to use with a tether system for external ship repairs, not fancy—

That's it.

She glanced at the back of Alex's suit. The technology was streamlined with little thought to what punches the technology packed. "Alex, does your suit have rocket boosters? Maneuverability?"

He didn't take his eyes off the crystal creature as he replied. "Minimal capability. Switched out the upgraded system for weapons."

Zurah double-checked her suit's rocket system, and the plan formed in her mind. "All right. Here's what we do. Finn said the gun was modified. I don't know for what exactly, but it should at least provide some kind of distraction. I'll shoot the creature then fire my rocket pack, which should be enough to shoot us up a good thirty to thirty-five meters, then you fire up your boosters and maneuver us over to the portal symbol back to Objer."

"Worth a try," Alex said, "but if it doesn't work, then we fall back. Clear?"

"Clear," Zurah said. But she was confident her plan would work. Alex's weapons were energy based, but the gun Finn had provided was old school. The fact Finn's great-grandmother had begun the research, put together with Finn's cryptic reasoning for the gun, gave Zurah the confidence to believe Finn was well aware that energy-based weapons weren't effective.

She pulled out the gun, took off the safety, and prepared to fire as Alex tethered his suit to hers. As her finger slid over the trigger, a piece of crystal broke through the platform and, before either of them could react, encased Alex's feet.

Alex's reaction was lightning quick, and he cut the tether before Zurah realized what he was doing. He shoved her to the side, and he grimaced as the crystal pulled itself up along his legs.

"Go, get out of here." He groaned.

"No, I'm not leaving you." Zurah turned her gun to aim at the base of the crystal holding him in place.

"Don't be a fool," he hissed as the crystal spread across his thighs. "The others have to be warned."

But Zurah fired. The bullet fractured the crystal around his feet, and for a brief moment, she thought she would be able to free him. But the shards reformed and created another layer on top of what was rapidly consuming Alex. Desperate, Zurah flipped the gun around and knelt, bashing the butt of the gun against the crystal. But her efforts had no effect. She spun around. "Let him go. We've done nothing wrong."

"The Timeless Sleepers see all. Justice has been called."

Zurah screamed in frustration and turned back to Alex. "Here, I'm going to wrap my arms around you. My suit may be old, but it should pack a punch. Maybe the burst will break you free."

"Don't." Alex groaned. "Don't touch me or it. I can already feel—" All the color had drained from his face. "Just go," he whispered. "Save yourself." The crystal continued to spread, moving across his torso and his arms.

Zurah didn't want to leave him behind, but with the rapid rate of growth, she knew there wasn't anything she could do. Not with the tools she had. Her suit was heavy and made her feel sluggish as she moved, trying to dart around the crystal creature. But its crystal spread, while other pieces pushed up through the platform, blocking her every move. She considered firing up her rockets, but without maneuverability, she had no way to ensure she could get to the portal symbol and not float off into space.

Damn. She holstered the gun and realized if she was going to save him, the only option she had was what Alex had suggested. She spared him one last look. The crystal was already to his neck, and she fervently hoped his suit was strong enough not to crack under the pressure. For a brief moment, Mexa was inside the suit, and when she blinked, Zurah saw Nissa next. She shook her head and stared at Alex's pale face. *I won't watch someone else die.*

"I'll come back. I promise," she whispered, and she took off down the staircase.

11

Crystals burst through the upper portion of the stairs, reaching out toward each other and effectively sealing Zurah below. Racing down the stairs, she tried to watch out for any crystals that had pushed through the walls and stairs. As she wound deeper into the darkness, the crystals stopped growing and instead began to produce an eerie orange light. Working to catch her breath, Zurah slowed down, taking note of what she was seeing.

There were several large clusters, along with single crystals sporadically placed throughout the facility. One particularly bright cluster made her heart race as she felt it stretch toward her when she passed. Once she hit the second platform, she wished for more light to dispel the dark which enveloped her.

There were crystals scattered throughout the floor and dotting the walls where the alcoves were located. Zurah questioned her choice to return to the space, but even if she wanted to go back up, she couldn't, not without finding a way to either destroy or at least temporarily halt the crystals. She was trapped.

Wrapping her fingers around the butt of the gun, she considered her odds of just shooting her way out and making a mad dash for safety. But that would leave Alex trapped in the cocoon of crystal. While the temptation to flee was strong, Zurah couldn't stop the rotating images of the dead and nearly dead. What she needed to do was clear her mind and focus. She had gone there to gather intel, and that was exactly what she was going to do.

Alex had insisted on showing her what was in the alcoves. In fact, Zurah believed whatever was down there was the one thing he'd felt she *needed* to see. Everything else had been window dressing meant to expose her mind to the possibilities of the impossible. But her answers lay here, trapped in an eternal darkness.

Cautiously, she approached one of the alcoves. The lights on her suit cut through the darkness, and Zurah screamed. Standing in the center of the alcove was a crystalline figure.

There was no soft halo of light emanating from the crystal, though. And as Zurah gulped in air and forced herself to step closer, she realized there was a *person* inside the crystal. *Just like Alex.*

She scanned the figure and was shocked when an alert popped up.

Crewman Halion Prophen, SubClass B, Engineer, First Shift of the Eagle's Nest, current status unknown

"Dear god," Zurah muttered, and she quickly moved to the next alcove. Even though she was expecting it, as her lights struck the crystal, she still felt a tingle of fear. She scanned the figure.

Crewman Kathleen Yule, SubClass A, Pilot, Second Shift of the Eagle's Nest, current status unknown

The next three alcoves held three more crew members. When Zurah moved on to the next, she wasn't sure what to think. This crystalline figure was missing half of its head, as if someone had taken a blunt instrument to the person's face. Zurah ran a scan, but the facial recognition program wasn't able to discern which crew member it had once been.

She moved back to the first alcove and studied Crewman Prophen, wondering if he could still be alive under the crystal. He didn't appear to be wearing any sort of protective suit. And she dearly hoped Alex's suit would be able to protect him until she could figure out how to free him. Her mind raced through a hundred different thoughts. *Am I witnessing the consequences of the crew from the* Eagle's Nest *somehow disturbing this alien place? Was this what the crystalline entity considered justice? If the research team discovered these lost crew members, then why keep it a secret?* Even though a handful of generations would have lived and died, undoubtedly, family members would be glad to have that facet of their lives come to a resolution.

Enough with the questions. This is a job. Approach it like any other. There was a system that needed to be hacked. She needed to understand how the crystals were able to replicate. Then she could find a way to break the bonds, free Alex, and make it back to Objer, where they could warn the others. Zurah scanned each of the figures in the alcoves, compiling data and cursing the antiquated suit. The SeeClear tech was helpful, but she needed to be able to cross-check information and run computations through a more powerful processor.

As she moved from alcove to alcove, the programs silently churning data, Zurah wondered why these particular individuals from the crew had been left here. The alien ship on the other platform held data on every single crew member. *Did the others not survive? Did the alien ship strip information from the* Eagle's Nest? *Or perhaps these were the only crew members who disturbed this place. But again, what happened to the rest of the crew?*

Not to mention the sand creature who had saved her life and the piles of the stuff scattered throughout the platforms. Once she had scanned the crystallized men and women, Zurah crouched and analyzed a pile of sand. Her working assumption was that the sand and the crystals were adversaries or at least entities who didn't see eye to eye. The theory made sense, considering the medic had defended her against Alex. *Were the sand creatures from the crashed ship? Or were the crystals?*

The programs finished running, and Zurah blinked to bring up the reports. There were biological conclusions, a breakdown of components, several hypotheses, and a lot of scientific jargon that meant nothing to her. Adding in the observations from Alex's weapon blasts and how rapidly the fragments of crystal were able to reform and grow, Zurah felt as frustrated as she had before. Angry and scared, Zurah moved around the perimeter of the platform, looking at each alcove for some sort of clue. Zurah wondered if Alex had wanted to show her the lost crew or if she was missing something. A piece of information that would help her combat the crystals. She needed to find an answer. She had no idea how long Alex's suit would be able to protect him.

Zurah found herself back at the individual who had been partially destroyed, wondering why the crystal hadn't grown back. Cursing herself, she moved as close as she dared and did another set of scans. *This was where I should have been focusing my time.*

Blinking, she magnified her vision as far as it would go. The internal structure was breathtaking, geometrical patterns within the hexagonal substrate. Several of the geometric patterns had tendrils with feathered ends reaching out from the center of a pattern to touch another offshoot from neighboring patterns.

A small text box popped up in Zurah's lower-right field of vision. *Comparative analysis among database sets show similarities between known neurological systems.*

Zurah considered the information. Biology wasn't her strong suit, but a handful of security systems and AI programs were patterned off neural networks. That was something she could work with.

Feeling a rush of excitement, Zurah stepped back without paying attention to where she placed her foot. Her boot slipped on a pile of sand, and she involuntarily swung out her arms to steady herself, grabbing hold of the crystalline figure. Once steady, she realized what she was holding onto and let go, fear gnawing at her belly. She shook her gloves and examined them for any signs of crystal. While the crystal encasing the crew members appeared to be inert, Zurah wasn't up for taking chances.

There were a few minute particles on her glove, but

the readout indicated they were not crystal but sand. *The sand.* If they were opposing forces, and what she had witnessed on the bridge was accurate, then perhaps she could figure out a way to use the sand to slow down the crystals. She wasn't worried about completely destroying the creature or its offshoots. All she wanted was to get Alex and get out of there.

Ignoring her concerns, Zurah scooped up a handful of the sand and analyzed it. However it functioned, she couldn't parse out any clues, no matter what program she ran. Frustrated but curious, she tossed the handful of sand at the damaged figure. No reaction. Not that she was expecting any, but she decided to try again. She gathered another handful of sand then decided to toss it at some of the glowing crystal. When the sand touched the crystal, Zurah heard the distinct sound of popping and sizzling, and the soft light within the crystal briefly flared then dimmed to half its previous strength.

Relief flooded her body. At least she had a workable idea, even if she didn't understand how any of it was possible. But these were the only tools she had, and without more intel or understanding of how the crystals and the sand functioned, this was her chance.

At first she went around scooping up sand until it was streaming through her fingers, then realizing how foolish that was, she stopped. *I need a way of carrying large quantities of the sand, of delivering it fast enough to at least distract the creature, grab Alex, and make a run for it.* Zurah didn't want to admit it, but if she couldn't free Alex, she would have to leave him. Even though she had only just met him, that thought made her sick.

She tucked a handful of sand into her only pocket, and her hand brushed up against the gun. Pulling out one of the bullets, she examined it. To her relief, Zurah discovered she would be able to open and repack each bullet with a small amount of sand.

By the time she had repacked fifty-seven bullets, sweat was running down her face from sheer nerves. She held the gun and took a deep breath. *One more sweep of the area, then it's now or never.*

Recording her last round through the platform, she gripped the gun and headed for the stairs. The crystals' glow illuminated her path but didn't appear to stretch and grow as she passed. Zurah reasoned whatever intelligence drove the crystalline creature must have dismissed her as a threat. When she reached the top, her hand was shaking, and she nearly decided to head back down and try to come up with a different plan.

As a security hack, her job was to find nonviolent solutions, ways to work around a system to get people in and out. If the worst happened, she could turn a security system on the people it was designed to protect. But that was a last-resort option that Zurah never wanted to use. And ever since the horrible job where innocent people had died because of her curiosity, she had done everything she could to make sure senseless violence didn't happen again.

She raised her arm, the tremor uncontrollable, and she had to holster the gun and shake her hands, steeling her nerve. Once more, she drew the gun and aimed at the crystal covering the exit. *Now or never.*

Zurah fired. The bullet exploded from the gun and

shattered the crystal. There was a brief flash of light, and pieces of crystal rained down around her. Zurah stepped back, careful not to let any of the crystal touch her suit. Where the bullet had impacted the crystal dome, the edges appeared to struggle to reform. She took a few seconds to observe the crystal, which had fallen. None of it seemed to grow. Satisfied, she fired two more shots, creating a hole big enough to let her pass, and she ran up the last few steps and away from the stairway.

The crystal creature hadn't moved, still blocking the best path to the portal symbol, and Alex stood as a sentinel, fully encased in crystal. A soft light sparked to life in a cluster of crystals to her left, and the light seemed to jump from crystal to crystal until it reached the creature. Not waiting to see what was going to happen, Zurah started firing. She emptied the chamber on the creature, watching as pieces crumbled off the whole. The majority of the creature still appeared to be alive and began to reform, but the edges around the impact areas weren't.

Quickly reloading, she turned, then with only a moment of hesitation, she fired at the base of crystal holding Alex. She shifted her weight and fired again, aiming the bullets so they grazed the sides of Alex. Cracks formed, and crystal splintered. Zurah started kicking at the crystal. She focused on freeing Alex's feet, and for once, she was glad for her outdated suit's heavy boots. With each swing, she was able to break off a piece of crystal.

A flash of light caught her eye, and she turned in

time to see the creature begin to repair the holes. Zurah once again emptied the chamber, trying to slow down the creature as much as possible. As she reloaded, she felt dismayed by how little progress she was making with Alex. Her supply of bullets was finite, and if she continued having to go back and forth, she was going to quickly be out of ammunition.

If only I could reach his controls, Zurah thought frantically.

"You have dared to disturb this sacred field of dead," the creature's voice loomed all around her. "Justice shall be dispensed."

Crystal shot out, pushing through the platform and racing toward Zurah. She leaped to the side, her foot narrowly missing being impaled. Desperate and out of options, she aimed at Alex's arm, just below the small rectangular protuberance where the rocket booster should have been. Through a small miracle, cracks formed, and pieces of crystal broke off. Frantic, she flipped the gun around and slammed the butt against the crystal, breaking enough off to get to the screen on Alex's arm. There was still power running through the suit, and Zurah brought up the menu, looking for the rocket controls.

A person-sized crystal broke through the platform centimeters away from Zurah. She yelped and stumbled back, tripping over another piece of crystal. She crashed against the platform with enough force that the suit couldn't mitigate all of the impact. Pain spread across her lower back.

The crystal towered over her. Its edges began to change, with smaller spears of crystal pushing through then seemingly sucked back in. Zurah realized the crystal was rearranging itself to look like her.

Sightless eyes stared at her, and a hole formed in place of the mouth. "Justice will be dispensed."

Another wave of pain pierced Zurah's leg, and she rolled onto her stomach, scrambling away from the crystal creatures. She gasped as her leg immediately felt as if it were on fire. Everything went blurry, and for a moment, she almost blacked out, but a fresh wave of pain pulled her back to reality. She forced herself to sit up, and she looked down at her leg. The suit had a dark gash running from the tip of her knee down to her ankle. The outer layer of the suit had been compromised.

Without thinking, Zurah pushed herself up, ran to Alex, and wrapped her arms around him. She turned and fired her last round of bullets at the creature attempting to look like her then powered up the rockets on her suit. Her body rose at an odd angle, and she fought to keep hold of Alex as her hands slipped up along the crystal. But she tightened her grip, and she felt a shift in Alex's crystallized body. Then with a jolt, he was free, and they shot up and away from the platform. The force required to break him free had spent the majority of her rocket's power, and she fumbled to turn on his rocket pack.

Shards of crystal were blown out into space as his rocket pack kicked on. Zurah's right hand slipped as her left tried to work the controls through the screen's interface. She wrapped her legs around his, and together, they tilted sharply with her shifting to hold on. With every last bit of determination, Zurah managed to guide them toward the portal symbol. They crashed into the symbol just as the platform exploded into a million different crystals.

Zurah coughed and rolled over off Alex. Ignoring the pain, she grabbed his legs and dragged him away from the strange pillars and portals, moving him toward the safety of the shield. Once they were through, she wasted no time and pounded on the crystal left around Alex's body. When only a minute part of the crystal broke, Zurah stopped, gasping for air.

She turned and hobbled down the corridor to where the researchers had set up camp. She grabbed the first thing she saw—a chair. Then she turned and smashed it against the cavern wall, taking one of the metal legs with her. She pounded against the crystal and at least got enough of it off to start prying Alex out of his suit.

His skin was gray and clammy to the touch, but she wanted him as far away from the crystal as possible. Once she had the suit off, she used it to gather up as much as the crystal as she could then threw it all through the shield into the cavern with the portals. Grabbing one of Alex's arms, she dragged him through the corridor and back into the area where the researchers had set up.

Once satisfied he was safe, Zurah ran back one last time to the edge of the shield's perimeter. She took aim and fired at where the corridor ended. Fissures ran through the rock, and large segments tumbled down. Dust billowed up around Zurah, and she covered her mouth with her arm as she backed up. She fired one more time, retreating farther down the corridor, before she turned and ran back to where the researchers' camp as the corridor's ceiling collapsed behind her.

The surge of adrenaline was wearing off, and Zurah dragged herself back to the cavern and fell down next to Alex. She rolled her head to the side, her vision going in and out. Relief flooded her as she watched his chest slowly rise and fall, but fear rapidly replaced the feeling. She knew helping him was beyond her abilities. She needed help. But Mexa was dead, and Nissa was in stasis. *Who would help me now?*

There was only one possibility left. She forced herself to move to one of the workstations then pulled herself up. Fumbling at the controls, she found what she was looking for and keyed in a coded message, set on a ghost frequency. *Injured. Need assistance.*

She rubbed her face, trying to keep focused as she made sure the signal got out. She fervently hoped Finn would get the message before anyone else.

12

Zurah collapsed to the floor, gasping for air. Her hands fumbled on the clasps throughout her suit as she started to panic. Once a clasp loosened, she ripped at the material, trying to free herself. Stripping off the suit and throwing it to the side, she lay there, panting, her hands clutching her throat as the sensation of being suffocated remained. Her breathing was labored, and her extremities tingled. Zurah thrashed, her feet hitting one of the chairs and sending it crashing to the floor, as strange voices filled the cavern.

"She's been infected."

"But not too far along where a course of treatment can't be started. If she's taken through to the—"

"And risk having them follow us? We're barely keeping this lot out of the gates. If we open it up now, they'll only follow us. Why risk our security for them?"

"Don't you remember anymore? Where we came from? What we've sacrificed?"

"More so than most," the first speaker snapped.

Zurah clawed at her throat, desperate for air, and her vision wavered from blurry to a shade of gray. A figured appeared, standing over her, their face wreathed in shadow.

"At least let me give her an inoculation. It might slow down the rate of infection." A second shadow appeared.

"And what about him?"

"Him, as well. We need them to fight back, unless you think we can win this war on our own." One of the shadows crouched. Their hand stretched out and hovered above Zurah's leg.

"We'll win. Only because we have to. But now who isn't remembering? That wasn't our original purpose. We're supposed to be guarding the gates. They will have to suffer the consequences of their actions. It isn't up to us to rescue them."

"Bullshit, and you know it. Now you're just spouting off her doctrine. If the humans fail here, it won't be long until the infection spreads, and from what I've gathered, the worlds are far more vast than what we ever dreamed of."

"It isn't our problem. We've already lost one to that foolish way of thinking. And for what? For her? Don't you ever want to see your family again? To be able to finish the transformation?"

There was a long pause, then one of the shadows moved out of Zurah's field of vision.

"You're right. I'm sorry." A shadow shifted, and

Zurah turned her head, trying to make sense of what she was seeing. She struggled to sit up and tried to call out. Her throat was like ice, though, and her voice had disappeared. Exhausted and confused, she collapsed back down. As the cold wore off, she was numb, and her fingers were puffy and stiff. Eventually, she regained some mobility and rolled over to her side, purging her stomach. Repulsed, she rolled back to the other side and reached out toward Alex. Her fingers brushed his face and discovered he was ice cold to the touch. But his chest was still rising and falling, and his skin had picked up a bit of color.

"Alex." The word was hardly there, more a raspy exhalation. She took a deep breath and tried again. This time, the word was stronger, but it had no effect. Alex's eyes remained closed. Zurah tried a third time, and when he still didn't stir, she turned once more to lie on her back.

Her vision was clearing, and she stared at the ceiling. The rocky interior had been smoothed at some point. She briefly wondered if the researchers had done it in an effort to carve out an area big enough to set up camp or if whatever had once crafted the portals had been the architect. Her thoughts drifted, briefly considering the bizarre nature of the job, if the *HighTail Flyer* was still waiting for them, what Nissa would think when she woke up...

Nissa. Her aunt. The words stung like a dermatex bite. *Why didn't Nissa tell me the truth? And what did she know about my parents?* With a sigh, Zurah closed her eyes and sought out the memory of the first time she met Nissa.

The Crescent Moon had been full of various species. The chatter of conversations mixed with the sultry alto of a human singer, mixing Old Earth melodies with Telt instrumentation. Zurah had ducked in, attempting to get lost in the crowd as she knew someone had picked up on her trail. The bar was an iconic location on Pielar's Station, and Zurah had used it as a way to dodge unsavory characters before. And the Glipglow who ran the establishment had an extremely low tolerance for the IGJ, who normally steered clear of the place on account of its owner.

Zurah closed the back door, took a few steps through the maintenance corridor, and stopped. A woman was casually leaning up against the wall, smoking. The faint odor of dried lominat leaves and the spicy hints of divo nuts wafted toward Zurah.

"Hard times," the woman said. "Especially for the likes of us."

Zurah stayed still, using her SeeClear tech to sweep the area. They were the only two in the maintenance corridor.

The woman took another drag off the cigarette then let it fall to the floor, where she ground it down under the heel of her boot. "Got a job that needs doing. And I was told you had the skills I'd been looking for."

"Don't know what you're talking about. Just trying to get back to my hab," Zurah said. Then with a shrug, she tried to brush past the woman.

But the woman turned and blocked her way. "I know the drill. Been at this game a long time." The way her eyes moved over Zurah, she knew the woman was using a bioupgrade to evaluate her. "Looks like you could use a credit boost. Your tech is a couple gens behind."

"Does what it needs."

"I'm sure you're resourceful, but upgrades never hurt no one."

"Depends on which side of the line you're on," Zurah countered.

The woman grinned then extended her hand. "I'm Nissa. Just Nissa. You can look me up on the whisper nets if you like. But my rep is solid."

There was something comforting about Nissa's demeanor, and Zurah succumbed to how at ease Nissa made her feel. "Will do. But if you know who I am, then you know my troubles."

"I do. And I'm willing to help you there. This job I've got, I need your skill set. Interviewed a couple others, and they didn't have what it takes when it came to the hack needed. But I've asked around, and I believe you do. Come with me for a trial run. Then if you're good, and I'm impressed, we'll make it formal. If not, no worries."

Zurah had been hanging on by a thread after the incident, and the offer was too good to refuse. She accepted, and when she passed Nissa's tests with flying colors, Zurah accepted the job and a permanent place on Nissa's crew. But not once had Nissa ever hinted at the fact there was a lot more to their relationship.

Zurah's eyes fluttered open, and she considered another possibility. Nissa might not have known. Yet as soon as she thought it, Zurah dismissed the idea as ludicrous, unless Nissa had no knowledge of her family history. Zurah had never hidden anything about her past. The information would have been tagged in her files.

"What happened?" Alex groaned.

Zurah turned her head to look at him. His eyes were open, and he was shivering.

"A mess," Zurah croaked. "That's what happened. One big old mess."

"I feel… I feel strange," Alex moaned. "And my ears are ringing."

"Just stay still." Zurah pushed herself up and gritted her teeth as she slid over to his side. "I don't know what all happened. That crystal… thing, it engulfed you. But you had your suit on, so…" She let the word hang between them. Then she opened her mouth to add on a comment about the shadows, but the memory was already slipping away, and she wondered if they had been real or some figment of her imagination.

"How are we still alive?" Alex asked, his eyes focused on hers. "I remember being… attacked. Of hearing the screams." He raised a hand and covered his eyes. "Oh, god. The screams. They were everywhere."

"Screams?"

Alex nodded, and he started to shake. Zurah looked up and around the room. She had seen the crates but hadn't thought much of them before. She made her way over to one of the piles and pried the lid off the top one. Spare parts filled the crate, all neatly packed in foam. The parts may have been useful, but not what she was looking for in that moment. The crate below it held more of the same, so she moved on to another stack. The next one she opened had more scientific instruments, several of which she couldn't identify. She moved it and eyed the bottom crate and the one next to it.

Cracking open one of the two, she was pleased to find what she had been hoping for—emergency rations and a standard field kit. She snagged the kit and grabbed two ration packs. She flipped them over and frowned. Zip pockets. Not her meal of choice, but they worked. She sat down next to Alex and opened up the field kit. There were basic medical supplies and exactly what she wanted—a thermal blanket. She broke the seal, and the blanket expanded. Careful not to touch the ID tag, she let it fall into Alex's hand.

"Grab it," she urged. When he didn't respond, she tapped his hand. "Grab the tag." His fingers curled around it slowly, and when the tag glowed green, she lowered it across his body. The sensors within the blanket paired with the small processor in the tag, reading Alex's biosigns, and worked to bring his body temperature back within acceptable parameters. Once it was working, Zurah dug through the kit. There were three doses of field boosters, some redi-wrap bandages, sealant, a basic repair kit for standard-issue suits, and an emergency beacon.

She took one of the field booster shots. "Where's your HalfLife chip?"

"Don't have one."

"What?" she asked. "Your HalfLife chip, which hand is it in?"

"Don't have one. None of my family does. But here." He pulled an arm out from under the blanket and tapped the left side of his neck below his earlobe.

"Same principle, just won't be picked up on the usual systems."

"You've got to be kidding me," Zurah muttered. "Those damned things are standard across the known worlds. If you don't have one, or at least one that can spoof your ID, no one lets you in."

"I'm a Goldsmith, remember?"

"Yeah, right." Zurah leaned over him and tapped the field booster against his skin. There was a flash of red light, then it blinked green. "Here. Hold on." She took his arm and plunged the shot into his skin. He jerked but didn't pull away. She had experienced the boosters a few times and remembered their bite. While the booster wasn't a cure all, the medicine would help his immune system and provide basic antibiotics to help until a medic could assess the damage.

Alex shifted, the blanket and booster already helping, and studied Zurah. "What happened?"

She sighed and took a booster of her own before giving him the rundown.

"And the screaming?" he asked.

"Didn't hear anything like that," she said. "Perhaps a hallucination? Or some unknown reaction to the crystal cocoon? Perhaps some type of feedback loop with your suit's sensors?"

Alex shook his head. "No. I would know. This was…" The look of fear in his eyes convinced Zurah he had heard something unsettling. More than any type of feedback loop.

"All right, I believe you." She shifted so she could lean against the table's support. "So, tell me. What the hell is really going on here? I saw the bodies, the crew of the *Eagle's Nest*. That's what you had wanted me to see all along."

There was a long, drawn-out silence before Alex answered her. "Finn is rather secretive with her information. And she has good reason too." Alex coughed then pulled himself up into a sitting position, scooting back until he was next to Zurah. "Her family has learned to guard their secrets well. Too many enemies or opportunists out there."

"Isn't that the truth," Zurah muttered. "We all learn to guard our trade secrets, and someone with her rep surely has to. But so what?"

Alex laughed then cringed at the pain it caused.

"I don't get why that's so funny. What's the deal with the two of you? Are you dating? Each other's ex? Lovers? What?"

"Oh dear gods, no. Finn's my cousin."

Zurah harrumphed to hide her surprise but knew she should have realized the connection. Finn and Alex working together, the resources she had access to, and her reputation—it all made sense.

"So the Goldsmiths have a lot to protect. I get it, but what makes *this* place so special?"

"Finn isn't a Goldsmith." Alex shook his head. "She's of the House of Zhu. She's the emperor's sister."

Zurah's jaw dropped, and she stared at Alex, gobsmacked. "You're kidding me."

"Nope. Afraid not."

The emperor's sister. Miles High's sister. The words went round and round in Zurah's mind. *I've been working with the emperor's sister.* The knowledge of who Finn really was added an entirely new dimension to the situation. "Wait, and you're cousins?"

"Yup."

Zurah listened to the whisper nets late at night when she couldn't sleep. There were several popular channels that touted the idea that the Consortium and the Emperor of Old Earth were in cahoots, but she had dismissed the idea as paranoia. Now she had proof.

"Finn's great-grandmother, from what I know, was determined to find out what happened to the *Eagle's Nest.* Why, I don't know. And if Finn knows why, she never shared the information. But she did at least share some of the journals her great-grandmother kept, and they helped us with being moderately prepared for what we might find."

"The portals?"

"No, not those. But those damnable crystals, what the researchers designated as the cryrot. The journals talked about a strange affliction which ravaged her crew and the potential source for that affliction. Except, none of us had any idea that it could take our shape. We just knew that any crystalline structure we came across to stay well away from."

"Great job on that," Zurah said. "So you all believed the ship was here?"

"Yes. That was the working theory. With the significant advancements in tech, Finn was confident we would be able to find it. But all of our scans turned up empty. So we started bringing in researchers from a wide variety of fields. Then the portals were discovered and the grisly secrets they held. But still no evidence of the ship, which then goes into my working theory."

Alex paused, and Zurah huffed. "Which is?"

"That the *Eagle's Nest* went through the gates."

The revelation wasn't as shocking to Zurah as Alex had set it up to be. "That would make sense, considering there are portals. Why not something large enough for a ship to move through? But how? These portals are active. I'm hazarding a guess the gates aren't."

"You would be correct. We haven't been able to figure out how the gates activate. When this chamber was discovered, Finn initially focused her teams here. Thinking if they could unlock the secrets of these portals, then perhaps they could activate the gates."

"But?"

"But," a sharp voice cut into their conversation. "We found something even better."

Zurah's hand went to the gun, and Alex tensed, then Zurah felt his whole body relax.

"Angelina."

"In the flesh." She clicked off her helmet, and the head gear retreated into the collar of her suit. "You two look worse for wear."

"Could be better," Alex said as he tried to get to his feet.

Zurah reached out and grabbed him, pulling him back down. "How do you know it's actually her?"

"Because I brought Angelina onto the team," Alex said, shaking off Zurah and getting to his feet. "She's the most qualified out of all of us to be here."

"Alex…" Angelina growled. "We don't know—"

"She saved my life when she could have left me. I think she's owed some information. Whether she likes it or not, she's a part of this now."

Zurah narrowed her eyes as she looked up at Alex. "What aren't you telling me?"

He extended his hand, and with a bit of trepidation, Zurah decided to take it. He helped her to her feet. "Zurah, I would like you to meet Angelina Adeyemi, second-in-command of the *Eagle's Nest*."

13

Angelina stared at Zurah, her dark-brown eyes searching Zurah's for a reaction. Instead, Zurah returned the stare, taking in Angelina's ebony skin, high cheekbones, and confident posture.

"Of course she is. A long-lost member of the crew. What a neat little way to wrap this all up," Zurah muttered. "But if she's who you say she is, then why haven't you gotten answers from her? Why all the research?"

"A valid question," Angelina replied. "And one easily explained."

"Oh yeah? Try me." Zurah sat down in one of the chairs and crossed her arms against her chest. "I can't wait to hear this."

"First," Alex said, "this information doesn't go any further than the three of us. Finn doesn't know."

This time, Zurah was genuinely shocked. "She doesn't know? How in the worlds is that possible?"

"Since Alex seems to trust you, I'll answer your questions. But we need to get a move on. This location isn't secure. Your suit?"

"Damaged," Alex said and glanced over at Zurah. "Both of them."

"All right, hold on." Angelina turned and darted out of the cavern.

"You're pulling my leg, right?" Zurah asked, turning to Alex. "This is just too much."

"I'm not. I was going to explain most of this on that last platform." He sat down next to her, running a hand through his hair. "Finn and I have a lot of pieces to this puzzle, but most of them don't appear to fit together. And Finn's driven by some kind of family obligation or remorse—I don't know. But I'm concerned about what we might find."

"Then why partner with her?"

"Because Finn wouldn't listen to me. She's always been stubborn like that. So the next best thing was to join with her and keep an eye on what she was doing."

"Family," Zurah said.

"Indeed," Alex replied. "And before you ask the next question I'm sure is turning around in your head, I'll answer it. When you showed up, I had hoped I might be able to persuade you to be a go-between for me."

"A spy, you mean."

"No. Not exactly. It's not that I don't trust Finn. It's just that I know there's a lot she's keeping from me, and in my family, you learn how to cultivate a wide variety of resources."

"So, a spy."

Alex grimaced. "Fine. Yes, a spy. I'll support Finn, but at the same time, we've uncovered something that should—"

"Nicked one of the supply rovers by pure luck," Angelina said as she returned and tossed two suits at them. "Here."

Not as outdated as what Finn had provided, the suit still wasn't as useful as the one Zurah had originally worn.

As they dressed, Angelina talked. "The problem is, I don't remember what happened. I remember my life, signing the contract to be a part of the *Eagle's Nest* crew, my admiration for the captain's bold approach to exploration. When we hit this area of space, we started having issues with various areas of the ship, and we were considering making an emergency landing. The captain issued an alert, then all hell broke loose. Next thing I remember is waking up, hundreds of years later, in an escape pod. A passing trawler picked me up, thawed me out, and tried to sell me to the highest bidder. Thankfully, that turned out to be Alex."

"You bought her?" Zurah asked.

"Well, I bought the pod, and she happened to go along with it. Turns out to have been a fortuitous purchase."

Angelina ignored the interruption. "One thing I know for sure"—she handed both of them weapons—"is that I never would have abandoned my post. I don't know why I was put in the escape pod, but I wouldn't have done it myself."

Alex looked over at Zurah. "Ready?"

"For what?"

"You kept saying you needed to get to the beta site. Well, are you coming?"

"Hold up," Angelina said. "The beta site has been compromised. We're headed north."

"On whose orders?"

"I'll give you three guesses, and the first two don't count," Angelina replied.

"Finn," Alex replied at the same time that Zurah asked, "What happened to the beta site? What about the ship?"

"Come on." Angelina started walking, but instead of the entrance to the cavern, she moved toward the door leading to the portals. When she pulled open the heavy door and looked down the corridor, she called out, "What the hell happened here?"

Zurah looked at Alex and shrugged. "Needed to make sure that thing couldn't follow us back."

Angelina poked her head back out and glared at them. "You certainly made a right mess of it. But if we work together, we might be able to clear enough of the debris away to access the portals. But it's got to be fast. Trouble is heading this way. You're lucky I picked up on your little signal before the others did. Come on, hop to it now."

Alex moved, but Zurah didn't. When he got to the door, he looked back over his shoulder. "What?"

"I have no desire to go through one of those things again. Let alone take the chance that creature could come through if we clear the way."

"Angelina knows what she's doing," Alex said, a hint of frustration in his voice. "Come on."

"No."

Alex stared at her, then he turned and vanished. Zurah was taken aback, but she knew she wasn't going to help. She had accomplished her mission. She'd gathered intel and knew enough to understand the nuances between the major players. And she'd experienced enough to know she didn't want to be tangled up any further in this ill-begotten adventure. Finn and Alex could do what they wanted, but Zurah was going to get Nissa, one way or the other, and get them off Objer. She'd had enough of exploring and space mysteries. She was a security hack, and that was all. Nothing else. And knowing what she did, Zurah highly doubted Finn would hold up her end of the deal.

Angelina had said she'd gotten there by rover, and that was good enough for Zurah. She picked up the field kit and stuffed several of the zip pockets in the bag. After a moment of indecision, Zurah reached for the gun and the remaining ammunition. Making sure it was secure, she engaged the helmet on her suit, swung the bag over her shoulder, and headed out to the rover.

The rover was built for unstable terrain and had back row seating, plus room for storage. Zurah slid into the driver's side and studied the controls. The operation looked to be standard, and she fired up the engine. A gentle thrum ran through the rover, and she brought up a map of the area. She picked a halfway point between where she was at the buried ship that had been turned into headquarters for the operation. She wasn't a fool.

Driving the entire way would be a red flag. But she would go partway, enough to have the rover ping the ship's sensors then send it off on its own while she hiked the rest of the way to the ship. The suit Angelina had so graciously supplied had enough tech Zurah could easily set up its systems to completely ghost the ship.

She plotted her course and shifted into drive.

"Zurah, wait!" Alex called out. He jogged out to the rover and caught the sidebar on the driver's side. He grimaced, and one hand went to his side. "What are you doing?"

"I'm getting out of here," Zurah said. "What does it look like? Let go."

"No. If you go out there like this, they'll find you."

"No they won't. I'm good at being able to hide in plain sight."

"Zurah," Alex growled then winced again. "When we get to safety, then I promise I'll help—"

"I'm going to stop you right there," Zurah interrupted. "I've had enough of other people's promises. This"—she waved at the landscape—"is your problem. Not mine. Never was."

Alex didn't let go of the rover, but he didn't protest or try to argue with her. Instead, he sighed then looked out in the direction of the ship. "All right. But if you're going to try and rescue your friend, then you'll need access codes."

"I'll get in how I got out," Zurah said. "And besides, don't you think they've reset your codes by now?"

"Maybe, maybe not, and yes. I'm quite sure they

have. But there's one thing I have that they don't. Come." He turned back to the cavern.

Zurah eyed the route she had keyed in and was tempted to just leave. Yet Alex was right. When she left the ship, there had been multiple explosions and undoubtedly other sabotage Finn had devised, not to mention how the fake Alex would have retaliated. Reluctantly, she climbed out of the rover and followed Alex.

When she returned to the cavern, Alex had already undone the top half of his suit and pulled it down to his waist. He rolled up his sleeve. "Angelina, hand me a whip."

"Alex, this isn't a good idea. We'll need those codes."

"We have plenty of other resources that Zurah doesn't have access to. She saved my life, and I owe her."

Angelina scowled but dug into her pack and handed Alex a small laser whip that was easy to conceal and even easier to use. He shook it, and the whip flared to life. He clenched his fist and, without preamble, cut the middle of his forearm. Blood dripped down his arm and onto the floor as he handed Angelina the whip. Digging into his flesh, he pulled out a small disc. "Here. Goldsmiths have learned to be resourceful. This is a flesh eater."

Zurah stared at the tiny disc in equal parts admiration and horror. "And you've just been carrying one of those around all this time? *Inside* of you?"

He shrugged. "It's got a propriety coating on it, so no ill effects from having it embedded. But this will—"

"I know what it is." Zurah took the disc with an almost reverent expression. The disc was the holy grail for security hacks. A golden ticket into any system, no matter the security setup. A lot of security hacks refused to believe they even existed, but Zurah had always held out hope that they did. Now she couldn't believe she was holding one. "And you're just giving this to me?"

Alex grinned. "Sure. Like I said, you saved my life, and if you're not coming with us, then the best thing I can do is give you an advantage. But just remember, you can only use it once—and know that it will completely fry whatever system you plug it into. There will be no salvaging or rebuilding. This annihilates everything. So decide wisely when and where. You'll have to get into the ship, but you're also going to have to get out of the security grid. And then hope they haven't tampered with your ship."

Zurah watched him with narrowed eyes. "What's the catch?"

Alex's grin slipped. "You asked me that question already. Not everything has a catch or a hidden agenda. I grew up with enough of those issues to find them insulting."

His words were hard for her to believe. All of her life, Zurah had known everything had a hidden agenda. Someone always wanted something from someone else. But there was a look of sincerity in his eyes, and for once, Zurah decided to believe the best instead of the worst. She closed the distance between them and gave him a hug.

"Thank you," she whispered, then before anything else could be said, she darted out of the cavern.

Once she was back in the rover, she tucked the disc into a side pocket then sealed it shut. She engaged the driving controls and took off. It wasn't long until Zurah hit the halfway mark, and she stopped. She switched the rover over to auto, double-checking the course she had lain in. The rover would continue on toward the ship at an angle then double back and head toward the beta site. With a few quick adjustments, she turned on the privacy mode and spoofed the system to make it look as if there were three life signs in the rover. Satisfied with her work, she watched it take off, and once it was several meters away, she headed off toward the ship.

Zurah engaged her SeeClear tech, enhancing her vision and zooming in on the ship. The entrance with the guard station was a pile of rubble, twisted steel with scorch marks streaking toward the top of the ship. At the midsection were two gaping holes with temporary shields engaged. A handful of suited individuals were moving around the top of the ship, undoubtedly working on repairs.

The terrain wasn't conducive for hiding, and Zurah had to trust in her work. If any of the suits working on the ship looked in her direction, they would be able to spot her. Making herself invisible to the naked eye wasn't possible. But if they were only running scans of the area, no one would detect her suit or her life signs.

Moving quickly, she headed toward the emergency hatch she'd blown, knowing it was the fastest route back to the medical bay. With each step pushing her closer to the ship, her heart rate quickened until the rapid hammering was all she could hear. Her hand strayed to the gun then to the pocket holding Alex's disc. *Focus on the plan.*

Zurah began running through scenarios. She had gathered intel on the security grid and was slightly more confident about being able to hack that system than hacking anything on the ship. Despite the three discs she had left behind, Alex's copy would be foolish not to have revamped access into the computer systems after Finn's sabotage. But there might be a slim possibility Zurah could still use them.

The real obstacle was going to be the medical bay, Nissa, and the stasis pod. There were so many variables, it was nearly impossible to conceive of a plan that could address them. *I'll have to improvise.*

Zurah slowed when she was a handful of meters away from her target. The hatch was ringed by dark scorch marks, but the cover hadn't been replaced. *At least that's a bit of luck headed my way.*

She enhanced her vision, looking for anything out of place, potential repair work, or traps. But the darkened interior appeared just as she had left it. Zurah reasoned that with the scant number of people combined with the turmoil over leadership, the teams were undoubtedly patching the critical systems first. From experience, Zurah knew maintenance tunnels were designed with temporary shielding or manual bulkheads to prevent atmo leaks in the event an emergency hatch was blown. But Zurah also knew they were easy to work around.

She grabbed the rim of the emergency evacuation opening and, with a grunt, pulled herself up. She pushed her feet against the side of the ship, using the grips on the soles of her boots to help provide an additional boost the rest of the way up. As she crawled into the maintenance corridor, she ran a brief scan for signs of anyone working in the area. Everything appeared to be clear. Not wasting any time, Zurah began the crawl back toward the medical bay, careful not to snag her suit.

When she reached the door into medical, Zurah stopped. The interior walls were thick, but she ran multiple scans to assess what might lay on the other side of the door. The scans didn't pick up on anything. Not even a life sign for the doctor, and Zurah wondered if the cryrot Alex had discovered the doctor's betrayal. But there was no way to know for sure, and the longer she debated, the thinner her chances at successfully retrieving Nissa became. If no one was there, she needed to seize the opportunity to get in and get out.

The door was easy to pop open. Zurah drew the gun and paused. Waiting for any sign of movement. She did one last sweep, and when it came back clear, she climbed out and immediately crouched behind one of the medical beds. The quiet was unnerving. Not even the sound of medical equipment softly running in the background. Everything had been shut down. The lights had been dimmed, and Zurah moved from one shadow to the next, working her way to the depression in the floor. Once there, she didn't waste time and crawled down into the nest, releasing the stasis pod. Air hissed at Zurah as the pod slid free of its compartment, and Zurah breathed a sigh of relief. She holstered the gun and wiped off the condensation.

Her blood ran cold. The pod was empty.

"Humans have a strange affinity for each other. An emotion I have yet to completely understand."

Zurah whipped around, drawing the gun to aim it at the cryrot. For the briefest of moments, Zurah was unsure if what she saw was the imitation or the real Alex. But he tilted his head as he studied her, and there was a faint glow beneath his skin. A decidedly unhuman glow.

The cryrot jumped down beside her then walked over to the stasis pod to finish cleaning off the condensation. "Your physical bodies are so frail, so dependent on technology to survive beyond your planet. I wonder if your species was meant for the stars, or if you should have stayed on your terrestrial home world, fighting and squabbling amongst each other until you would undoubtedly cause the human species to go extinct. Yet…" He reached out and brushed his hand against his cheek. "Your physiology is not without merit. We do appreciate the nutrients you provide in being able to replicate. We have been starved for far too long."

Zurah took a step back but bumped up against the edge of the nest.

"Not even curious where she's been taken? Or if she's still alive?" he asked.

"Of course," Zurah snapped.

"Good. Then I will share with you that she is alive. Or at least in a suspended semblance of life."

Zurah slowly moved along the perimeter of the nest, trying to create as much space between them as possible. "What do you want?"

"What do I want? An interesting question. Perhaps it would be more apropos to ask what *we* want. The answer to that question is justice. But in regards to what *I* want? That becomes a bit more complicated. But surely you can suspect the direction I've been taking." The cryrot lifted a hand, pointed at Zurah, then lowered it slightly to indicate the leg that had been injured. "Like calls to like." He took another step closer and began to hum. The throbbing in Zurah's leg intensified, but the cryrot frowned. "It would appear someone has interfered. But makes no matter, the Timeless Sleepers see all."

Zurah fired the gun, then she whirled around and climbed out of the nest. Laughter followed her as she ran for the door, then something shot past her upper arm, millimeters away from ripping through her suit. She spun around and watched as the cryrot climbed out of the pit, the hole in his chest closing rapidly.

Zurah raised the gun and fired again and again. Each time the bullet struck, it caused the cryrot to jerk, but it didn't slow his progress. All it did was impede his recovery time. When she had fired her last bullet, she stood there, shaking.

The cryrot reached up and touched the latest wound. Some of the sand stuck to his fingers, and he rubbed them together then looked up at Zurah. "Clever. But I am not without the ability to adapt." Then to her horror, he began to hum again. The melody sounded disjointed but his tone as clear as a bell.

Afraid and unsure what the cryrot was trying to do, Zurah whipped around and waved her hand in front of the door's sensor. When it didn't open, she slammed the palm of her hand against the control panel, and when that still didn't trigger the door, she pried off the cover.

The humming intensified, and pain tore through Zurah's leg. She crumpled to the floor and grabbed her knee. A deep vibration filled her calf, strengthening the pain, and her leg began to glow.

"Like always calls to like," the cryrot said. "Due to the interference, growth has slowed. But in time, you will understand the call of the void. The more you fight it, the greater the pain."

Zurah tried to scoot away, but the copy moved too fast.

He crouched and grabbed her arm. "I am not without some form of mercy. I will allow you to see your friend one last time." He hauled her effortlessly to her feet and hummed once more

The door opened.

14

Crystals jutted out of the ship's wall at odd angles, and Zurah had lost count of how many by the time they reached the deck above medical. They passed a few individuals, and her stomach rolled and twisted into knots at the sight of them. Each had crystals that had burst through different areas of their bodies, some on their jaws, through their cheeks, neck, or arms, with dried blood crusted on the gemstones.

The cryrot who had copied Alex ignored them all as they passed by, but each individual stopped and made a peculiar gesture as he passed. As they made their way up another deck, the cryrot stopped in front of one of the doors. The sign indicated it was a research lab, and Zurah tried one last time to twist out of his grip. But his fingers dug into her arm, and for a moment, she was afraid he had pierced her suit.

Then the door opened, and a blast of hot, humid

air hit them. The lighting had been dimmed, and a soft song was playing in the background. A few individuals sat at the different workstations, each with their head bent over their work, studiously ignoring the intrusion.

"Devon, will you prepare a holding cell for our new guest? She doesn't require treatment, just a comfortable spot in which to await the changing."

A young man stood up and bowed. "Yes, Awakened. It would be my honor to serve." He scurried off to a darkened corner and started moving things around.

"It is useful to have those with their minds still intact," the cryrot mused. "Gifted with just enough understanding to know resistance is useless and to understand their place in this new world."

"New world?" Zurah asked.

"Yes, well. I admit my mission parameters have changed since I was awakened and commissioned with the task of justice for the disturbance of the dead. May the Timeless Sleepers bestow their benevolence upon me when they realize what I am creating. But I fear you are not quite ready to hear this. Your body and mind need time to adjust to the changes." He pulled her with him, toward the area where the young man had gone.

As Zurah's eyes adjusted to the dim light, she realized a row of makeshift cells had been constructed along the back wall. Portable shield generators had been set up, and to her right, she saw Dr. Ordotham, his tentacles firmly wrapped around his body. In front of his cell was a stasis pod.

"Nissa," Zurah cried out.

"Yes. I do uphold my promises. As you can see, your

friend is still safe and secure. And I am gracious, as you will come to understand. Here you can maintain vigil over her body until you are ready," the cryrot said. He forced Zurah to step over a makeshift frame, and there was a pop and a zap as a shield went up around her.

"And you will have the good doctor to keep you company. Well, as long as he proves to be of interest to my work. Once we can understand his biological resistance, I fear he will have no choice but to succumb to the inevitable. Oh, and if you experience any undue pain, please let Devon or one of the other researchers know. While we must be careful with how many sedatives you might be exposed to, one or two to help dull the pain is not without reason. Now, if you will excuse me, I have work to see to."

Zurah watched Alex's copy make his way from station to station, bending over like a benevolent teacher checking up on his students. He clapped each of the researchers on the back, and when finished with his inspection, he left without a backward glance. Zurah turned to examine her cell and noted a cot had been placed in the center, along with a rectangular platform. Upon closer inspection, it was a portable replicator and waste disposal unit. *How cozy.* She limped over to the cot and sat down, bending over to rub her leg where it hurt. The second she started kneading the area, she felt a lump underneath the suit. She stopped kneading. Not caring where she was or who was watching, she immediately stripped out of the suit and rolled up the leg of the undersuit. There was no mistaking the three distinct lumps in the middle of her lower leg, and enhancing her vision, she knew what they were. Crystal fragments. Without thinking, she started clawing at her skin, desperate to get them out.

"I wouldn't do that if I were you," a familiar voice said.

Zurah twisted around to stare at Dr. Ordotham. "I don't care. I don't want these things inside me."

"I would agree, but causing yourself bodily harm won't help the situation, and I can assure you, the crystals have already begun to replicate and embed themselves in your nervous system and circulatory system. You will not be able to simply pull them out."

"What would you know?" Zurah snapped, but she stopped clawing at her leg and felt embarrassed. "Sorry. I didn't mean to say that."

"An understandable outburst, given the situation. But I am as much a prisoner now as I was then. Only, under a more watchful eye."

"Right. And how do I know you didn't sell me out? Or Finn, for that matter?"

One of his eyes rolled to the side, watching one of the researchers get up and move to another station, voices hushed and unintelligible. But his other eye stayed fixed on Zurah. "Because you are young, I will forgive the ignorance. Yet, given your profession, I would assume you had some awareness of my kind."

When Zurah didn't move or respond, the doctor continued. "Once a Neetho chooses their pod, they are sworn to uphold the laws and regulations of their chosen profession. When I decided to swim against the current and turned my interests to the larger medical community,

I took an oath to protect lives, no matter the personal cost. I would not and I will not break that oath."

Zurah rubbed her leg then slowly rolled down the undersuit. "I didn't know. It would seem there's a lot I don't."

"Understandable. Most individuals only glimpse a tiny fragment of the known worlds, and that is usually relegated to their immediate area. Very few travel too far beyond the shores of their home. And if they do, they are still biased by the unconscious habits that were patterned as young."

"Will I turn into one of these or the... what? Drones?" Zurah asked. "The ones I saw when he brought me here."

"I am unsure. I have studied the journals and log entries of those who came before us and was a part of the original research team who was aware of potential issues. But even after all of our studies and theories, we were unable to unravel the mysteries of the cryrot. How long have you been infected?"

Zurah paused. She wasn't sure how to answer that question. "How long since Finn and I left?"

"Two days."

"What?" Zurah was stunned. *How was that possible?* She shook her head, trying to piece together the events since she'd first left the ship. She was quite sure she hadn't been gone for two days. The only answer she could come up with was that the portals somehow messed with her understanding of time. "Then I guess, maybe a day? Or a little over a day?"

"And you still have control of your awareness? You don't feel compelled or confused?"

"No. Just rather ticked off, to be honest. And a lot scared."

"A database of infection timelines along with when various effects started to appear would have been helpful," the doctor mused. "But from what I can tell, it would appear there are no consistent timelines for when an individual will be fully compromised. And there may be other factors at play here, as well."

"So, no idea how long I've got until I'm one of them?" Zurah asked.

"No, I'm afraid not. Some individuals appear to succumb rapidly, while others take more time."

The researcher named Devon stood up and moved to stand in front of Zurah's cell, stopping their conversation. He scanned her then consulted the readout on a handheld pad. After a look of surprise, then concern, he scanned her again.

"Why did you do it?" Zurah asked, standing up. "Why are you working for him?"

A strange mixture of fear and unease crossed his face, but Devon didn't respond. Instead, he simply turned around and went back to his station.

"It won't do you any good. They won't communicate with us. I have observed them long enough to ascertain they are a mixture of their original selves and the cryrot. There is enough left of their biological functions to continue with their research but still carry a potent amount of the cryrot, which binds them to the cryrot who has taken on Alex's appearance. Exactly how this is accomplished, I'm not yet sure. The crystalline structures we studied were intricate and beyond my comprehension of what a biological system would appear to be. If it wasn't for the threat we face, I am certain this would be the next big breakthrough in medical science across the known worlds."

Zurah sat back down on her cot. "When I was… Well, I don't know where I was. But I got a chance to analyze some of the crystals. My scans showed an internal structure that had a comparative analysis with neurological systems."

"That would corroborate my initial research. Highly unusual and quite fascinating." The doctor continued to ramble about the unusual nature of the crystals and theorize on how they were able to cannibalize other biological systems, but Zurah was only half listening to him as she stared at Nissa's stasis pod.

Why did the cryrot let me live? Or keep Nissa in the pod? Why not use her like he's using the rest of the researchers? Were Nissa's injuries too severe? Or did he know I would return and that he could use Nissa against me? And what in the worlds am I going to do now?

At some point, the doctor had stopped talking, and Zurah laid back on the cot. The shielding generators weren't hard to hack, and Zurah could easily break free. But that wasn't the problem. The researchers and Nissa's pod were.

"If we were able to make our way out of this place, do you have a secure location?"

Zurah jerked her head to the side to stare at the doctor. "I won't leave without her."

"I would expect as much."

"And what if I do?" She wasn't sure she did. But there

were options. They could head north and find Alex and Finn, or they could head for the *HighTail Flyer*. She knew which option she preferred.

"I believe our odds of surviving are acceptable with the two of us working together. I am able to produce enough *sheiol* to cloud this room, plus another burst if need be. If we could make our way to one of the decks below residential, there are rovers there."

Zurah sat up and considered his offer. "The effects of your... *sheiol* didn't seem to last long. It wouldn't give us much time. And making our way through that many decks would be risky. Too many people we might bump into, and once these guys come out of it, they'll set off an alarm."

"You received a fraction of what I can produce. The effects would last for far longer with these individuals."

Zurah considered the idea. She could short-circuit the shield and engage her suit so she wouldn't be affected by the *sheiol* this time. She glanced at the pod. Taking Nissa with them would be the biggest challenge. *How would we explain what we're doing if we have to talk our way out of a situation?* She had used the last of her ammunition on the copy of Alex, and the suit Angelina had provided didn't have any built-in weapon's systems. Not that she wanted to try to shoot her way out.

The more she considered the idea, the more she wanted it to work. Her suit was already set up to ghost the ship's sensors. She slowly stood and stretched, walking the small perimeter of her cell. Then, as if considering the idea, she bent down and pulled on the suit. When finished, she stretched again, facing Nissa's stasis pod.

She used her SeeClear tech to zoom in and noted the control panel appeared to be a standard model, and in a stroke of luck, she also saw the pod had built-in grav-boosters. Moving it would be easy.

"Does the pod have shielding tech?"

"I believe so, although my knowledge of the technology is woefully lacking. Finn had the stasis pods installed as an afterthought when she had my nest designed."

"Any idea why?"

"No. I did not question her. It was her credits and her project. If the pod does not have shielding capabilities, will you not agree to my idea?"

Zurah chewed on her lower lip. "No, it's not a deal-breaker." She turned to look at him. "How many of the crew know that you've been arrested, so to speak? Do you think you could bluff your way past anyone, once you're out of your *sheiol*? Since you're the doc, moving the pod wouldn't be out of your job description. Maybe even moving it on his orders. Think they would buy that? Give us enough time to get to a rover?"

"And what about you?"

"I'll just be a tech you asked to help with the pod. My suit is set up so the ship won't register my movements, but I can modify the spoof to make it look like I'm a part of the crew. But you don't have a suit. Once we're outside the safety of the ship's environment, what will you do? If we make it to a rover, that's not a great solution. Anything could go wrong, or we might have to ditch the rover at some point."

"Neethos have learned to adapt, both biologically and technologically to a wide range of environments.

I will survive long enough until we can find a more permanent shelter."

Zurah wasn't convinced, but she didn't know enough about Neethos to argue. "Fine," she said with a shake of her head. "Give me a few minutes, and I'll be ready."

Zurah turned back to her suit and got to work. The plan had more than a few holes, and there wasn't a fallback or anyone else to provide support if things went wrong. She was quite sure Nissa would disapprove and advise Zurah to take more time to consider all the possibilities. But the throbbing pain in Zurah's leg was a constant reminder that she was running out of time. She wasn't going to hang around and wait to become one of the cryrot's lackeys.

"There, got it," she said. "You ready? I'll follow your lead on getting around the ship."

Dr. Ordotham waved a tentacle. "Yes. Ready."

Zurah knelt and, with practiced ease, pulled out two control nodes from the bottom of the food replicator. Overloading the node, she sent it spinning toward the shield generator and watched with smug satisfaction as it popped then went dead. Quickly engaging her suit's helmet, she sent the second node spinning toward the generator maintaining the doctor's shield. There was a second pop, then without any need to give the all clear, he burst forward—far faster than Zurah realized he could move—and a cloud of *sheiol* rained down around the researchers before they could raise an alarm.

Rushing over to the stasis pod, Zurah engaged the grav-boosters and followed the doc out into the corridor. After every step they took, Zurah waited for an alarm to be raised. But they were halfway to their goal before they even ran into another worker. Zurah kept her eyes down, focused on her job of guiding the pod, but she couldn't ease the tingle of anxiety in her chest. In her periphery, she watched for the doorways, considering alternate options if the worker stopped and created a problem. The doctor, though, didn't appear concerned. He didn't slow down or speed up but, as they passed, waved a tentacle at the worker, who didn't even turn to look their way.

Once they were safely out of earshot, Zurah hissed at him. "Why did you do that? We're not supposed to draw attention to ourselves."

"I have always greeted my fellow workers. To do otherwise would be out of character."

Zurah clenched her jaw in annoyance. She wasn't happy about it, but she couldn't argue with his logic. They passed three more workers without incident, and as they moved down to the deck with the rovers, Zurah was beginning to think they were going to make it, when they ran into a small group of security guards.

"Halt," the guard in front said, raising a weapon. "What are you doing down here?"

"I was given orders to move the pod to this location," Dr. Ordotham said. "I had issues with the grav-boosters, and this tech was told to assist."

"This area is off-limits. Who issued the orders?"

The doctor slid forward. "My apologies. I was unaware, but I can assure you—" He abruptly rose onto two of his tentacles. The other six whipped out, knocking all of the guards to the ground and pinning them in place. "You must hurry. With their suits active, the *sheiol* will have no effect. You must deactivate their shields and helmets."

Zurah hurried around the pod and knelt next to the nearest guard, who was struggling under the Neetho's tentacle. She pulled at the guard's arm, trying to gain access to the suit's screen, but the guard ripped their arm out of her grasp. She stumbled back then reached out, trying to grab the arm.

"You must hurry," the doctor said. "I cannot hold them for long."

Zurah wrestled with the guard and finally was able to grip their arm. She half straddled the suit while the doctor's tentacle moved to wrap around the suit's neck. It took her far longer than she liked, but she was able to gain access to the system and shut it down. Then she bent forward and clicked the trigger for the helmet. The woman inside the suit wasn't entirely human, not any longer. Crystals traced a path across her forehead and down her face, with a large cluster embedded at the base of her neck. Zurah fell back in shock and disgust then scrambled to her feet.

"The Timeless Sleepers see all," the woman spat, but Zurah was up and moving on to the next suit. She was able to disable three more before a shot rang out, and the doctor quivered with rage. Thick, coppery-colored blood spread across the floor. Zurah raced over to the guard who was already aiming for a second shot, and without thinking, she kicked at the helmet, again and again, until the suit's arm dropped, and the guard lay still. She dove for the last suit, but either the doctor was beginning to wear out or the injury was more severe than Zurah realized, as the last guard managed to free themselves just as she launched herself at them. They rolled across the floor, neither of them finding purchase as their boots slipped on the doctor's blood.

Zurah grabbed the suit's arm, but the guard was too strong, and within a few moments, they had her pinned to the ground. They raised their arm, the glove quickly becoming encapsulated by a small Vulture, and they aimed directly for her head. A wailing cry filled the room, and in the blink of an eye, the suit's head was gone. Blood ran down the headless body as it toppled to the ground. Zurah wiped the blood that had dripped onto her suit's visor and looked up at the belly of the doctor. Two razor-sharp beaks had descended and held the head of the suit.

Zurah scrambled back in shock as the doctor released the last of his *sheiol*. Once the suits were still, he lifted his tentacles and slid back into the shadows.

"Doc?" Zurah called out softly.

"Go, I… I have committed the gravest of offenses. I am no longer worthy to be within the waters of the deep. I must make atonements."

Zurah got up and glanced at the stasis pod, down at the suited security personnel, then over to the doctor. Careful with where she stepped, she made her way over to him. "I don't know exactly what that means, but you saved my life."

"And does that justify the taking of another? To save yours?"

She shook her head. "I don't know. I don't like to

think about those sort of questions. But right now, we've got to go. And you're coming with me. After what we've done, I highly doubt that they're just going to put you back in a cell. No matter how valuable you think you are to them. This is our chance. If we make it out, you will have saved not only my life but Nissa's, as well."

The doctor would not meet her gaze, and slowly, his tentacles started to wrap around his body. But Zurah jumped forward and grabbed the edge of one, trying to hold it back. "Hey. Listen to me. We've got to go. You want to make amends for what just happened? Then do it by trying to get us to safety, then use that medical knowledge of yours to figure out how the crystals are able to do this. Maybe you can figure out how to reverse the effects."

The tentacle she was holding jerked free, and for a second, Zurah thought the doctor was going to ignore her. But instead, it moved to gently nudge her toward him then wrapped around her. Part of her felt a tingle of fear at what might happen, but then she realized the doctor was imitating a common human form of comfort. He was giving her a hug.

"Yes. We will find a way to undo the damage." He released her. "But first, I must ask you to look away. I must deal with this injury."

"Tell me what to do. I can help," she said.

"You will not understand. We do not have the necessary equipment to begin the healing process, nor can I leave my flesh behind."

"But we can—"

"Please, turn around, Zurah. I do not wish you to witness this."

Slowly, Zurah turned. There was a deep inhale then the sound of flesh ripping. Bile rose up in her throat as she realized she had a fairly good idea what the doctor was doing.

"It is finished. You may turn around now."

The doctor now had seven tentacles, and the eighth one was nowhere to be seen. Without asking any more questions, Zurah grabbed the pod, and they hurried off to one of the cargo bays where there were still a handful of rovers.

15

The doctor barely fit into the back of the rover, his tentacles wrapped securely around the stasis pod and the seats. Zurah slid into the driver's seat, taking only a moment to familiarize herself with the console. As the rover came to life, Zurah hacked into the system and forced the cargo bay doors to open. Lights illuminated the path and the side of the ramp up to the exit as the rover picked up speed and shot out into the desert landscape, dust billowing up behind them. Their exit wasn't careful, but Zurah didn't care. The time it would have taken her to fully ghost the rover was too risky. She wanted to put as much distance between them and the ship as possible. But as they sped off, Zurah sent the ship a parting gift.

She blinked, activating the SeeClear tech, and scrolled through the menu. She blinked again and activated the three discs she had left behind. A green light appeared next to each disc's identifier, and Zurah couldn't help but smile. Her own unique set of codes would worm their way through the system, scrambling systems and files, leaving a general mess that would take time to clean up.

Her hand reached up and touched the pocket where she'd tucked Alex's disc. She knew what she was going to do with that one. The security grid wouldn't stand a chance against it. All Zurah needed to do was find a control station. The grid couldn't operate without them and had to have been placed at regular intervals along the perimeter of the grid.

Blinking again, she brought up a different menu then set the tech to start scanning the area. The energy signatures would be easy to spot as the base coding would all be the same, with unique codes stacked on top only to identify the control station.

Dr. Ordotham leaned forward. "Where are we going?"

"We're getting off this miserable little planet. We left the *HighTail Flyer* geared up and ready to go."

"But you can't leave," the doctor said.

Zurah almost slammed on the brakes, but she gritted her teeth and switched the controls over to autopilot. She twisted around in her seat to stare at the doctor. "What the hell do you mean I can't leave this miserable shithole?"

"You can't leave in your present condition. Leaving might inadvertently spread the crystalline entity. There is still so much we don't know about how it functions. A solution needs to be found, a way to neutralize and destroy the cryrot. Until then, it isn't wise for any of us to leave. We must be free of contamination."

"Shit." Zurah turned back to face the front, slamming on the brakes. She punched the steering wheel. "Shit!" She hadn't even considered that, and she wasn't sure she even cared. All she wanted was to get away from this mess and find medical help for Nissa.

"Once we get to the *HighTail Flyer*, you could knock me out. Find a way to contain me. Then figure out what to do," she said.

"Potentially. But I do not understand how the crystals are able to spread nor their source of energy or nourishment. And it would be preferable to have samples I could work with before having to extract those which are embedded in you. Removing them forcibly might cause more harm than not."

"I don't care," Zurah hissed. "I want nothing to do with this, and Nissa needs help. What if she stays here and is infected? Even in the stasis pod?"

There was an uncomfortable pause. "I fear it is too late. When I scanned her before placing her in stasis, Nissa's body was already infected. There were minute traces of the cryrot in her wounds. Not only will the stasis pod suspend her body until she can get adequate medical attention, but I also believe it will temporarily stop the cryrot from growing inside her."

"Why the hell didn't you tell me?"

"Finn's instructions were clear. You were not to know, but you are a part of this now and need to know."

Zurah unclenched her jaw and slumped forward, feeling defeated. All of the possibilities her mind had considered vanished in wake of the doctor's news. Yet still, all she wanted to do was leave.

A tentacle snaked forward and gently touched her shoulder. "I am quite sorry. But I am afraid you must stay here until this issue is resolved."

She shrugged off his kind gesture and took back control of the rover. Grudgingly, she admitted the doctor was right. Even though she wasn't a xenologist or a medical professional, every child was taught the procedures to help reduce the risk of exposure and contamination when so many different species mixed and lived together. Technology aided in that endeavor by scrubbing atmospheres and providing decontamination zones and the like. Even most clothing and suit manufacturers embedded tech that helped prevent horrible epidemics from rapidly consuming worlds. But that was only possible when they had a fairly good idea of what types of viruses, bacteria, and mutations they were looking for or could extrapolate what might show up.

The crystals were a whole other scenario. One no one had planned for. *Would I really want to be the one responsible for spreading them to other parts of the known worlds? Could I live with myself?* No, she knew she couldn't.

"What if we got to the *HighTail Flyer*, input coordinates, and sent Nissa off with it with some kind of warning?" she asked in a last-ditch effort to at least be able to do something to protect Nissa. "We could program it to orbit Objer or at least stay in the area. But put up warning signs of contamination, like a radiation leak or something."

"I appreciate what you are trying to do, but if we do not survive, then we will not have found a solution to destroying the cryrot, and so the same problem still remains. Not to mention the speculation amongst the researchers what this planet had once been."

"What's that got to do with anything?" Zurah asked, turning around once more to look at him.

"What was here that made this planet ideal for such technology? Was it simply a way station? A stopover? Or was there something important here? Or perhaps there is something intrinsic to the chemical makeup of this planet that scientists are simply unaware of? Could any of our ships or materials have been exposed to some of these contaminates?"

"If you're going to look at it from that angle, then no one should ever leave their home world. Besides, other individuals have come and gone from this place. You have to get supplies in, and Finn and Alex have both come and gone."

"That is true. But that was before the crystalline entity was able to produce a copy of Alex and embed itself into other individuals. This was not anticipated. We had believed what we were examining was dead. The leftovers from an unknown alien civilization."

"Really," Zurah said with a heavy dose of sarcasm. "Somehow, I have a hard time believing your proposed ignorance of what the researchers are doing here. Not after what I've seen."

One large eye stayed focused on Zurah, while the other rolled to the side and stared off into the distance. "The project knowledge was compartmentalized for security purposes. Finn in particular has been most cautious in how she approached it."

"Doesn't surprise since she's the emperor's sister," Zurah muttered.

Both eyes moved together, and a ripple of dark blue crossed the doctor's skin. "You are aware of this?"

She shrugged. "Alex told me."

Another ripple of blue spread across the doctor's skin and settled around his eyes. For a moment, the color appeared to seep into the white sclera of his eyes, but when Zurah blinked, the color was gone.

"Only a few individuals know of Finn's true identity. I would advise you to not let anyone else know or even allow Finn to know you are aware of who she truly is."

"Then how come you do?" Zurah asked.

"Perhaps we should continue on our way," the doctor suggested, deftly slipping around an answer. "Sitting here is probably not the best course of action."

The doctor was right. Staying put only created an easy target. With a building sense of anger directed at the one person responsible for the mess, Zurah hissed. "Fine. Then we only have one option. We head north." Bringing the rover back online, she adjusted the coordinates, and they changed directions. "You have any idea why we're heading north? Anything out there to be aware of?"

"There were untouched rock outcroppings to the north of the ship. The earlier teams decided the area had not been touched nor the rocks quarried from that area. My assumption would be that Finn has considered the area a reasonably safe fallback position. No prior contamination from the research teams nor supposed ruins from the unknown civilization or crystalline creatures."

"All right, sounds logical. But don't think you're getting out of answering me."

"I cannot betray a trust," the doctor replied.

"Then tell me how you became involved in this project," Zurah said.

The doctor shifted his weight, a tentacle moving to hang over the front passenger's seat. "My choice in profession was not... welcomed. When a Neetho comes of age, they are expected to leave their birthing pod and choose the pod they will become a part of for the rest of their life. The choice is not to be taken lightly, nor are any who delay the decision tolerated. There is a strict adherence to this way of life, which has not changed for millennia. There are a handful of Neethos who swim against the currents to choose careers outside of the established pods. Those of us who do, we are left drifting, unwelcome in the majority of pods, and while driven with the need to find one, often become resigned to the reality of living outside of a pod."

There was a long silence, and Zurah wondered if that was all the doctor would confide. But a second tentacle slid over the passenger's seat to join the first.

"I was on a transport to Seli Prime, where I had been accepted into a medical extension program. None of the major schooling branches were interested in sponsoring me, but on Seli Prime, I would be able to begin classes and demonstrate my competence to look for sponsors. I won three sponsors after four years on Seli Prime, two of which were quite generous and one-time donors. The third indicated they were willing to commit to a reoccurring sponsorship if I would agree to work for their company after graduation. I eagerly accepted."

"Let me guess. Finn."

"No. Quite the opposite. It was a sponsorship from the Kietho-Y-Quipo."

"Who?" Zurah asked. "That doesn't ring any bells."

"Nor would I expect it to. Pod names are not generally spoken outside of the shoals."

"Wasn't that a good thing, then? A pod had accepted you wanted to be a doctor?"

The two tentacles on the passenger seat flipped over, and Zurah glanced at them. The underside with the suckers was riddled with scar tissue.

"Yes. At first, I believed so. Finally, a pod had recognized the importance of the medical profession and how I could enrich the pod with my knowledge. The Kietho-Y-Quipo holds a significant stake in all the gaming establishments on the Lunar colonies, and I thought I would be put to work on one of them. But I wasn't. Instead, I was transferred to the abyss. Where I was conscripted into our Holy War against the darkness."

Zurah couldn't help but turn around and stare at him. "Um, what?"

"This is an ongoing, internal struggle on my home world, between those of my species and another sentient race we consider the darkness. This information is not known outside of my kind. But because we have shared the *sheiol*, and I no longer hold to the tenants of my kind, I do not feel the riptides any longer."

"So, because they hated the fact you wanted to be a doctor, they tricked you then forced you to fight?"

"Put so bluntly, yes. At first I refused to fight, but after a cycle of torture, I took up the weapons of the Neetho and fought against the darkness. And in doing so, I cursed the part of me which only wanted to learn how to heal. After I served ten cycles of fighting, the Kietho-Y-Quipo allowed me to leave. For another cycle, I served in their gaming dens on Lunar 2, under close supervision. When it was believed I could be trusted, I was allowed leniency. It was then that I met Finn."

Zurah could put two and two together, and as the doctor recounted his first meeting with the woman, a deep sense of sorrow for the horrors Dr. Ordotham had been forced to endure overwhelmed her. "So, she tricked you too."

"No, I wouldn't say that. She presented an opportunity to free myself of the Kietho-Y-Quipo in such a way they would not be able to retaliate. It was my only option. And so I took it."

They rode on in silence for quite some distance, eventually skirting the perimeter of the shield as the rover continued north. With each kilometer they sped through, Zurah's anger grew. *Who was Finn to think she could just use anyone she wanted without consequence?* Time and time again, Zurah had seen or heard stories of the rich and famous not caring who they stepped on or abused to get what they wanted. One of the reasons Zurah enjoyed her line of work was being able to poke back at people like that, whether through subtle thefts or large jobs, as long as it caused a serious problem for the target.

The rover's screen blinked and switched over to the long-view screen. There were several rock outcroppings roughly five kilometers from their position. Zurah brought up the ship and noted they were ten kilometers away from it. The shield was far larger than she had anticipated, which was fine with her. That meant there was more distance between her and the ship.

"We'll be there soon," she said. "So far, I'm not seeing any activity from the ship or surrounding areas that would indicate anyone is coming after us."

"I would not count on that," the doctor said. "If there is one thing that I've learned, it's that whatever the crystals truly are, they are tenacious."

Justice. It's all about justice, Zurah thought. "Hey, doc. Can you promise me something?"

"Ask, and we shall see."

"When we get to wherever it is that Finn is hiding out, can you make sure that Nissa is taken care of? That her stasis pod is protected?"

"I have already made this promise. I will not abandon it."

"Thanks," Zurah whispered. "You know, she never told me."

"If I hadn't experienced the hatred of the pods and the need for quiet separation, I wouldn't have come to have a small understanding for why some species choose to keep their pod affiliations a secret. But knowing what I do now, perhaps there is a valid reason for keeping her familial connections from you? A reason that was to help keep you safe. Or she has experienced her own sense of shame or guilt and wished to keep that from you."

Everything that had happened since she'd landed on Objer was a blur, and Zurah hadn't gotten a moment to truly try to digest the information that Nissa was her aunt. The realization had been both infuriating and overwhelming. And Zurah couldn't deny the fact that one of the reasons she wanted Nissa to survive was so that she could get answers. But there was more to it than that, Zurah admitted silently. Nissa had believed in her and given her a job when so many had turned her away. All things that Zurah had deeply appreciated. Yet, an edge of doubt had wormed its way through that comfort. *Did Nissa only do those things because we're related? Did she keep her opinions to herself, secretly wondering if I was truly worth the risk? Did Nissa actually trust me? Or did she only keep me on because we're related?*

Zurah shook her head, trying to dislodge the growing darkness. Dwelling on such things would only make her dull, and she needed all her wits about her. When everything was over, then she would talk with Nissa and figure out the truth. Glancing down at the screen, she was surprised to see the rover had covered more distance than she'd thought. She took the rover off auto-pilot and slowed down.

"Can you keep an eye out on the notifications? Let me know if we start picking up any activity from either where we're going or the direction of the ship. So far, everything has been quiet… too quiet."

The doctor shifted and leaned up against the seats, his tentacles working the controls. "The rover isn't detecting any incoming traffic nor any unusual signals."

"What about life signs? Or a shield? They've surely

got to have some kind of protective shielding or shelter set up where we're going."

"We're either too far for the rover to pick up on anything, or else there is nothing."

A new knot of anxiety added itself to the rest in Zurah's gut. "There's got to be something."

The doctor ran another set of scans, and Zurah did the same with her SeeClear tech. But both of them came up empty.

"Are you certain we were supposed to go north?" the doctor asked.

"Yes," Zurah replied. She had no doubt about that.

"Then I'm sure we will eventually find what we need to find. If this location truly is secure from the crystalline creatures, then no doubt Finn has initiated some type of shield which does not register on the scans."

That sentiment, Zurah was less sure about. Technology always left a trace, and her SeeClear tech was top-of-the-line. Even the copy of Alex had given off strange readings. If Finn's research team had developed a type of shielding that didn't emit any traceable signatures, then it would be a game changer for every kind of war waged and thieving imaginable. The more plausible explanation was a shield paired with some type of ghosting network—that was an idea she could buy.

"Any chance you could drive this thing and let me do a little bit of hacking?" Zurah asked.

"Of course."

She switched places with the tentacles and tucked herself in the footrests. Her fingers moved over the bottom console until she found the edges for the control panel. Popping it open, she took a look at how the rover's system was laid out. The nodes were placed in a standard configuration. She swapped the second and third nodes then pulled herself up. Bringing up the menu, she muttered, "You'd think these tech companies would pay more attention."

"To what?"

She chuckled. "How easy it is to find the weakness in their systems. See?" She pointed to the lower-right corner of the menu, where a small override code was blinking. In less than a minute, she had wormed her way into the system and was rewriting the codes. Once that was complete, she reset the nodes then ran another scan. "Gotcha."

There were two anomalous blips on the screen in the rocky outcroppings in the north. Zurah turned to grin at the doctor, but one of his tentacles snaked toward the screen and pointed at another blip. "What does this indicate?"

Zurah watched the third blip move and cursed. "It means we've got trouble."

16

Zurah slid back into the driver's seat and pushed the rover to its limit. "Keep me updated."

"It would appear they've increased their speed, as well."

"Great," she muttered. *Rule number one: never let your guard down. And I did.* She cursed herself for her complacency. When they'd been able to leave the ship, she had been so focused on getting off world, then so angry at being unable to, that she hadn't gone through the most basic routines of ensuring she was scouting for possible threats.

"I would estimate we will hit the rocky outcropping before they catch us," the doctor said. "But it will be close. They must be using a different type of vehicle to be gaining on us."

Zurah bit her tongue. If it had been Nissa or Mexa saying that, she would have shot back with a not-so-kind response. But she was quite sure the doctor was simply stating a potential fact and not subtly commenting on her lack of thinking ahead.

The jagged spears of rocks appeared before them as the rover's lights bounced off the black rocks. They were only a kilometer out from the nearest blip, and Zurah was forced to slow down.

"What are you doing?" the doctor asked. "If we reduce our speed—"

"I don't know what type of shielding Finn might be using. If it's anything like the shield they've got over this sector, then we'd bounce right off it when we hit it. But if it's military grade or worse, then we run the risk of being incinerated. Without a read on the perimeter, I don't know where it's at. Our hope is that they've spotted us and will give us a signal."

"And if not?"

"Then… I don't know. We could make a run for the second blip, or… I don't know. Hopefully, it won't come to that." They were close enough now that Zurah had slowed the rover down to a crawl. *Surely the edge of the shield is out here. Unless there is no shield and the blip isn't them at all.*

"Zurah, we may have another issue," the doctor said. "Look."

Zurah glanced over at the screen. With a sinking feeling, she watched as the second blip began to move toward the first one. "Dammit. They're not shielding signatures. No shield tech is going to move that way."

"Then what are they?"

"I don't know," Zurah said, frustration and fear increasing rapidly. "Just hang on." She stopped the rover and got out, staring at the rocky outcropping. She used her SeeClear tech to run another scan, hoping the proximity would produce clearer results, but it merely reproduced what the rover's sensors were showing. She climbed back and started the rover once more. "If I had more tools to work with, it would help. The signals are registering, but nothing is able to identify what they might actually be."

"I believe our best option is to continue toward the signals," the doctor said. "We know what the ones pursuing us want, and it is not good."

Zurah walked to the back of the rover and ran another scan. *Damn.* The SeeClear tech pinged the unusual energy reading it had identified as coming from the copy of Alex.

"You really trust her?" Zurah asked as she scrambled back into the driver's seat.

"I do. Despite your misgivings, Finn is an honorable human. I don't make those statements lightly."

Zurah was sure the doctor didn't. "All right. Then we continue on."

A flash of light appeared in the rearview mirror, and Zurah revved the rover's engine. The tires spewed sand as they took off. The terrain changed, and she shifted to semiauto control, allowing the rover's system to compensate for the adjustments needed to navigate the increasingly rocky landscape while she continued to steer it toward the first blip. It wasn't long until the rover's screen flashed a warning. The incline had grown too steep, and huge pillars of rock jutted up out of the ground, making it impossible for the rover to go any farther.

"Looks like this is as far as it'll go." Zurah went to the menu and scanned the list of options. "Of course this unit isn't equipped with anit-grav units. Just my luck," she mumbled. "Come on, we've got to get out." She twisted around. "Can you walk? I mean, I know you can walk… but can you walk around in this environment without any other kind of protective gear?"

The doctor's skin shifted to a dull black and hardened. Zurah could only stare wide-eyed at the change.

"As I said before, Neethos have learned to adapt to a wide range of environments, not least of which was how to utilize that knowledge for combat situations. I may have been able to retain the natural coloring of my species, but I wasn't able to escape the bioupgrades necessary to fight. My bioarmor will protect me for now. It is not a permanent solution but will hold for now."

The answer wasn't solid, and Zurah didn't feel much relief about the vague timeline, but she knew sitting around dithering over his answer would only waste what precious time they did have. "Can you—"

Dr. Ordotham had wriggled free of the rover and had two of his tentacles securely wrapped around Nissa's stasis pod. "We should move."

Zurah blinked and activated the SeeClear radar. She pinned the location of the first blip, which, thankfully, had remained stationary. The second blip had altered course and was no longer on a trajectory with the first blip but was making its way toward the advancing rover.

"Doc, we may have gotten ourselves tangled up—"

But the doctor had moved past Zurah and was quickly

scaling the rocks. She scrambled to keep up with him. "Doc, hey, wait!"

But he didn't slow down, and within minutes, the doctor was out of sight, his darkened exterior blending into the rocks.

Zurah twisted around to watch the bouncing lights of the rover. *They're not far away.* She crouched between two boulders as the headlights lit up the rocks above her. Her heart hammered, and her hand moved to her side, but she had no weapons. If she stayed, she was relying on the suit's ability to ghost whatever scanning tech they had brought with them. Zurah didn't consider her odds favorable. The suit wasn't bad, but she wasn't familiar with it. Nor was it a model she would've been inclined to purchase for work. The only other option was to climb as fast as she could.

She turned around and scrambled for the next rock that was just beyond the lights of the rover, but her fingers slipped and came away coated in a slick substance. There wasn't any time to determine if it was a naturally occurring phenomenon or artificial.

Voices drifted up to her, and she could hear the cryrot's orders to fan out and start searching. She tried again, this time reaching for what appeared to be a crevice in the rocks. She forced her fingers into the small opening and, through sheer willpower, pulled herself up. Her feet skidded along the rock face, trying to find purchase. Dangling by one arm, she swung her body, trying to grab the ledge just above her head. Her fingers touched the rim but started to slip. Panicking, she tried to get her feet underneath her, but they continued to slip, as well. The fingers tucked into the crevice burned, and seconds before she lost her grip, a hand reached down and grabbed her free arm.

"Hold on," a voice whispered.

"Alex," Zurah said as relief flooded her body. Without thinking, she pulled her hand out of the crevice, grabbed hold of Alex's forearm, and held on as he hauled her up onto the ledge. She tried to stand, but even the top of the ledge was slick, and without Alex's steadying grip, she would have tumbled down to her death.

"You okay?" he asked. "We've got to move."

"Yes. But how are you here?" She shook her hands in disgust. "What is this stuff?"

"Hold on to my shoulders then lift one foot up at a time."

Zurah did as he said, and he coated the bottom of her boots with some type of substance.

"Now stand still."

With an immense sense of relief, Zurah was able to do just that.

When he didn't move, she asked, "Alex?"

There was a strange sort of day-dreaming expression on his face.

She leaned forward and touched his arm. "Alex?"

He shivered and blinked. "Hold out your hands."

She frowned but did as he said, and he coated her gloves then instructed her, "You'll need to pair the nano-bots with your SeeClear tech. Hurry. Once complete, you'll see the handholds. Make sure to grab exactly where you see them light up." And without further explanation, Alex turned and started climbing.

As quickly as she could, Zurah followed his instructions. Relieved to find glowing hand and footprints leading up the side of the rock face, she reached out and touched the first one. Thin filaments reached out from her glove and embedded themselves into the glowing pad. Fascinated, Zurah gave an experimental tug. To her delight, her hand was firmly in place. She reached up, and as her hand made contact, her other hand loosened, allowing her to move it forward. Once she had the rhythm of moving her hands and feet in order, she made short work of following Alex up the side of the rock face.

When she came to the last couple of glowing pads, she realized they were right below a large ledge, and Alex was waiting for her. He helped her up then motioned for her to follow. She glanced back down the cliff, and the rover was still there. Zurah picked up five different life signs milling around the base of the cliff and the abandoned rover.

"Come on," Alex said.

"I'm coming." She hurried after him. Alex disappeared into the rock face, and without a second thought, so did Zurah. The other side was something entirely different. The rock vanished, and in its place was a highly polished metal flooring, along with walls and a ceiling.

"Welcome to the *Capsia*," Finn said as she stopped to stand next to Alex.

The thrill of what Zurah was seeing vanished immediately. She marched forward and punched Finn. No one stopped her, and Finn didn't back away or try to defend herself. But the moment Zurah's fist connected with Finn's cheek, the anger inside of her burst. Embarrassment and shame crept forward to replace the fury, and Zurah quickly backed off.

"I'm—" She couldn't finish the statement, but she needn't have tried.

Finn did so for her. "Sorry. I should never have involved you and the others."

"Then why did you?" Zurah asked.

"Out of necessity. I made you a promise, that I would get you and Nissa out of here, and I will. But being able to make good on that promise is going to have to wait. When this is over, you may ask anything of me."

Zurah stared at Finn, trying to ascertain the sincerity behind those words.

"She will make good on her promise," Alex softly assured her. "But right now, we have other things to worry about."

"Alex is right," Finn said. "I tried to keep any information from leaking into the wrong hands, but we're to the point where I have no choice but to tell you exactly what's going on. We should have enough time for that at least. For the moment, we're secure here."

"And where is here, exactly? Are we still on Objer?" Zurah asked.

Finn glanced at Alex and frowned. "Yes, we are. This was my personal ship I used to transport the more sensitive items when we set up the research team. But only a few personnel were aware of its location."

"So much for trust," Zurah muttered.

"Rather a healthy dose of discretion," Finn countered.

"What makes us any more safe here than anywhere else?"

"Let's just say I have access to proprietary military-grade tech that most of the known worlds aren't aware of. Before I received the distress calls," Finn continued, refusing to add any further explanations, "a handful of the researchers were already aware of the cryrot and the potential concerns for contamination. We moved a select few of their labs to this location as a backup. Once contamination was confirmed, protocol was enacted, and those researchers moved here. When I had your team enter the ship, I was confirming their status and the level of contamination throughout the rest of the teams. There were only a handful left who hadn't been exposed, and I needed to make sure I got them to safety."

Zurah took a step back. "Then you need to know that I've—"

"Yes, we're aware. Dr. Ordotham informed us, but we were already aware while you were making your approach. The cryrot emits a particularly strange energy signal, one we are able to identify but not quite fully understand."

"Then why let me come here? Won't I spread the contamination?"

"To be blunt, you are turning out to be a bit of an anomaly. You should have already succumbed to the cryrot's influence. But you haven't, and we need to know why. But beyond that point, it's too late. The cryrot has bled into even this environment, and my ship's sensors have indicated minute crystal fragments in the air recycling system. At this point, we are simply trying to ascertain how to slow the spread of contamination and reverse its effects."

"So I'm to be a guinea pig for you all," Zurah snapped.

"No," Alex said. "You're not. And I'll make sure of it." He glanced at Finn, who had an unreadable expression on her face. "We simply need your help. I've asked the doctor to work with you, and I would also like you to help what is left of the tech teams. They're working on trying to gain control of the ship's systems."

"Why can't you just—" She started to reach for the pocket where she had hidden the flesh-eater disc Alex had given her.

But he interrupted her. "We've already tried a wide variety of methods, but with your creative outlook and background, you might see something that we've missed."

Zurah got the hint and finished the gesture by scratching at her suit. "I'll do what I can."

"Good," Finn said. "Come with me. Alex, go and check on the doctor and tell him when he's ready, Zurah will be on the bridge."

"Wait, where is the doc? And where's Nissa?"

Alex gave her a reassuring smile. "The doctor immediately took the stasis pod to the medical bay. It's not as expansive as what he worked with on the ship, but he's already put together a temporary holding area for the pod."

Zurah believed Alex, and she believed the doctor would watch over Nissa. "Thanks."

Alex nodded then left.

"Now, let me try and put all the pieces together for you," Finn said as they began to walk. They moved through an expansive cargo bay and headed off through one of two doors leading into the rest of the ship. "As you are aware, this research expedition was put together with the goal of understanding what happened to the *Eagle's Nest* and their crew. Research that was originally done by—"

"Your great-grandmother. Yes I know," Zurah said. "Why don't you just skip to the part and explain why? Why is this research so important?"

Without missing a beat, Finn turned left then came to stop in front of a door. "Because her son had her executed for it."

17

"Excuse me?" Zurah said. The door opened, and they stepped into a moderately sized hab-unit. "Executed?"

"Yes, under the guise of treason." Finn took a seat behind an oak table. Tapping the top, she brought up a screen. "I am Zhu Ekadzati, the Serene Tempest of Night. The sister to the Emperor of Old Earth."

Zurah feigned shock, allowing Finn to believe it was a revelation. She wasn't going to betray Alex's trust. "And sister to Miles High, then. So the rumors are partly true."

Finn scowled. "Insomuch as I must tolerate him, yes. But Miles does what he wants, while I work to try and make—" She stopped herself. "That is a topic for another discussion. There are many secrets at the heart of the emperor's throne, and this is one I'm determined to unravel."

"Why?" Zurah couldn't help but push.

"Why don't you have something to eat first?"

Zurah eyed the bowl of fruit sitting to the side and took a hard, round purple-skinned ubu, one of the only fruits she could identify in the bowl. She took a bite of the nutty, aromatic fruit as Finn opened a file, and the face a kindly looking older man appeared. His long hair was snow white and tied at his neck with a leather thong. The unmistakable crown of the emperor rested on his head. The golden circlet gleamed, and the emeralds and rubies shone with a bright light.

"My popo was a kind man and often would care for me when my parents were called to handle matters of state. By the time I was born, my brothers were well into their teenage years and had little interest in anything to do with me. And even if they had, I doubt they would have been permitted to play, as they were already well into their schooling on how to govern. Popo told me several stories, some of which were a combination of Old Earth mythology and his own creative imaginings. But many were based in reality, and when I was older, he would often whisper what he termed 'the forbidden' stories to me. And on a few rare occasions, he allowed me to accompany him to the vaults.

"But the forbidden story he shared with me more and more as he grew older was the story of his mother and how his brother had given the order to have her executed. If you're at all familiar with the throne of Old Earth, I'm sure you're aware that my popo overthrew his own brother to take the throne."

Zurah shook her head. "Haven't had much use for that kind of information."

"Fair. The simple explanation is that my popo's

brother was a cruel man, and besides having his own mother put to death, he had a string of atrocities linked to his name. If my popo hadn't overthrown him, there undoubtedly would have been an uprising from the people. Instead, he was able to calm the growing anger and resentment, and he is widely regarded as one of the most benevolent emperors.

"But he had always wanted to know why his brother executed their mother. What crime could have been so horrible, or what knowledge could she have held to have led to such a horrendous act? It was a question he never solved and one he passed on to me."

Zurah considered what Finn was telling her. She empathized with needing to understand why family members had done certain things and needing to get to the bottom of that mystery. But she couldn't figure out what was so important about Finn's story. *Why would this question take priority above so many others? And why expend so many resources?* "So, this is just about family?"

"How far can I trust you?" Finn asked.

"If you uphold your end of the deal in making sure Nissa stays alive and gets medical help, then you can count on me," Zurah said.

"I appreciate your honesty." The image on the screen was replaced by images of Old Earth. "How much do you know about the Cricade Wars? And the upheavals on Old Earth in its wake?"

Zurah shrugged. "Just what you hear on the vids and whisper nets."

"My brother, the esteemed emperor…" Finn pushed back from the table and stood. She moved to stand beside a view screen, looking out over the desolate landscape of Objer. "Has already sent a team through the gates."

Zurah stared at Finn, her brain stumbling to catch up. "The gates? You're confirming those two gigantic slabs of rock are really another portal?" She kicked herself for not making the connection earlier.

"Yes. Big enough to accommodate a ship. Alex doesn't know this, and I am asking you to keep it a secret."

Great, now I've got secrets on both sides. But it does give me options if worst-case scenarios start happening. I wanted intel, and now I've got it.

"My brother sent a team through the gates at the tail end of the Cricade Wars. I only learned about it a little over a year ago, and I haven't been able to figure out why, what he was hoping his expedition would do. My brother is many things, but taking on such an enormous undertaking at a time when humanity was reeling from the devastating effects of the war means there was a very important reason to do so. And I'm certain, whatever it was, wasn't in the best interest of the known worlds."

Zurah sat up, realizing a connection. "So, when that cryrot creature was talking about desecrating the dead and all that, they weren't talking about what your researchers did. But what your brother's team must have done." And as soon as the revelation hit, she saw the holes in the idea. "But that wouldn't make sense. Not unless your brother's teams also went through the smaller portals. Do you know where the gates lead?"

"No, but we are fairly certain each location isn't bound to a single portal. We theorize there was once an intricate network of portals connecting a wide range of alien sites. The teams have found fragments of what we believe to be other portals on the platforms, but so far, none of them have worked. We believe they have been either destroyed or purposefully disconnected."

"So, your brother had to have had researchers out here for quite some time, then."

"Yes."

Zurah chewed on the information. "Then you'll need to go after your brother's team."

"Yes. But before we can do that, we have to stop the cryrot. Turner was on the verge of activating the gates. I was already making the final arrangements to come out here and prepare to go through the gates when I received the distress calls. And that is why I believe the cryrot killed Turner and has worked at contaminating so many others. It wants to protect the gate or at least stop us from going through."

"From desecrating the dead," Zurah muttered. "Are you sure this is something you should do?"

"If it wasn't my brother we were dealing with, then I would be hesitant. I have no desire to dishonor another culture or civilization, but I can't let this go unchecked. I need to know what my brother is attempting to do and why. And how this is related to what happened to my great-grandmother."

"What exactly are you hoping I can do?"

"As I said, I need you to hack into the ship. I need control because we're close to understanding how to neutralize the cryrot. Your ingenuity on escaping the cryrot and freeing Alex has been extremely helpful. Any other questions?"

Zurah shook her head.

"Good. Then if you'll follow me, I'll take you down to where Angelina is working. You'll be assisting her."

Zurah merely nodded and kept her expression neutral. She had been good at keeping secrets before, and now she felt she was becoming an expert. She couldn't help but wonder if this was what Finn and Alex did every day—compartmentalizing information from a wide variety of sources and always having to live behind a mask. She shuddered at the thought. There were times when she needed to do so, but when a job was over, she relaxed and had enjoyed the company of the crew. But she couldn't imagine having to live that way all of the time.

When the door opened, Alex was leaning against the wall opposite the door. He straightened up when he saw them. "Good to go?"

"Yes," Finn said.

"I can take her to Angelina," he said. "The doc would like a word with you before he joins Zurah on the bridge." Finn hesitated for a moment before she threw Zurah a strange look but turned and left them be.

"How you holding up?" Alex asked. "Sounds like you had quite the ordeal with the doc."

Zurah was a little startled by his concern but appreciated it nonetheless. "Just don't give me a chance to sit down," she joked. "Not until this mess is over. I don't think I could keep it together if I had to dwell on it all right now."

"I know the feeling." Alex ran his hand through his hair. "Come on. The doc's down in… No sorry. I mean Angelina's on the bridge."

"Are you all right?" Zurah asked, a twinge of unease at his obvious mistake.

"For the moment." Then he asked quietly, "Can you hear them?"

"What?" Zurah stopped. "What are you talking about?"

"Nothing," he said quickly with a shake of his head. "Forget it."

"No. What did you mean?" she said, refusing to move.

Alex sighed then looked up and down the corridor. "When I was encased in the crystal, I thought I heard"—he rubbed his forehead—"god, it was horrible. The whispers, all the voices clamoring to be heard on top of each other."

"What did the doc have to say?"

He shook his head. "Haven't talked to him. Haven't talked to anyone."

Zurah narrowed her eyes and studied Alex. With a few blinks, she activated her SeeClear tech and ran a quick scan. A routine sweep didn't bring up any red flags, but Zurah dug deeper until she found a faint, but still unusual, energy signature. There was a seventy-three percent match to the energy signature from the cryrot.

Why isn't it a match? Because Alex wasn't infected by our particular cryrot? These questions were beyond Zurah's field of expertise. "We need to tell the doc. Can you still hear them?"

Alex looked at her, and his guard dropped. There was a healthy amount of fear in his eyes. "Yes."

"Then we're going to see the doc. Tell him what's going on."

"Can't. He's loyal to Finn. We tell him, and he'll tell her."

"At this point, I don't think that should matter," Zurah said.

"But it does. If Finn gets a whiff of a hint that I'm compromised, she'll pull me off the team. Lock me up until all of this is sorted."

"Because what? She doesn't fully trust you?"

"No." Alex frowned. "Nothing like that. She trusts me… as far as anyone in our position can trust another person, but out of all of our family, we can get along, work together. The same can't be said for the others."

"I see. What about Angelina? Could you tell her? Someone needs to know, Alex. What you've heard or are hearing might be important."

"I know. I just wanted to see if you'd experienced anything similar since… well…" He blushed and waved at her leg. "You were contaminated too. I can't find any mention of the phenomenon in any other reports."

"I get it," Zurah said. *Just another secret to add to the pile.* "Look, I'll keep monitoring you. If things get worse, or you start acting like someone is forcing you to do stuff, I'm telling the doc."

For a moment, Zurah thought Alex was going to argue. But a small amount of tension drained away from his face, and his shoulders relaxed. "Deal." He gave her a slight smile. "Thanks. Now, let's get you to the bridge."

They walked the rest of the way in silence, only passing two other people along the way. Both wore haggard expressions and didn't even seem to notice Alex or Zurah as they passed. Zurah wondered if she'd made the right decision. But she understood Alex's need to remain a part of the team, to be able to work freely without suspicion.

I'm just giving him the same courtesy that Nissa afforded me. After everything went wrong with the job on Cloud-11, there were so many who didn't want to work with me. But Nissa looked past all of that and did. Even if she wasn't telling me the whole truth.

Zurah reminded herself that she had a backup plan. If anything went wrong, she was going to the doc. When they got to the bridge, Angelina was the only one there. She was sitting down and bent over a console, furiously working.

"Hey, I've got—" Alex started to say, but Angelina whipped around, her weapon drawn. "Whoa, easy now," Alex said and raised his hands.

A flutter of confusion passed across Angelina's face then quickly disappeared as she holstered her weapon. "Sorry. We're all a bit jumpy right now. Perimeter scans show they haven't left. They're trying to find a way up the cliff, and once they do, it won't take them long to realize what we've hidden up here."

"Don't sweat it," Alex said. "What can we do to help?"

Angelina glanced at both of them. "Zurah, get started on cracking the security codes popping up on the main ship's interface. We need to get control of their systems. Alex, monitor the perimeter for me, will you? And I'll go back to analyzing the cryrot's energy signatures. There's got to be something in there we can use against it."

Zurah sat down behind what would have been the

security officer's console and got to work. The ship's interface was easy to work with, and before long, she was lost in the codes. She'd done substantial damage to their system and could easily see where someone had been repairing issues. Yet, despite the advantage it gave her, she couldn't quite crack the mainframe. She had access to several systems but not the override controls. She could start shutting things down from her end, but any competent security personnel could override her work. The hack needed to be foolproof.

She leaned back and twisted her sore neck first one way than the other and realized that Angelina had left at some point. Alex was sitting a level below her, still monitoring the sensor sweeps.

"Have they figured out how to get up the cliff?" Zurah asked.

"I'm not sure. That was Angelina's contribution. Not even sure what the stuff entirely is. But it looks like both of the rovers have left, and there are three individuals still out there. My guess is they are headed back to the ship for supplies. So we've got roughly thirty, maybe forty, minutes if they're pushing those things at top speeds. Any luck on your end?"

"Not as much as I'd hoped. I'm having trouble with the last firewall. I need access to the final set of codes that could override anything that I do." Zurah stood and stretched. "Why not just tell Finn about the flesh eater?"

But Alex had closed his eyes and turned away from her.

"Hey," Zurah snapped. "You've got to stick with me. Just try to block it out."

Alex shivered then glanced at her. "Sorry. What did you say?"

With a huff full of more concern than irritation, Zurah ran a quick scan, but she didn't detect any changes in the energy signature. "Why not just tell Finn about the flesh eater?"

Alex grimaced. "She'd be furious. Do you know who manufactures those things?"

"No. Never thought I would ever see one. So many think they're just a fancy story."

"Yeah, well. They're manufactured by the Eeri."

Zurah gaped at him in disbelief. "You've got to be kidding me."

Alex shook his head. "No. I'm not. The Goldsmith Consortium worked with the Eeri before the war, and we managed to keep a few of the more… exotic pieces of tech for ourselves."

"Why in the worlds are you telling me this?"

Alex shrugged and looked away. "You saved my life. Figure that counts for something."

"I have no doubt anyone else would have done the same," Zurah said.

"You have no idea how lonely a life of my position can be. You can have all the workers in the worlds who sign loyalty contracts and pledge their lives for the Consortium, but when it's all boiled down, they're there because you're paying them. You didn't have to rescue me. You could have left and continued your deal with Finn. She would have seen you right."

Zurah blushed and took her seat. Trust was a hard commodity to earn in her line of work, and it took quite a while to cultivate. But she also understood the feeling of being isolated and alone, and when someone appeared to throw you a lifeline, you grabbed hold, no matter what.

"That and the odds of us getting out of here alive are pretty slim. So if I end up telling you all my family's secrets, I don't think it's going to matter much." Alex grinned, and Zurah appreciated the levity. "But the flesh eater wouldn't be a solution anyway. Finn wants control of the ship, not to fry its systems. If we can neutralize the cryrot, we still need to try and help the others, and that also means we still need a base of operations. Finn's ship is adequate for now, but it would be too small if we're able to save the others. Not to mention the databases and the information that are still on that ship."

"No, I know. I just wish that was going to be the simple solution to this all. A flesh eater could go in and just strip it all down, and we would have access in seconds." Zurah stopped then considered what she just said. "But I wonder if I could mimic…" She leaned back over the console, her mind already several steps ahead.

Alex walked up the steps to peer over her shoulder. "What are you thinking?"

She swatted at him to keep silent as she worked. "I think I've just about—"

An explosion rocked the ship, and Alex and Zurah tumbled to the left. She groaned as she untangled herself from him and tried to get to her feet.

"Damn." Alex scrambled to get back down to the sensors. "Looks like they took a page out of your play-book. They must have spoofed the system. Switching over to the overlays." Alex swiped up on the console and flung the images up to the main view screen. "My best bet is they took the fuel cells from one of the rovers and jury-rigged them into a type of bomb." He hit the comm button. "Finn? What's the damage?" Then he turned and gestured for Zurah to take the console next to him. "What's the ship saying?"

Zurah glanced down and read through the scrolling reports. "Not too much damage it looks like. The field generators have taken a hit, they're down to fifty-one percent capacity, and it looks like whatever shielding tech Finn had set up has been compromised. But everything else is reading in the green."

Finn's voice crackled through the comms. "We're getting the same reports. Except it looks like one of the engines might have sustained structural damage. Can you confirm?"

Zurah sorted the reports to only display engineering. "Yes. Confirming. Engine three has been damaged. Looks like it's going to need some repairs before it's functional."

There was a round of swearing through the comms. "Then we're sitting ducks. Had to pull out the second engine just to set up the ghost field. This thing can't fly on one engine alone. Zurah, we need control of that ship. Now."

"I'm almost there. I—" Zurah's back arched as a white-hot searing pain ripped through her body. She screamed in agony as her vision blurred. Then the whispers began. She slapped her hands over her ears, trying to block them out, but they only got louder. Through the tears, she saw Alex curled up on the floor, his hands also covering his ears.

"What's happening?" Finn's voice sounded small and distant. "Zurah? Alex? Do you copy?"

Zurah collapsed and crawled over to Alex. He was crying tears of crystallized blood.

Zurah touched her eyes, confident they would come away stained with her blood. But they weren't. "Alex," she whispered. "You've got to try and block out the noise."

But as soon as the words escaped her lips, the whispers grew louder, and another jolt of pain tore through her injured leg, spreading throughout her body. Grunting through the pain, she forced herself to sit up in order to take a look at the leg. What she saw chilled her to the bone. A faint orange glow had encased her leg. She turned back to look at Alex. The same light was wrapped around his arms.

The whispers were there, gnawing on her thoughts. But there were also the sounds of individuals shouting and heavy boots pounding against metal. She lay back down and reached out to touch Alex's shoulder.

"Listen to anything but them, Alex. Try to focus on my voice or the noise around us. Don't let the whispers take over. Can you hear me? Alex?"

There was a small, almost imperceptible nod on his part, and Zurah pushed herself closer. "Have you ever played Triple Luck? It's usually only run by Neethos. Each player gets five different rounds, and they have to toss this orilic cube into baskets to score points. Except there's one basket that moves around the board, the golden one. If you hit that, you've about won the game.

I almost had Nissa beat this last time before the IGJ raided the place. I guess I lost 'cause they were looking for Finn."

The edges of Alex's lips curled up, and in a weak voice, he said, "Bet I could beat you."

"Bet you can't. Tell you what—when we make it off this hellhole, I'll play you a game. We'll see who does better. Deal?"

He nodded. "Deal."

"Have you ever been to a Rockerton's?" Zurah asked, trying to find another topic.

Alex shook his head.

"Then you're in for a treat. Better not let any of them know who you are, though. I bet they'd charge you up one side and down the other just to breathe a drop of their air. But if you can pay, they've got everything—"

A tentacle wrapped around her body and lifted her when another explosion reverberated through the ship. The background noise of chaos increased, but the whispers quieted momentarily. Zurah attempted to twist around to look at the doctor, but a burst of orange light at the front of the bridge caught her attention. Crystals were pushing through the ship's hull. Hundreds of them.

Someone shouted a series of orders, and without warning, the tentacle unwrapped, and Zurah fell to the floor. She groaned in pain as she landed the wrong way on her left arm and rolled over, hugging it to her body. The whispers shifted from anger and fear into a swelling chorus of voices that she couldn't block out. A pair of hands grabbed her legs, and she kicked back, trying to get them off.

Movement caught her eye, and she glanced over to see Alex sitting up. His eyes were wide open and staring at nothing in particular. "Alex?" she cried out. "Alex!"

When he didn't respond, she gave one last furious kick at the hands, freeing herself. She crawled over to him and shook him violently. "Snap out of it."

But a burst of wrongness erupted in her mind, and the hands were back, grabbing at her legs and arms, trying to pull her away from Alex. She twisted back and forth. "No, you can't have him!" But this time, she wasn't able to free herself. The song of the crystals intensified until all she could hear was their deafening roar.

"I hear you," she whined. "But you… can't… have him."

Pain nipped her neck, and her body relaxed immediately. Her head rolled back, and she looked up at Alex's face. A line of crystals had pushed out from under the skin along the injury down his cheek.

Zurah shook her head. *That's not right. Alex didn't injure his face.* Then she realized she was staring up into the face of the cryrot.

"I'm happy to know you can finally hear us. But you should know, I don't care about him. As it turns out, it's you that I want."

18

Zurah was helpless against the sedative. The hands lifted her, and the cryrot turned toward the crystal, which had burst through the hull. As they neared the brightly glowing crystals, the largest crystal in the front produced a distinctive hum. As the humming dropped in pitch, the crystal increased its size until it engulfed Zurah, the cryrot carrying her and Alex, who had stood and walked with them with no prompting.

Her world was overtaken by warmth, and millions of fractures formed and reformed as the cryrot moved them through the crystals. Thousands of geometric shapes twisted and twirled around them, with feather-like tendrils reaching out then retracing to stretch toward a different one. The air pressure changed, as if something were pressing down on her from all sides, and the whispers that had been angry turned into a gentle breeze carried along by the low-pitched humming.

They moved past the ship, the crystal-like cocoon moving with them. The pitch changed from a continuous smooth flow into disjointed staccato notes. With each new note, a piece of the crystal punched into the rock, anchoring the cocoon, as it gradually made its way down the side of the cliff. Once they were safely to the bottom, the cryrot moved to one of the rovers, placed Zurah in the back, and slipped into the driver's seat. Alex sat on the passenger's side. Zurah tried to move her legs or her arms, but her limbs wouldn't respond. All she could do was move her eyes, looking from the back of the cryrot's head to Alex's.

Why does he want me? I'm nothing special. Zurah's panicked thoughts rotated through an increasingly chaotic set of reasons. Each one was more nonsensical than the last. The rover bounced over a rough patch of rocks, and the sudden movement jarred Zurah back to a semblance of reason. *I've got to find a way to stop this. But how? Finn's teams were working on this issue for how long?* Zurah felt a sense of hubris, believing she alone might be able to figure out a solution. She wasn't a biologist or scientist. She was a security hack. *What skills could I bring to this kind of situation?*

Eventually, she closed her eyes, feeling the weight of hopelessness settle around her. She'd experienced that feeling too many times before. When she'd realized her parents weren't coming back for her, Zurah was lost, and the feeling she was sinking into a deep abyss had been nearly impossible to defeat. Then after fleeing Harold and his crew, she had felt the darkness settle over her again. If she were honest with herself, the darkness had never truly left. The questions of who she was, who her parents had been, and why they'd left her always had an oily darkness clinging to them that tainted every other thought. Despite her immobility, Zurah cried until she had no more tears left. Her heart heavy, she lay there, wondering if this was how she was always meant to die. Alone.

The rover eventually came to a stop, and Zurah opened her eyes. The cryrot stepped out of the rover and issued orders before returning and picking up Zurah as if she weighed nothing. Alex quietly followed the cryrot back to the ship, moving swiftly through the decks until they reached the room where she and the doctor had been held.

A medical platform had been brought into the room, and the cryrot laid Zurah down on it while Alex moved to stand to the side. Zurah slowly looked around the room, as far as she could. The interior had completely changed, with pillars of crystal spread throughout the room, and it gave Zurah the feeling of stepping into an alien landscape. The cryrot moved over to the nearest one and placed his hand on the crystalline pillar. The faint orange glow emanating from the structure intensified around his hand, and a low-pitched hum filled the room.

"The Timeless Sleepers shall awake," the cryrot said, "and they will discover new worlds for their vengeance."

The words washed over Zurah, and she desperately wished she could speak or do something to stop what was happening. She looked to the side and stared at Alex, silently willing him to do something, anything but stand there like a slack-jawed idiot.

For crying out loud, you're the idiot, Zurah chided herself.

She blinked, activating her SeeClear tech. Having a screen to pair with would have made the work easier, but where there was a will, there was a way. She navigated the menu, looking for potential networks in the vicinity. A handful pinged her system, but she finally found the one she was confident was Alex's own SeeClear tech. It took her longer than she liked, but Zurah synced with Alex's system then hacked into it. She forced his menu to activate then input the codes for a hard reset.

Zurah had been forced to reset her tech only once before, and the process had been less than pleasant. In fact, there had been several warnings issued when she had opted to add bioupgrades to avoid a hard reset at all costs. As long as the user stayed up-to-date with the updates to the system and followed any additional procedures that might be initiated, a hard reset could be avoided.

She watched Alex's face, and if she could have leaped for joy, she would have. He winced, blinked, then shook his head. Zurah maintained the link and quickly flashed a warning sign. *Don't move. Don't do anything. Just stand there and look dumb.*

Alex complied so well that for a split second, she was afraid her idea hadn't worked. But when he started to blink and his eyes began to move in the telltale way a SeeClear tech user's did, she sighed inwardly.

Encrypted user 157.C.X.87.210: *What's going on? I don't remember leaving Finn's ship. Are you okay?*

Non-specified user: *I'm okay for now. I don't know what the cryrot has planned. Do you still hear the whispers? Or the humming?*

Encrypted user 157.C.X.87.210: *I do, but they're like a dull background noise right now.*

Non-specified user: *Good. You've got to try and keep it that way. Just try to ignore it. I know it's hard, but somehow the whispers and or the humming are connected with helping the cryrot take over.*

Encrypted user 157.C.X.87.210: *What about you? Can you hear them?*

Non-specified user: *Just background noise is all. We've got to figure out how to stop it.*

Encrypted user 157.C.X.87.210: *I know. If only we had access to the research files. Maybe there would be something in there that we could use.*

Non-specified user: *Think you could get to a workstation under the radar?*

Encrypted user 157.C.X.87.210: *Can you create a distraction?*

Non-specified user: *Yeah, I'll blink him to death. Hold on.*

Zurah tried to move an arm or a leg then a finger. But her body still wouldn't cooperate. She swallowed then realized she could grunt. Trying to be as loud and annoying as possible, she grunted and groaned until the cryrot turned toward her. She glared as best as she could, and the cryrot simply smiled.

"You are an impatient creature, too bound by the constraints of your understanding of time. But perhaps that will be to our advantage. We are ageless, we are patient, and we do not carry the burden of time."

Zurah grunted, hoping the cryrot interpreted it as she meant it.

The cryrot laughed. "I believe the Timeless Sleepers

will agree with my assessment and alterations. There is a quality within your species that harkens back to the time before our sleep. Perhaps your kind will be a vehicle for a renewing. Long before the sleep, there were ideas which flowed, calls for such a thing. But the ground was not yet ripe, and we were too raw from the sundering."

Alex remained slack-jawed and dreamy eyed as he slowly made his way toward a workstation, but the cryrot shifted his gaze from Zurah toward Alex.

"It would appear I have more work to do before the Timeless Sleepers can join us," the cryrot said with a sad shake of his head. "You are fighting us but not in the same way as she has fought us. I wonder what the differences are."

A low hum filled the room, vibrating through every inch of the space. Within a few minutes, the door opened, and three researchers entered. Each one had crystals in various places along their body, and each one made a strange gesture when they saw the copy of Alex.

"Restrain this one." He pointed at Alex. "And I want samples from both of them. I want working hypothesis only."

The gesture was made again, and the three converged on Alex before he could react. His hands were bound, and a temporary restraining collar was placed around his neck, immobilizing his suit and body.

Zurah grunted again, trying to draw the cryrot's attention. He looked over at her then gave her a small nod of encouragement. "Do not fear. We are not here to destroy, merely to rearrange and rejuvenate." The cryrot moved to each of the three researchers, whispering further instructions before he left.

Non-specified user: *What in the hell is going on? Rearrange and rejuvenate?*

Encrypted user 157.C.X.87.210: *I don't know.*

Zurah closed her eyes for a moment, trying to keep calm. She felt a small prick of pain in the crook of her arm, and when she opened her eyes, one of the researchers was drawing blood. All she could do was watch as they filled three vials with her blood. Then the researcher picked up her arm and scraped the top of her hand until they left a small red patch of angry tissue behind. When she looked at Alex, another researcher was doing the same to him.

The darkness was threatening to overwhelm her. The feeling that she was going to die was overwhelming. *If I die, then Nissa dies.* The thought surfaced suddenly, and its simple cause-and-effect concept sent a jolt of renewed fervor throughout her body. *No. I'm not going to give up. Not here. I won't give him the satisfaction. He's intrigued by humans? Then I'll show him exactly what we're capable of.*

Zurah slowly looked around the room, mentally taking inventory. *Focus on what you have and on what you know.* This was no different than any other job. She was in a tight situation and needed to find a back door, a way to break into the system. She glanced at Alex. *He is a resource, another system of information to be used.*

Non-specified user: *Alex, run me through what happened when you arrived.*

Encrypted user 157.C.X.87.210: *I landed but was told my presence wasn't required, that there had been an error in the system and the distress call had been false. I played along but requested a refuel and update and said I would leave the next day. The response wasn't great… but they didn't put up a fuss. I requested a meeting with Turner but was told he was busy. When I did a little investigating, I discovered he was dead.*

Non-specified user: *Why? Why kill him?*

Encrypted user 157.C.X.87.210: *I don't know. Turner was a good guy. Both Finn and I had worked with him on numerous occasions as a liaison with the Telt trade governance. He was a good bureaucrat and knew how to get the job done without burning out his workers.*

Non-specified user: *Wait. Turner wasn't human?*

Encrypted user 157.C.X.87.210: *No. Why?*

Non-specified user: *What was he?*

One of the researchers looked up from their station and moved over to stand in front of Alex. When the researcher leaned forward and held up his palm pad next to Alex's face, Zurah's heart sank.

The researcher turned toward one of his companions. "I've found the signal."

"Shutting down," the other researcher replied.

Non-specified user: *Alex?*

But there was no response. Zurah's first impulse was to scream in frustration, but she couldn't. So she didn't.

All right. I need to tunnel a different path in the system. Zurah considered what she had learned from Alex and how knowing Turner wasn't human might fit in with what she did know. The doctor was an issue for the cryrot, and Zurah made the assumption it was because the crystals weren't compatible with his biology.

But why leave the doctor alive, then? Why not just kill him?

Zurah considered several different possibilities. There was something else that the doctor knew or a skill set that the cryot considered valuable. *Could it have something to do with the doctor's military history? The bioupgrades he had acquired?*

There were too many possibilities and not enough information for Zurah to come up with a solid theory, except that human biology appeared to be extremely susceptible to the cryot, while other biological lifeforms weren't.

The cryot was right about one thing—he was patient. He had taken on Alex's form and first tried to convince the researchers to simply follow his directions. When that had created too much division, that was likely when the cryot began to infect others or at least openly allow that process to be seen. Perhaps Finn's appearance and subsequent sabotage had caused the cryot to speed up his plans.

Zurah moved on. Endless speculation would get her nowhere. She needed to figure out how to shut down the cryot, how to worm inside of its coding and... She stopped then considered what she had discovered when hacking into the ship's systems. Someone had gotten there before her, hacking into three areas. The ship's internal biosensor's, remote access, and the comms—or more specifically, the ambient noise controls.

As she considered these three systems in light of what she knew, the hack made sense. If the cryot was able to target only certain species—for example, humans—then being able to track and identify potential targets using the biosensors made sense. Gaining access to remote access was a smart move, if the cryrot needed to be able to keep tabs on what was happening in the ship if he had to travel to the other research sites. And most importantly, sound was key for the crystals, and having access to the ambient noise controls meant the cryrot could create an environment suitable for his purposes.

Zurah blinked and scrolled through the SeeClear menu, finding the programs controlling the three discs she had left behind. The worm codes were spent; they were a one-time deal. But she still had the ability to gain access to the ship's systems through the discs. Two of the discs were offline, meaning they had been discovered and removed. But she only needed one.

The disc she had attached to the station on the residential deck was still active. She blinked and activated the disc. A green light lit up beside its files, and though tedious without the use of her hands, Zurah navigated the hack, working through the ambient noise controls. Just as she had suspected, the programming had been altered. Instead of the mainly human white noise, a rotating set of low-pitched frequencies were being played.

She paused to consider the implications. When she had heard a similar noise before, the crystals had responded. Furiously, she tried to remember. Zurah believed the crystals had responded by either growing or being able to reshape themselves. So she did what she felt was the logical choice. She flipped the coding, to play a series of high-pitched frequencies.

The second she initiated the altered program, the three researchers doubled over as if in a tremendous amount of pain. The crystal pillars throughout the room stopped glowing, and a darkness spread throughout them, tiny fissures appearing. Inwardly, Zurah shouted for joy. *Take that.* But her joy was short-lived as the cryrot's pain did nothing to improve her situation or Alex's.

Now what? Zurah scanned through the ship's systems, trying to find something of use.

The door opened, and the copy of Alex stumbled into the room. "Clever," he said through gritted teeth. "But not quite clever enough."

He made his way to a workstation, and within minutes, Zurah's hard work had been undone. The cryrot turned to face her and looked at her appraisingly. "I was correct in my assessment of your skills. Once I am successful in ridding you of your resistance, you will be a key asset." He took a step toward her. "I look forward to the day when you are—"

One of the researchers abruptly got up and ran head-first into the cryrot, tackling him down to the ground. Zurah tried to see what was going on, but her position on the platform didn't give her an angle. All she heard were a series of grunts and shouts of anger.

A flicker of movement caught her eye, and another researcher got up and quickly freed Alex from the restraint collar. The third researcher, an older woman, her graying hair coming loose from what had once been a neat bun at the nape of her neck, made her way to Zurah and looked down at her. Her eyes were fearful, but her lips were pressed together in determination.

"I'm sorry," the woman whispered and jabbed something into Zurah's neck.

A distinct burning sensation traveled across her chest

and down through her limbs. Then the tingling began, and Zurah found she could curl her fingers and wiggle her toes.

"Destroy them," the woman said. "Destroy them all." Then she turned, and with a scream of both anguish and fear, she leaped onto the cryrot, helping her fellow researchers.

Zurah half rolled, half fell off the medical platform, but Alex was there and caught her, lifting her arm around his neck, and weaving his own around hers to give support.

"We've got to go," he said.

Zurah didn't need to be told twice. Together, they headed for the door. As it slid open, she glanced back over her shoulder, and bile rose up in her throat. Blood coated the researchers, the floor, and the cryrot as they ripped it apart with their bare hands.

19

Zurah's strength and coordination returned quickly, and by the time they turned the corner to head to the next deck, she no longer needed Alex's support. He turned toward the main exit, but Zurah stayed focused and kept going straight. When Alex realized Zurah wasn't behind him, he skidded to a stop, turned, and jogged to catch back up with her.

"What are you doing? We need to get out of here. Now's our chance."

Zurah didn't slow down. "Go if you want, but I'm heading for the bridge. I know how to stop the cryrot." She picked up speed, running through the corridors and decks until she reached the command level, only slowing down when she reached the door to the bridge. Zurah knew it was a race against time and the unknown. Changing the ambient noises had freed the researchers long enough to regain control, but how long that control would last, she had no idea. Nor did she know if those effects were ship wide. Even if they weren't, Zurah wasn't going to stop. She was ready to barge onto the bridge when Alex shoved her out of the way.

Her protest died on her lips as Alex said, "Stay behind me."

He activated his weapons, and grateful for the assistance, Zurah moved into place. When the doors opened, Alex charged forward, weapon raised and ready for combat. But there were only two individuals on the bridge, and neither one raised a weapon. As if the two individuals were in perfect sync, they turned around to stare with a look of mild disdain at Alex and Zurah.

"Back away, slowly. Keep your hands where I can see them," Alex growled as he advanced, quickly making sure the bridge was clear save for those two. Zurah rushed over to one of the consoles and got to work. Within minutes, she was in the system once more and found that the cryrot had tried to create a defensive wall around the ambient noise program, but Zurah attacked it viciously and made short work of his code's defenses.

As Zurah worked, she couldn't help but glanced up at the two individuals. Neither wore a suit, and their clothes didn't match the typical jumpsuits the researchers wore on their downtime.

"Who are you?" Alex asked.

The two individuals shared a look, but both stayed silent.

"If you're concerned about who I might be, I'm not the cryrot. I'm the real Alex Goldsmith. Run a scan if you need to, but you can stand down. We've figured out how to stop the contamination from spreading."

"Doubtful," one replied. He had sandy hair cut close on the edges but long on the top and pulled back into a tight topknot. His bright-blue eyes watched Alex then turned to Zurah. "Gregori died for you."

The strange statement gave Zurah pause, and she glanced in his direction. "Excuse me?"

"What makes you so special? Why would he do that?"

"I have no idea what you're talking about," Zurah said. "I don't know any Gregori."

"Enough. This is neither the time nor the place," the other individual snapped.

"No? I thought you were the one with the soft spot for them. You wanted to help them. Don't you want to know why Gregori did what he did?"

"Of course, but they've got support inbound. We can't stay here."

"You're not going anywhere," Alex said.

Zurah frowned and turned to get a better look at the two strange men. From outward appearances, they seemed to be human males. Something about their voices was familiar, yet she couldn't quite place where she'd heard them before. "Do I know you two? Have we met before?"

"No." The other one shook his head, his dark hair falling into his eyes. "We're no one."

"They're just playing mind games, probably still under the influence of the cryrot," Alex said. "Have you finished?"

"No, but almost there." Zurah turned back to the hack.

The cryrot had skills, and if there had been more time, Zurah would have wondered where the cryrot had learned to hack. But there wasn't, and Zurah homed in on the small mistakes here and there, taking advantage and inserting her own codes. She broke through the wall, and as she built it back up with her own defenses, she reprogrammed the ambient noise once again.

Satisfied, she leaned back. "Now I'm done. My best guess is if we keep the ambient noise programmed to emit these frequencies, we'll be able to help everyone who was contaminated."

Alex wasn't paying attention. "What the hell?"

She turned and watched as the two men appeared to vibrate, the edges of their bodies coming in and out of focus. She stood and moved to Alex's side. "Who are—"

But the door slid open, and a rush of confusion spilled onto the bridge, as armored suits ran in and took up position throughout the room. Zurah whirled around, fear flooded her body, and she desperately wished for a weapon, until she saw the flash of tentacle.

"Doc!" she cried out and rushed forward.

Dr. Ordotham moved through the doorway and wrapped several of his tentacles around Zurah in a near-crushing hug. "You are alive!" he exclaimed. "May the sun warm the sand upon which you rest."

Angelina squeezed through the doorway and stopped to ask Alex for an update.

"Commander?" the man with the sandy hair asked.

Angelina's jaw dropped. "Johnston? You're… You're alive?"

The doctor released Zurah, and she turned just in time to catch the incredulous look on Angelina's face.

"Shouldn't we be asking the same question of you?" the man with the sandy hair asked.

"What are you—?" But Angelina wasn't able to finish her question. The two men abruptly exploded into sand, spreading across the bridge, then gathered back together in a stream of particles and escaped through one of the ventilation grills.

Sand people, just like the one who—Zurah corrected herself as she realized. *Just like Gregori saved me from the cryrot.* Zurah turned to Alex with questions, but he shook his head, motioning for her to stay silent.

"Update." Finn marched forward, her helmet retracting. Two of her people scrambled over to the workstations.

Alex holstered his weapon as he walked over to her. "Zurah figured out how to get back at the cryrot. Listen." He paused for a moment. "They must use sound waves to aid their growth, but at the higher pitches, it appears to force them to shrink or retract. I don't know the details, only that it appears to be working."

"That is interesting," the doctor said. "I don't believe we had considered that aspect yet." One of his eyes turned to stare at Zurah. "Well done."

"Sir, it appears that the cryrot has reduced in quantity since our last scans. We're still showing concentrated amounts in most of the crew still on board but not at the previous levels."

"Good, get the data over to Hels and their team. I want this information modified and into a weapons system."

"Yes, sir."

Without holstering her weapon, Finn turned her attention back to Alex. "And you?"

Alex shrugged. "I'm in control, if that's what you're asking. We'll need to figure out how to completely purge ourselves of the cryrot, though."

Finn pursed her lips and nodded, then she turned to look at Angelina, who had moved off to the side, quietly working at a console. "And what about you? Commander."

Finn shifted her weight and aimed her weapon at Angelina. Zurah took a step back as Alex went completely still.

"So far, the reports show a reduction in the contamination in the ventilation system, although I'm not showing any traces of—"

"No, that's not what I'm asking."

Slowly, Angelina turned around. "Then I will need clarification, sir." Angelina's eyes flickered to Finn's weapon then back to look Finn directly in the eye.

Finn looked at Alex then back to Angelina. "Who are you?"

"Finn, what are you doing?" Alex took a step toward her. "Are you concerned that she's—"

"Compromised? No. I don't think so, at least not by the cryrot. But we've now witnessed the fact we have a second unknown entity, which has been cleverly hiding in plain sight, like the cryrot. Or am I the only one who witnessed our two friends here just up and vanish?"

"I saw them, too, but why are you singling out Angelina?" Alex asked.

"And why are you so quick to her defense? A characteristic you've always had since we brought her on to this project. Your special hire. And now I want to know why."

"Then perhaps you can tell me why you're so bound and determined to figure out what your great-grand mother discovered?" Alex shot back.

"Zurah? Care to answer that question?"

Alex turned to stare at Zurah, a brief look of concern and betrayal in his eyes before he schooled his expression back to neutral.

Zurah swallowed and felt a knot of anxiety in her chest. Keeping secrets usually came at a price, and now she was caught in the middle. *And Finn knew exactly what she was doing to me too.* "The emperor has sent an expedition through the gates. Finn needs to know why."

"What?" Alex exclaimed and whirled around to face Finn. "Your brother did what?"

"Everyone out," Finn snapped. "Except the doc, Angelina, and Zurah."

The team who had come with them retreated hastily, and when the door closed, Alex let loose.

"This is what you've been hiding? Why didn't you tell me? Good god, woman, this is information that needs to be passed on to the Consortium. If your brother has sent a team through the gates, then we're so far behind, it isn't funny."

"I didn't tell you because I suspected you were working for him. Or rather, she was." Finn waved her weapon toward Angelina. "You brought her on to the project, vouching for her when any idiot could see her HalfLife credentials were faked. But I kept quiet and watched, hoping one of you would make a mistake."

"You crazy idiot," Alex snapped. "I wouldn't work with your brother, not if the whole entire galaxy was on fire. He's a traitorous fool."

Zurah swallowed and took a few steps toward the doc. She had witnessed plenty of arguments before but never before with people who could decide the fate of an entire world, let alone people who were responsible for the majority of humanity.

"Then who is she?" Finn pressed. "The first distress call I received wasn't an accident or a setup like the one I supposedly received from you. Turner had his suspicions about Angelina, and when I got here to try and figure out what was happening, I discovered he was dead."

"Because of the cryrot," Alex said. "Not her."

"Then, again, I'll ask, who is she?" Finn ground out the words.

"I'm Commander Angelina Adeyemi, second-in-command of the *Eagle's Nest*."

There was a brief pause, then Finn responded. "If we were in any other place or situation, I'd shoot you on the spot for a seemingly nonsensical response. But given recent events, I believe you."

"Thank goodness for small miracles," Alex muttered.

"Why hide that from me?" Finn asked.

"I think that's a bit like calling the kettle black," Alex

said. "Let's just chalk it up to the fact we're both good at keeping secrets, maybe even when we shouldn't be."

Finn finally lowered her weapon and powered down. "Perhaps." She asked Angelina, "Why are you here?"

"Because I want to know what happened to my ship and my crew."

"You don't remember?"

"No."

"Do you know how to activate the gates?" Finn asked.

"No. But I believe Turner was close. He stopped sharing the research notes from the gate team a couple of weeks before everything went to shit."

"All right." Finn stared at Angelina for a few moments. "We need to strip the ship of our files, anything and everything that is of use. While that is being done, we need to ensure we've got the contamination under hand. Zurah has provided a start, but we have to make sure it's a permanent solution or at least a beginning to which we can create a permanent solution. Doc, I need you to update what's left of your team."

Two of Dr. Ordotham's tentacles rolled out from underneath the bulk of his body and gently waved back and forth in excitement. "I will see to it. I've also been contemplating why the cryrot believed I was important enough to keep alive. My assumption was that my biology presented an obstacle that it wanted to understand. What allows humans to be susceptible, where I am not? I have a working theory, which, thanks to Zurah, I am confident I can build upon."

"Me?" Zurah asked with a hefty dose of skepticism.

"Yes," he said with another wave of his tentacles.

"You were infected, and even accounting for individual biology, I've wondered if perhaps there was something in your immune system which was more resistant. As I pondered this question, I made a connection between my unique resistance and yours. You alone have partaken of my flesh. You ingested a part of me, thus boosting your own immune system with my unique biology. Somehow that action allowed you to resist the effects of the cryrot."

Zurah blushed and refused to meet anyone's eye. She wasn't particularly happy about having to remember what she'd done. While she might have had a semblance of understanding of the importance of the custom, she still didn't relish the experience.

"I'm not even going to ask," Alex muttered.

"Good. Don't," Zurah said.

"And," the doctor said, "it now appears we have more data we need to study. You also were infected." His gaze moved to Alex. "But remained undetected by the sensors we had put in place. Why is that, I wonder? I will need to study your differences, as well."

"Not to mention, explain to me why you put us all in danger," Finn said. "You and I, cousin, are going to need a heart-to-heart."

Alex glared but didn't say anything.

Finn turned to the doctor. "Can you make a serum? Or an inoculation based off what you know from Zurah's experience?"

"I believe so, if Zurah, along with a few more, will allow me to take samples. I believe I have a strong working theory to build from."

"Good. Do it," Finn said. "Once we're sure we've

gotten the contamination eradicated on the biological level, we're going to scrub the ships then blow them."

"What?" Zurah asked.

"The methods we're discussing are to help make sure biological individuals have been cleared of the cryrot, not the ship itself. We can purge the ventilation systems, the air tanks, the water recyclers, but we have no way of sterilizing the actual material of the ship. And we don't know at what level it might have been contaminated."

"Then how are we going to get off Objer?" Zurah asked.

"We'll initiate standard contamination procedures. We'll remote in to the *HighTail Flyer*'s navigation and contact one of our long haulers. Once contact is made, we bring the ship back down. When the long hauler arrives, we'll set up a decontamination zone. We'll destroy the ships and any equipment. The long hauler can bring in suits, anything we might need, and start evacuations."

"While you go after your brother's research team," Alex added. "Don't think I've forgotten about that little tidbit."

"If you're going through the gates, then I'm coming with you," Angelina said. "I need to know what happened to my crew and why some of them are… well… different, for lack of a better word. Those two men you saw? That was Ethan Johnston, chief engineer, and Montgomery Harrison, one of our pilots."

"Done," Finn said without hesitation. "Alex?"

"Yes. I'm on the same page with you. We need to know what's going on and be prepared."

"Good, doc?"

"I go where you go," he said.

Then Finn turned to Zurah. "I keep my promises. Once the long hauler is here and decontamination has been started, I'll make sure the appropriate amount of credits have been transferred. You and Nissa will be free to go. And I'll ensure she gets the best medical care, all expenses taken care of." She turned back to the others. "Any questions?"

"Time table?" Angelina asked.

Finn considered the question. "Rough estimates, at least a two-week cycle Old Earth standard. It will take the long hauler time to make sure they have all the necessary equipment for a decontamination zone. And I'll need to contact a few of my people to ensure everything is discrete."

"Then I would suggest limiting activity to only one deck," Angelina said. "Medical, perhaps? There is enough room for the researchers to work alongside the doctor, and we can set up temporary living quarters. I would also suggest our own decontamination zone, checking everyone going in or out."

Finn nodded. "Do it. Anything else?"

Angelina shook her head.

"Good. When the basics are set up, you and I are going to have a long talk." And with that, Finn turned and left, already issuing orders through her suit's comms.

"Well," Zurah said, not quite sure how to respond to the whirlwind that was Finn.

"That's my cousin for you," Alex said with a heavy sigh.

"If you're through on the bridge, then I suggest we

head to medical," the doctor said. "I would like to get started."

"Of course. Just give me a moment," Alex replied and motioned for Angelina to walk with him.

Zurah shrugged and followed the doctor, sparing only a glance at Alex and Angelina as they discussed something in hushed tones. She gave herself a little bit of a shake then hurried to catch up with the doctor. They moved through the corridors in an awkward silence until Zurah couldn't stand it any longer.

"How are you?" she asked then immediately regretted asking the inane question after all they had been through.

"I will regenerate within the month," the doctor said. "An advantage of both biology and technological improvements. If you are inquiring about my mental state, that may take a bit more time. I feel… adrift after recent events. I did not expect to have to kill again."

Zurah's embarrassment at the question was only compounded by the intimate nature of the doctor's response. "I think I understand. This wasn't at all what I expected either." She added hastily, "Not that I'm trying to equate my experiences with yours."

"There is no need for polite societal niceties. Not where I am concerned. We have shared the *shieol* and exchanged ourselves with each other. You and I are bound by the tides now."

Zurah wasn't sure how to respond to that statement, but she did feel a warmth toward the doctor and was grateful for his support.

"But I don't believe any of us expected this research expedition to turn out as it has," the doctor continued.

"But perhaps if Finn and Alex had been a bit more trusting of each other—" He stopped. "No, reverse thinking does nothing to break a rocky shore."

The rest of the way to medical was spent in silence, and Zurah couldn't help but wonder how many aspects of life would be made easier if feelings of mistrust or the need for secrets vanished.

Of course my job would vanish, Zurah thought with half a chuckle. But the idea stuck, and Zurah seriously considered what kind of job she could pick up if she decided to get out of the life. She could easily do cyber security, but explaining her previous job experiences would be a bit tricky. *No, this life is mine. It is what it is.*

"If you wouldn't mind taking a seat, I need to consult with who is left of my team, prep a few items, and then we shall get started."

"Sure." Zurah shrugged as she hopped onto a medical platform. As she watched the doctor move around the medical bay, talking with the two other medical staff and gathering various items, a wave of exhaustion rolled over her.

How long since I last slept? Zurah wasn't entirely sure. Objer didn't orbit a sun, and she hadn't been keeping track of the time based on Old Earth standard. *Probably at least a day or two.* Her record was four days and five hours without sleep. A few of the bioupgrades she had paid for helped her push past her biological need for sleep when the situation called for it. But the need for sleep would eventually become so overwhelming, she would be forced to crash for a few days.

A young-looking female Telt walked over with a tense

smile. "My name is Chali, and the doctor would like to draw a few blood samples to get started."

"Sure, do what you need to," Zurah said.

Chali nodded and moved to the side of the platform as Zurah worked on getting out of the top half of her suit. She rolled up the sleeves of her undersuit and patiently waited as Chali drew her blood. Dr. Ordotham wheeled a mobile workstation over to the platform as a screen appeared above the small, rectangular table.

"The first step will be to collect our samples and begin building a database. Ideally, I'll be able to draw blood from a few individuals who aren't fully free of the contamination. It would be best to have samples in various states," the doctor said. He continued to ramble on about the types of tests they could run, the various methods they could use to test his own biology against the cryrot, and developing some type of immunity booster for the researchers. But the technical side of things didn't interest Zurah, and most of what he said made little sense to her.

At one point, when there was a brief moment of silence, Zurah interrupted to ask, "And Nissa?"

"She is still safe. I promise you," the doctor replied. "I've requested that her stasis pod be transferred to this ship with the next load of supplies."

"Thanks," Zurah said, a small knot of anxiety unwinding. But she knew she wouldn't fully relax until she could lay eyes on Nissa. "Do you really think this is all going to take a couple of weeks?"

"At the best, yes. At worst, more than that. The research will need to be verified. And any inoculations we develop will need to be thoroughly tested. It might be that the teams will need to remain on the long hauler for quite some time before they are cleared to return to their homes. I will also need to designate another set of doctors to continue the research when I am gone. Not to mention the fact, Finn will need to request fresh supplies before we travel through the gates. It will all take time."

"Provided they are able to get them to work," Zurah added.

"Yes, of course."

"Where there's a Finn, there's a way," Alex said as he entered the medical bay and hopped up onto the platform next to Zurah. "Don't doubt her tenacity, especially when it comes to keeping tabs on her brothers."

"You really going with her?"

Alex nodded. "Yes. If I'd known about Hiro, I would've pushed us harder to get the gates functional. She should have told me."

"What do you think he's doing?"

Alex shrugged then leaned back on his hands. "Don't know, but I doubt it's good. Hiro's never been stable. Always a bit of a loose cannon. But bureaucracy has always slowed him down, and he's got a decent set of advisers. The reality is they're the ones that make most of the big decisions. Hiro, or rather the throne, has become more of a public relations job than anything else. And he's certainly failed at that part. His ratings are at an all-time low."

"When is the monarchy ever popular?" Zurah muttered.

"It has its moments," Alex replied with a shrug.

Chali came over and drew blood from Alex, and when she finished, Alex shivered. "Never liked needles." He hopped down. "You hungry? We haven't had a decent meal in quite a while. I know the food replicators are up and running."

Zurah shook her head. "No thanks. I'm good for now. I'd like to stay here for a bit."

"Okay. Come find me when you're finished with the doc." Alex winked.

Zurah smiled back and decided she liked the relaxed version of Alex. Without the pressure of the past events, she could begin to see the real Alex underneath. She watched him leave then turned so she could lie down, feeling the overwhelming need to simply relax.

She closed her eyes and tried to picture leaving Objer. Perhaps they could head to Rockerton's on the far side of Mandarin's Rhine. Out of all the different Rockerton's, that was her favorite. There were three different levels for gaming, a whole level dedicated to a bar and restaurant, and a top dome for gazing out at the stars. A handful of nights would cost a small fortune, but Finn and Alex both owed her more credits than she could count. Blowing some of them on at least a month's stay wasn't going to be out of line. All Zurah wanted to do was to relax and have the last couple of days fade into a memory.

"Did you need some—?" Chali started to ask, then a crash cut her off as something dropped to the floor.

Zurah's eyes popped open, and she sat up, turning to stare face-to-face with a very battered and bloody Alex.

No, not Alex, but the cryrot, Zurah realized.

Strips of skin hung off his face, revealing crystals where bone should have been visible. Blood oozed from the wounds, running down his face and neck, staining the top of what was left of an undersuit.

Zurah was paralyzed, unable to scramble out of the way while the cryrot slowly advanced on her.

"I am finding myself less and less tolerant of your species. I had hoped to be able to build upon your kind, creating and molding them into glories they barely can conceive of. But at every turn, you continue to resist what we have to offer. And so I find myself considering the wisdom first visited upon me. That of justice. A total annihilation of your kind. We have learned enough to know there are several species throughout this galaxy who may embrace what we have to offer."

"And what is that?" the doctor asked calmly as he moved behind Zurah. One of his tentacles slowly made its way up the platform and wrapped around her waist.

"To rebuild what was destroyed. To call anew what should never have been forgotten." The cryrot smiled. The majority of his teeth were missing, and there were a few small crystals embedded along his gumline.

"Perhaps you can answer a question for me," the doctor continued, as if nothing were amiss. "You have taken on the form of Alex Goldsmith but are not him. Yet you appear to be constructed not only of the crystals but of flesh and blood. How did that come to be?"

"Clever doctor. I would enjoy the opportunity of working with more of your kind, if only you weren't resistant to what we offer," the cryrot said.

"I think you would be sorely disappointed. I am not like most of my species." Slowly, he moved Zurah to the edge of the platform as the rest of his body moved around the side and put himself between her and the cryrot. "Although there are some who possess the majority of my unique upgrades." His tentacle whipped Zurah off the platform and across the medical bay. She hit the wall, pain erupting along her back. Her vision swam as she watched the doctor leap toward the cryrot. Razor-sharp crystals flew out of the cryrot, ripping through the doctor's body. Blood coated the floor as his tentacles lashed out at the cryrot, attempting to grab him and pin him down.

Zurah struggled to her feet, her mind a confused muddle, but she knew she had to help the doctor. She stumbled as she took a step. Pain shot up her leg, and she fell forward, grabbing the edge of a workstation.

A tentacle shot out and crashed into the cryrot, sending him spinning back against the medical bay door. There was the distinct sound of a crack. The cryrot got back to its feet, crystal ribs poked through what was left of its flesh, and its back lurched to the left at a horrendous angle.

"We are not easily defeated. We will rain down our vengeance and our wrath upon you and all your kind. We will spin the worlds in fire and see them reborn in our image," the cryrot cried. He flung his arms forward, launching crystal darts at the doctor.

Dr. Ordotham tried to move out of the way, but one of his tentacles was shredded in the process and hung lifeless from his body. Without hesitation, the doctor ripped off the tentacle and flung it behind him.

"You will find that I am also not easily defeated," the doctor snapped. With his remaining six tentacles, he pushed himself up until he towered over the cryrot.

Zurah wanted to shout at the doctor, to tell him not to expose his underbelly, but the words only came out in a sickening croak. She fumbled along the edge of table, watching helplessly as the doctor charged the cryrot. Tentacles wrapped around him, squeezed, then twisted, pulling the cryrot in two. The lower half spun across the room, skidding to a stop at Zurah's feet, while the upper half fell in front of the doctor.

The cryrot grinned. "We cannot be killed by conventional means." And then he laughed, a sickening, deafening laugh. Low and deep and long. It wasn't until it was too late that Zurah realized what he was doing. The sound wasn't laughter, but a low frequency tone, encouraging the crystal shards, which were now scattered throughout the medical bay, to grow. The pieces that had fallen off when the doctor had ripped the cryrot in two began to vibrate. Then they grew, sharp points reaching up and piercing the doctor. He stumbled back then fell as two more of his tentacles were pierced to the floor by the crystals. In a sickening move, the doctor ripped them off, falling sideways. The remaining four tentacles reached out, dragging his wounded body across the floor until it was able to tumble into his nest.

"No!" Zurah screamed, her eyes frantically searching the room for something she could use as a weapon.

The room was full of various medical equipment, but Zurah didn't have a clue as to what each piece did or how it might be useful. Her eyes swept past one of the larger workstations then stopped. Chali had crawled behind it, desperately trying not to be seen.

Zurah ducked down and hurried over to her. "What pieces of equipment in this room can emit high-frequency sound waves?"

When Chali didn't respond, Zurah grabbed her shoulders and shook the woman. "What equipment can produce—"

Grimacing, Chali looked around the room and finally pointed to a rolling cart with a piece of equipment on top. "The ultrasound. It can."

"Tell me how to use it!"

"Turn it on and pick a transducer," Chali said. "Then just press it against the part of the patient you're trying to—"

Zurah was up and hobbling for the ultrasound, ignoring the pain ripping through her body with each step. She grabbed the cart and wheeled it over to the upper half of the cryrot. She flipped on the machine and grabbed the larger of the three transducers.

"You are clever, but you can't—"

Zurah didn't wait for the cryrot to finish his speech. She slammed the transducer against his temple and squeezed the trigger. The pitch was too high for her human ears, but the effects were instantaneous. There wasn't even time for the realization to dawn on the cryrot's face before it shattered into oblivion. But Zurah didn't stop there. Doubled over in pain, she scooted along on her knees, placing the transducer on each piece of crystal that she could find until nothing remained but a fine layer of orange dust coating everything in the medical bay.

She heard shouts on the other side of the door but ignored them as she crawled toward the doctor's nest. She hadn't realized there was a retractable ceiling to the depression, and she pounded her bloodied fists against it. "Doc! It's Zurah. The cryrot is gone. Let me in. You need help. Doc!" But the nest didn't open, nor did she hear anything to indicate that the doctor was still alive down there.

A pair of hands gripped her shoulder and spun her around. Alex stared at her in horror. "Are you okay?"

But Zurah shook her head and pointed at the nest. "The doc is severely wounded. He needs help."

Finn crouched beside her. "I'll see to the doc. Alex, take her out of here."

Alex nodded and wrapped his arms around Zurah, forcing her to her feet. She tried to resist. "I need to make sure he's okay. He saved my life." But the pain was too much, and she couldn't stop Alex from lifting her and carrying her out of the room.

"I need help," he called out. Two individuals rushed over and gently took Zurah from him. "We need to assess the extent of her injuries."

"I've got her," Chali said, hobbling over. "She saved all of us." She nodded to the two workers, and together, they made their way down the corridor to one of the rooms that had been set up as temporary quarters.

"Lay her down over here." Chali listed off several pieces of equipment and sent the two workers scrambling to find what they could. She reached into her pocket and pulled out a small pouch. Unzipping it, she found what she was looking for and handed Zurah a small pill. "Put this under your tongue. It will dissolve, and you'll feel the effects in a few moments." Chali twisted around and looked at Alex. "Go find some fresh bandages and a new undersuit."

He nodded and rushed off.

Chali gently brushed Zurah's matted hair out of her face. "I was impressed with what you did back there," she whispered. "We all are."

Zurah rolled her head to the side to stare at Chali. To Zurah's horror, Chali's face dissolved into fine grain sand that rearranged itself to resemble the face of the medic who had saved her life on the bridge.

"Gregori?" Zurah asked, trying to scoot away.

"Yes." He reached out and held Zurah still. "Don't try to move. You've received considerable trauma, and I need you to heal."

"Why? No. I mean, what are you?" Zurah asked, her words beginning to slur as the medication began to do the trick.

"We were once human, but I'm guessing you were beginning to figure that out. We were the crew of the *Eagle's Nest,* and we stumbled across something which should have remained forgotten. But unfortunately, humanity has a way of repeating history, and there are forces that are being awakened which should have been left alone. What you call the cryrot isn't even a fraction of what's to come if you and your people don't stop the others. You must go through the gates."

Gregori shifted and pulled out a small metal container. "This is everything you need to know in order to activate the gates. Gather your strength, supplies, and people you can trust. Then go through and stop the others. We're all running out of time."

"What do you think you're doing?" an angry voice called out. "We thought you were dead."

Gregori pressed the container into Zurah's hands. "Keep this information safe." He stood and turned around, facing Johnston and Harrison. "I'm sorry I had to deceive the two of you."

"You know our mission. We're not to help them. The gates must stay closed."

Gregori shook his head. "It's too late for that. We need their help if any of us are going to survive what's coming."

Johnston took a step forward, anger plain on his face. "That's not up to you to decide."

"We don't have the luxury of a tribunal. Not now," Gregori said. Then in a blink of an eye, his body turned to sand. The other two followed suit, creating a furious sandstorm in the room.

Zurah closed her eyes and moved her arms to protect her face. For a moment, she believed she could hear voices arguing with each other, but then it was over. Nothing remained of the three men. *If they are even men anymore.*

The door opened, and Alex came in. "Where did Chali go? I got the bandages."

Zurah tried to shake her head, but the medication was taking hold, and everything felt fuzzy. She tried to speak, to tell Alex what had happened, but he sat down next to her and shushed her.

"It's okay. Don't try to speak. We'll get you patched up. Don't worry."

Then Zurah fell into a peaceful and dreamless sleep.

20

When Zurah woke, she had been moved to a different room. Someone had dressed her in a fresh undersuit and placed her on a rather comfortable mattress with several blankets. Her first inclination was to stretch, but as soon as she began the movement, she stopped, feeling something uncomfortable pull along her spine. Instead, she carefully sat up and took a look around the room. It wasn't a spacious hab-unit but large enough for the bed, a workstation, Dash 'N Wash, and a couch. And sleeping on the couch was Alex. There were a couple of blankets wrapped around his legs and one on the floor. As he lightly snored, she studied him.

The whole experience had been overwhelming and unexpected, but perhaps the one that puzzled her the most was Alex. Never in her life would she have dreamed she would have worked with a Goldsmith. They had always been at the top of humanity's society, far out of her circle. But a Goldsmith trusted her and worked with her. He was nothing at all like how the media or the whisper nets portrayed him.

With a small smile, she shook her head in disbelief as she tried to stand. The action was painful but not nearly what it had been. Slowly, she moved over to the Dash 'N Wash then splashed cold water on her face.

"Need help?" Alex asked.

"Sorry, didn't mean to wake you," Zurah said, carefully turning around.

Alex grinned. "You've been out for over four days. I've caught up on my sleep." He stood and helped her back to the bed.

"Four days?" she asked, grimacing as she sat.

"Took your body a bit to take to the wraps, but once it did, it just took time for everything to heal. You had quite a bit of trauma to your spine."

"What about the doctor? How is he doing?"

A cloud of grief shadowed Alex's eyes. "We don't know. We haven't been able to get into the nest. Finn finally told everyone to just leave it alone."

"What?" Zurah tried to get up but had to quickly sit back down. "How can she just leave him there? He was really hurt and needed medical attention."

"I know." Alex sat down next to her. "It's one of the few times I've ever witnessed Finn crying. And if you tell her that, I'll kick you out an air lock someday."

"Crying?" Zurah asked.

"She and the doctor were close. I don't know the whole story, but they have both been through a lot together. They've worked together for years. He was one of the few individuals she completely trusted."

"And so she just leaves him in there to rot," Zurah snapped.

"I don't know," Alex replied. "The doctor always seems to have a trick or two up his sleeves. He sealed the well for a reason. Just give it time."

But Zurah had a sickening feeling she knew why the doctor had sealed the well. When he was injured as they got to the rovers to escape the ship, he hadn't wanted her to see what he had done to his injured tentacle. *Could he really come back from what happened?* Zurah had no idea, but she could only hope.

"Hey, so I don't mean to rush you or anything," Alex said, changing the subject. "But…" He pulled out the metal container Gregori had pressed into Zurah's hands. "What's this?"

Zurah stared at it then looked at Alex. Her first instinct was to make up something. But after everything that had happened, Zurah knew one thing. What was happening on Objer was far bigger than anything she had ever handled. And she didn't want to do it alone. She needed a team. And right now, that was Alex.

"Did you ever find Chali?" she asked.

Alex shook his head. "Nope. Finn is pissed. She doesn't like loose ends."

"Well, then at least I can help tie that one up for her." Zurah proceeded to tell Alex what had happened.

When she finished, he gave a long, low whistle. "Wow. That is unexpected but extremely helpful. Finn's going to be pleased."

"Why is that?"

"They dug into Turner's computer and all his files. His notes, everything related to the gates, had been wiped. The teams have had to start over from scratch. Finn hasn't been happy."

"The crew members must have done it. Johnston and Harrison."

"That seems likely. I'm a bit concerned about what your friend Gregori had to say, that there's something worse than the cryrot on the other side of the gates."

Zurah shivered. "And you're still going through?"

Alex nodded. "Yes. I've got no choice. We need to know what's happening."

"Can you help me lay back down?" she asked.

Alex stood, and gently helped her, then pulled up the blankets for her. Once she was comfortable, he sat back down.

"I'm going with you."

"What?" he looked at her in surprise.

Zurah nodded. "I want to know too. And we already know there is more of the cryrot out there. What we encountered on the platforms. What we destroyed here isn't enough. I want to make sure that it's all destroyed. That no one else can ever be hurt by it again." As she said the words, a strange sense of purpose filled her. Revenge. The cryrot had killed Mexa, taken Nissa from her, and more than likely killed the doctor. She would find what was left and destroy it, just like she had the cryrot in the medical bay.

"Are you sure?" Alex asked.

"Yes."

He stood and tapped the small comms panel on the wall beside the door. "This is Alex. I need Finn to come to Zurah's room as soon as possible."

They sat together in silence until Finn arrived, and when she did, she looked worn out. She glanced at them both, flopped down on the couch, and stared at them. "Well? What?"

Zurah repeated her story a second time, and Alex handed over the metal container to Finn. She cracked it open, and a renewed sense of purpose filled her face. "And he said this is what we would need to operate the gates?"

"Yes."

Finn bounced up, but Alex was faster and caught her arm. "Wait. There's one more thing. Zurah's coming with us."

Finn's dark eyes studied Zurah, then she nodded. "Make sure to get her added to the list and find out what kind of gear she needs. The long hauler will be in range tomorrow, then it should take roughly nine days for it to pick up our supplies and return. When it does, we gear up, and we go through the gates."

"Thank you," Zurah said.

The door opened, but Finn paused and turned back. "He was important to me too," she said quietly then disappeared.

Zurah and Alex spent the next few days together. Zurah rapidly got her strength back as she helped Alex work with Angelina on the supplies list. The researchers had adapted the ultrasound machine's technology and modified a whole range of weaponry that was able to recreate the sound waves. Multiple tests were run, and each one had the same result. Higher frequencies delivered at close range with a powerful burst completely destroyed the crystals. A few of the researchers were tasked with gathering up some of the remaining crystals. They placed the samples in a secure room and started work on measuring the crystals every way they could. Nothing showed that the crystals had the ability to regenerate after they were reduced to dust. Armed with that knowledge, the majority of the researchers who were left systematically made their way through both ships, going over every inch with the new weapons.

Finn was still cautious, but she'd downgraded the idea of blowing the ships to at least leaving a small team behind who could continue their research, now that they felt they could defend themselves if the need arose. There were a few arguments over who was going to stay behind and head up that group, but Finn made the ultimate decision. And in the end, she chose one of the lead scientists.

Nissa's stasis pod was transferred over to the ship, and when it was brought to the new medical bay, Zurah asked for a few moments alone. She sat down on the floor next to the pod and peered through the view port. "I know I could stay here while they help to make sure you're free of the crystals. But you're still going to need medical support that they're not equipped for here. I believe Finn and Alex, as they've both assured me that you'll get the best of care. Their own personal medical doctors, actually. You're going to be able to spend time at one of Alex's homes. Can you imagine that?"

Zurah sighed and laid her hand on the view port. "I've got so many questions for you. I just wish you would have told me the truth. But those questions are going to have to wait, for now. I promise that I'll return, and when I do, I want to know everything. Why you never told me, what happened to my parents, why they left me. All of it. But I've got to go with them. I'm a part of this now, and I want to make sure that no one else can ever be hurt by the cryrot or whatever other monsters might be on the other side of the gates."

She stood, still feeling a slight hitch in her back. "But I promise you that I'll come back. You take care of yourself, boss."

Before Zurah left, she gave the pod one last look. She could picture Nissa's expression, her eyes full of concern and her chewing on her lower lip. Nissa would no doubt advise against joining the team. She would tell her to take the credits, pay off her debts, and find a place to lie low for a long while. Or perhaps, Zurah had never really known what Nissa would do after all. Maybe she would shake her head with a soft smile and tell her that she'd always known Zurah was meant for more than just being a security hack.

Zurah wasn't sure. She left and smiled at Alex. "You're turning into a bit of a stalker, you know?" she teased.

Alex shrugged. "Just wanted to make sure you're okay."

"I'm fine, or at least I will be. Any updates?"

"No, everything is quiet for now. But Finn would like us to join her on the bridge. You're going to regret coming with us, you know," Alex said.

Zurah stopped and threw him a concerned look.

He only laughed. "You're now going to have to sit through all of her debriefings. And she doesn't miss a single detail. If you don't get bored and fall asleep during one of them, then I'll owe you a trip to any place—your choice."

Zurah grinned. "I'll take that bet."

"But if you do, then you'll owe me a round of that game you were telling me about before. What was it called?"

"Triple Luck, and no matter what, I'm taking you to Rockerton's one of these times. And we'll play the game, but I'm still going to beat you."

"Yeah, right. We'll see about that."

Zurah was sure she could beat him at the game, and she was quite sure she could stay awake through all of Finn's meetings. There were so many different places throughout the known worlds that she would love to see, and if Alex was going to pay, she wasn't going to turn down the offer.

Thank you for embarking on this adventure with Zurah in *Abandoned Echoes*.

Zurah's adventures will continue in the second installment of the Black Gates of Objer series:

Echoes of Revenge

Zurah's about to discover not everything is as it appears to be!

If you haven't checked out the other adventures within the Embedded Universe, or if you'd like to explore my other titles, and stay up to date with what's happening, visit my website and sign-up for the newsletter!

elizabethknollston.com

You can also follow me on social media at:
facebook.com/elizabethknollston
twitter.com/EKnollston

Thanks again for going on this journey with me and all the crazy characters in my imagination!

Acknowledgements

In my wildest dreams, I've imagined filling a bookcase with my creations. In reality, I wasn't sure I would ever get there. But as hard as it is to believe, here I am working on my second series, with my mind brimming with more and more stories for the Embedded Universe. Who would have known!

In every book, I have to somehow thank my parents. Without their love of reading and encouragement I never would have gotten to this point. So, thanks mom and dad.

And of course, a huge thanks to my family and friends who continue to support me as I continue in my author career. Without their unfailing support, I wouldn't have gotten this far.

This book wouldn't be where it is today without all of the fantastic editors from Red Adept Editing. I've appreciated all of their hard work, their great feedback, and all the work they did to help these books shine. Thank you so much!!

A huge thank you goes out to the ladies I work with at the library. They have been supportive and encouraging as I've learned to balance the day job with being an author.

And as always, a gigantic thank you to all of my readers for taking a chance on my books. I'm so grateful for each one of you, with your kind words of reviews and encouragement. I hope to bring you more stories of far-off adventures!

About the Author

Elizabeth Knollston collects dragons. No, they're not real. But if you know of a mad scientist or genetic engineer who's working on the real deal, be sure to let her know. She would dearly love to collect star ships too, but those won't fit in her garage.

Her (overactive) imagination is credit to her parents, who outrageously encouraged her poor spending habits of buying too many books. And just a side note—if you ever plan on moving, book collecting isn't helpful.

In another life, Elizabeth dreamed of becoming an archaeologist, but a fascinating and rewarding job as a therapeutic horseback riding instructor derailed those plans. When Elizabeth isn't wondering about being on a manned mission to Mars, she enjoys bugging her dog, battling the weeds in her garden, and being a productive member of society.

www.ingramcontent.com/pod-product-compliance
Lightning Source LLC
Chambersburg PA
CBHW032358310726
48973CB00007B/2061